…andma & Grandpa
Jessee

Love,
Katie♡

# Copyright

# Six Keys

by

Kate Copeseeley

**This is book is dedicated to the wonderful folks over at NaNoWriMo. Without you, I never would have known that I'm a writer.**

~~~~~

**This book is also here with great thanks to Meg Cabot, whose pep talk taught me that I can, for once in my life, finish a book!**
~~~~~

## Prologue

She stepped with the grace of a ballerina, oblivious to the fact that most people would only be able to do so through years of training, staring up at the beautiful beige Victorian conversion in front of her. Walking up to the steps, she hesitated, then stopped as she noticed the small wooden sign at a set of stairs leading down to a basement apartment. *Sibilant Bedgood: Guidance*. It was reassuring, she needed guidance, but also worrying. She'd come so far and waited for a moment that she hoped would occur today.

Her tap on the door was light and polite, her expression schooled and distant, as though she was off in another world altogether. Pale hair sat glistening on either shoulder, and she felt no nervous urge to touch it, or brush it back. Instead, she waited, listening for the tap and scuffle of feet on the other side of the door and when she heard them she tensed, clenching her fists as the door flung open in front of her.

A short woman answered the door. She was sweet and round, with curling maple hair and light beige skin, reminding her of molasses from the jar. Her voice, when she spoke, was as dusky and sweet as brown sugar.

"Come in," she said and Elicia felt the calm that flowed from her blue eyes -still water at dawn. Elicia followed her through the door, staring at the worn, eclectic mix of antique and Country French furniture fixing her gaze at the plump green chair which Ms. Bedgood was gesturing toward. She sat, staring across the table at the self-professed purveyor of guidance.

"Okay," Elicia said, and waited. Ms. Bedgood looked at her for a few moments.

"Was there anything you wanted to know?" Ms. Bedgood asked, hesitating before her next movement.

Elicia shook her head, saying nothing. She had nothing to say. She'd explained herself before, strings and strings of endless words leaving her mouth, emptying her soul before each of the supposed spiritual leaders and cleansers and gurus.

"Alright then, " she said, "Place your hands in mine and try to relax."

Elicia took a long slow breath and put her hands in the ones laying on the table in front of her.

~~~~~

I gasped, my hands tightening around hers. There is a process to my work; guidance is what my sign says. When I touch hands with another person, and concentrate with my long years of experience, I get a feeling about where to probe in a person's life. It is then that I receive what I like to think of as a message, unique to that person and their situation. It always comes, and it's second nature to me now, but it does take effort to reach a person.

In this woman's case, there was nothing like that. It was like I was standing on solid ground one moment, then was sucked away into a tornado the next. Her mind was a whirling maelstrom, but I was having a hard time seeing the substance of it. Instead, I was drawn to another place altogether and the longer I looked inside her, the better I understood what she was. She was a sinkhole; she drew people to her. She couldn't help it, she was someone who was always noticed in a crowded room. People could feel her around the corner or in the dark.

My hands tightened again. And then, something happened to me that had never happened in any session before. I was sucked in further and fell into the middle of her blackness. I felt a curious pull from all sides as though I were
~~~~~

in the middle of a funnel cloud. I could feel the whispers of spirits around me- people near and far. I was standing on the soft gray ground of a gray world. The air was cool and moist, a damp washcloth. I spent a few moments trying to see more than five feet in front of me, but it wasn't possible through all the mist.

I turned, jerking my head. What was that? I could sense something near me, outside my range of vision. I peered off toward where I thought I could feel it, but it was hard to see anything in the fog.

Whatever it was, it was coming closer, drawn to where I stood. It was moving faster now, honing in on me. I swallowed. It almost felt as though I were being… hunted.

The world around me swirled and felt like a merry-go-round spinning out of control. I swayed, dizzy and disoriented, then tried to move, tripped over my own feet, and fell to my knees. Glancing up, I saw it speeding toward me, close enough now that I could see the whites of its eyes and feel the evil blackness of it.

To say it was demonic would be misleading -it had none of the hallmarks of a demon from folklore. Its eyes were black, not bulging and yellow. Its teeth weren't large and pointed -as a gargoyles might be. No, they looked much like human teeth, only larger in its face, and they were tinted with a dingy cement color -but that might have been because of the light around us. It did not have a forked tongue or a long tail. I say it was demonic because of the evil I mentioned earlier exuding from every fiber of its being, and because it floated like an apparition -something I've always pictured demons doing.

It approached, skimmed around me then slowed, staring me in the face, its breath putrid and filled with death.

"What are you?" I asked, pushing up to my feet. It cocked its head and I shivered. I could feel the malevolence flowing from it. The purity of its wickedness was both inspiring and horrifying. It looked at me like a spider considering the prey at the edge of its web.

"What are you?" It asked, echoing my voice back at me, head still cocked as it inspected me. "What are you? What are you?"

I shrank back, heart pounding. I was both terrified and fascinated. I knew that I should flee as fast as I could go, but a part of me wanted to know what the message was in this place.

"What are you?" It asked once more. I raised my hand towards it and it echoed my movements. I lowered my hand and it did the same. What a blankness in its eyes, I thought. Like the woman's. I jerked as I realized that I was still back in my apartment holding that woman's hands. What was I seeing here?

I started to turn away from it, but it moved, lurching in front of me. "What are you?"

I backed up, it moved towards me. "Go away!" I screamed. "Back off!"

"What are you? What are you? What are you?" It grabbed my arms and leered into my face as it continued to mimic me. It opened its mouth wide and I saw its large teeth and black tongue. It leaned in and I started screaming.

"What are you?" It asked as it started to chew on my neck.

I gasped as I was pulled out of her inner world.

Panting, I could feel the sweat trickling down my neck, and sobbed as the familiarity of home poured into my consciousness. It took several minutes to penetrate -I was alive, and unharmed.

I looked at the woman across from me, who for the first time since she walked into my house, had an expression of interest on her face. Her eyes were pale green and lit up from the inside as she leaned forward.

"Tell me," she said.

For a minute I was silent, trying to gather my thoughts and figure out what I wanted to tell her.

"You attract evil- like a magnet for every wicked and malicious force in your vicinity. They can't help themselves, they feel you near them like an empty canvas just waiting to be painted on. Drawn to you out of curiosity, they sense your vulnerability and pounce, devouring you."

"Yes," she said.

"All your life, you've lived like this?" I was appalled.

She sighed, leaned back, and pulled her hands from mine.

"Finally," she said. "Finally."

She stood up and laid four times my fee onto the table in front of me.

She took my hand and gave me a tired, yet warm smile.

"Thank you," she said. Then she left.

# Chapter 1

I was having an argument with my mother about selling out. She maintains that I should never accept money for using my gift. It's not fair: I can't blame her for feeling that way, since Grandma Wanda was a hippy wanderer, scamming people out of cash in return for telling them their fortunes.

Thanks to Wanda, my mom moved from place to place until they landed at a commune in the age of free love. She was the epitome of crunchy when she met my dad more than 30 years ago in Northern California. It's easy for her to talk; she's a happily married housewife who makes a hobby out of reading Tarot. Not all of us are so lucky. And this is what I told her.

"Some of us actually have to pay our own bills, Mom," I said.

I come from a long line of gifted *Readers*. My mother does Tarot readings. My grandmother read tea leaves. My great-grandmother practiced numerology and astrology. And up until Grandma Wanda, our family has always lived in Louisiana. "All gifted Readers come from the southern states," my mother always says. This makes me laugh because she's never lived there. The joke in our family is that none of us has ever taken our gift seriously.

My mother's biggest clientèle comes from her local garden club and the occasional referral from a friend. My Grandma Wanda, as I mentioned, was something of a gypsy -wandering hither and yon with her young daughter Honey in tow. I'm the only one who works at it everyday and tries to live off of it. Too bad I can't seem to earn more than a pittance.

My problem is that I don't lie well -I'm horrible at it. Everyone knows that to be a successful, money-making psychic, you have to keep them coming back for more. You tantalize them and give just a hint of things to come, without actually telling them anything of substance. Modern day psychics with their 900 numbers have the real money dialed in. They live off of other people's hope, you see. That's the smart way to make money.

I, on the other hand, live in a cramped little apartment that I feel lucky to have. I have enough money for my bills and a little bit more to buy food with. It's my own fault. I don't bring in return customers. When a person comes in it's a one time shot. I tell them what they need to hear and then my work is over.

"You don't even have enough money to buy a plane ticket home for Christmas," she shot back, "You should get a real job and then do your work in your free time."

I sighed, counting to ten. For a woman whose greatest gift was perception, she could be so obtuse sometimes.

"Mom, we've discussed this before," I said, coming back to the present. "I can't help as many people if I have a real job. I tried and it didn't work for me. The universe won't curse me if I get some money for it. I have to go, Mom."

"Sibby, you know I love you. I just don't want you to get to the end of your life and feel like you've wasted the wonderful gift you've been given."

"I know, Mom. I love you, too."

We said good-bye, I snapped my phone shut and set it on the table next to my dying fern. I have a black thumb, but somehow I always end up with plants scattered around my house, fading slowly into oblivion. I slumped in my chair and reached for the cup of tea next to me on the side table. I stared at my wood floor and watched the curls of dust waft across it.

They slowed for a moment and I saw the outline of a face. It was her, the blank woman. The dust motes swirled away, becoming dust again.

I kept thinking of her, in my still moments, wondering what happened to her. Her empty eyes and blank soul seemed like a part of me. I sipped my tea and jumped when the doorbell rang. I peeked through the peephole and saw a man on the other side, tall, thin and handsome with light brown hair, a pencil thin mustache, and a charming smile.

"Hello?" I said, through the door.

"Am I speaking with Sibilant?" he asked.

"This is Sibilant. How can I help you?"

"My name is Jordan Long. I'm a lawyer with Harper, Jensen and Roman. I wanted to speak with you regarding Elicia Ford. I have an I.D.," he said, holding it up so I could see it.

I opened the door. "I'm sorry, who?"

"Elicia Ford. You met her briefly when she came in for a reading, uh… " He looked down at a stack of papers. "Five days ago."

My breath caught, could he mean my mystery woman?

"Is there a problem?"

"Elicia passed away 2 days ago. Before she did, she came to me and changed her will. You are mentioned in it and I was wondering if you would be willing to discuss it."

"Um… sure, I guess," I said, holding open the door and gesturing him inside.

I followed him into the living room, sat in my usual chair, and waited while he took out a set of papers and laid them on the table in front of us. I was dying to know what was going on, what had happened to the mysterious woman who'd left without even giving me her name.

He looked up at me, and I studied him again, taking in his expensive suit and the sixty dollar haircut his light brown hair was trimmed with. His gray eyes were impassive, looking at me with the impartiality of a scientist studying a specimen.

"Thank you for letting me in. I can see you're used to having clients in here, based on the sign outside, but it's always a risk, letting a strange man in your house."

I smiled.

"To tell the truth," I said, "I'm not used to seeing men in my line of work. Other than the occasional delivery man, of course. I admit, I'm puzzled as to why you're here. Would you mind if..." I hesitated, then straightened, holding out my hands with a gentle smile.

"What? Oh, you want to 'read' me?" he asked, amused. That was okay -it was for me, not for him.

His hands were soft, and I was mesmerized by the clean lines of his manicured nails. It was these that I focused on while I held his hands.

"Oh," I said, welling up with tears, feeling the emotions that were roiling behind his professional, neat as a folded napkin, demeanor. "You *loved* her. Deeply. Oh, I'm so sorry for your loss, Jordan." I looked up at him and his face seemed to melt in front of me as he hunched forward, harsh sobs shaking his entire frame. I wanted to hold him, but settled for squeezing his hands and murmuring comforting words. After a few minutes, he sat up, wiped his eyes and put all his impeccable walls back in place.

"You're not here about her will," I said. "What are you here for?"

"Five days ago, the same day she came to see you, I got a call from Elicia, she had some things she wanted to drop off for me to keep in the file with her will. One of them, I noticed right away, was a letter for me. The other was addressed to you. I brought them both with me today."

He slid the papers across the table towards me, and I picked up a soft peach envelope with my name written across the front in a loopy scrawl.

*Sibilant-*

*I know this letter a must come as a surprise to you. We met for such a short period of time in both of our lives. However, you should know how long I searched for you, for someone with your abilities. Psychics, mediums, shaman, gurus, and other people associated with the spirit realm, they were all at a loss as to how my life became so torn apart. No one could tell me what I wanted to hear: an explanation of the terror that has followed me all of my life. I'm not sure where my life took a bad turn, but I do know that at some point I became what you rightly labeled me as -a magnet for evil. Again and again, I've been faced by terrible things that have haunted me and shadowed my steps with their malice.*

*I've become so tired in the past few years. I feel like the life has been drained out of me. I think I must be cursed.*

*I tell you all this, because I think that I still need you. In the past year, I've felt death's vise around my throat. I know I don't have much time left, but I need someone to help get me out of this blackness. If you are reading this, I'm hoping it's not to late for me, even after death. My intention is to see you again, when I have gathered up all my years of research and you can properly help me track down my spiritual illness and prepare a cure for me. If that is the case, then this letter will be destroyed. If somehow, I don't live long enough, then let this letter be my plea.*

*When I met you, I knew that I had found the person who could help. I need you to find out how to give me rest. Please. I sensed a kind heart in you and I know that you will not let me down. If you have any questions or need information, please talk to Jordan Long. He knows more about me than anyone else does.*

*Thank you once again. I wish you all success, in fact,*

*I'm depending on it.*

*Sincerely,*

*Elicia Susanne Wakefield Ford*

I finished reading and looked up.

"I don't understand," I said, still trying to sort through all of what she had written.

"Here, this will explain it better," Jordan said, handing me his letter, already opened.

*My dearest friend,*

*You have been my confidant and best companion for the past years since Jack's death. I've always regretted that I couldn't give the love you desire, and deserve. I'm so tired these days, as you know. I don't have it in me to give that kind of love any more. But if I die, I want you to have this letter to look back on. I want you to know that I understand how you feel about me, and that I hold you in the highest regard.*

*As you know, I've left everything to charity, but recently I met a woman, Sibilant Bedgood, who I believe can help me with that problem we've tried to solve for so long. In the case that I die, I want you to give her time to look through my things and read my research. As executor, you have that power. I would also like you to pay her for it, out of the estate. Call it a debt, so there is no question. I do owe her a debt.*

*The reason I write this to you, instead of just telling you to make the necessary changes, is because I hope that you'll never have to read this. It's my plan to see her again in a few days, when I will get her to cure me of this disease I've been plagued with. When that happens, I will request the return of these letters and no one will be the wiser. However, I can't take anything, even a few more days of life, for granted. I've learned that, through hard lessons.*

*So if you are reading this, I know you will do what you*

*can to make sure she succeeds.*

*Yours,*

*Elicia*

I felt more confused. "Okay, so basically, Elicia wanted me to cure her of some spiritual problem she's had for years, if that's even possible now that she's dead. This sounds like something a medium would do, not me."

He leaned forward. "Up until a few minutes ago, I wasn't even sure I wanted to come to see you. I think, after meeting you, that I'm going to take a chance, despite my skepticism. Elicia has believed for years that she is haunted by something evil. I always thought it was a load of crap, but then she died and they're saying it's suicide. Now I ask you, a woman like this, searching for a cure for years believes she has found it. Then she kills herself? I don't think so. Elicia wanted a cure, but I want answers. She was murdered. I want to find out who did it and make sure they pay."

I felt my mouth twist. "I'm a *palm reader.* You see what I did when you came in? That's what I do. I don't see dead people. I don't cure diseases. I don't perform exorcisms. I can give you a few referrals, if you want."

He blew a frustrated breath.

"I don't want a referral. I want you. Elicia wanted you. I'm willing to pay you a lot of money, here. Can't you at least give it your best shot? I'll pay up front, whether you figure out what happened or not."

"You want me to solve a murder. I'm not a detective, unless you're looking for something linked to the spiritual plane, and even then, I'm an amateur at best. The best I can do here is muddle around in her papers and research and give you my best guess."

He slid down in his chair, laying his head against the back for a moment before bending down to open the briefcase he'd brought with him and took out a set of keys and a paper with an alarm code on it. This was going to be my geas until I figured this out, I could just feel it.

"How can I possibly refuse a request from beyond the grave? Helping people is what I do. I can't very well stop now," I said, grabbing the keys in my hand, "How am I supposed to prove that I've helped her or that I know how she died? It's such an outlandish thing to ask of someone."

He frowned, silent for a moment. "It's a good question, Miss Bedgood. It's one that I've asked myself several times since she died. I wish you could have seen her the day that she came in with these letters. She looked so tired, and yet there was a hope I saw in her eyes that I haven't seen in years.

"Elicia was an intelligent woman and determined. She moved out of her parent's house when she was only 17, to make it on her own. She worked as a waitress in New York City, putting herself through college and got her Bachelor's and Masters' degrees. She met Jackson while she was hostessing one night during her school career and I guess he just swept her off her feet. When he died, she collapsed in on herself, but it was more than that. She looked ill, down to her very soul.

"If she thought you could help, then I'm confident that her trust was not misplaced. I am the executor of her estate and that gives me some legal power. If you can convince me that you even put your best effort toward helping her, that would be enough for me."

~~~~~

The house loomed before us, a stately, Edwardian-style mansion stretching out from the brick-paved driveway, where a series of tall elms ran along, pacing the drive. Between them I could see a lake off to the left. It seemed more like an show piece than someone's home. Then again, I didn't know how long Elicia had lived in the house.

I stepped up to the door and stuck the key marked house
~~~~~

into the front door lock and stepped inside. Jordan stepped up behind me and disarmed the alarm set against the wall to our right.

"Did she die in the house?" I asked, stepping inside after him.

"Yes," he said.

"Can you please show me where?" I asked. I needed somewhere to start. I felt a little like I was playing Crime Scene Investigator and laughed at myself. What was I going to do, pull my black light out of my bag and skim the room for blood residue?

He ushered me up the shining staircase and down a long hallway. When we had passed more doorways than I could count, he opened a pair of intricate stained glass doors to our left. They opened up to a large master suite decorated in antique furniture. The sunlight caught the patterns of the stain-glass windows and placed colors across the hand woven carpet covering the hardwood floor.

Jordan started to say something, but I shook my head. I preferred silence.

I walked towards the bed, trying to get an idea about who Elicia was. I turned to the tall rectangular window that looked down into the English style tea garden. I felt movement from the corner of my eye and jumped. It was only the curtain. Feeling silly, I walked into the next room.

This room, pale lavender, was a sitting room of sorts with a delicately tiled fireplace on one side of the room. Most of the chairs were antiques, but there was one armchair near the fireplace that was sunken in the seat -a favorite. There was a doorway on the left and I walked toward it, followed by Jordan.

The light pooling in the doorway -yet another beautiful stain-glass window- was what had drawn me, but then I saw the dressing table centered in the large closet, polished light wood and Edwardian styled -in keeping with the rest of the house.

There was a mirror set against the wall, a long low tabletop scattered with various objects and a high-backed chair placed askew of the center. I don't feel things and I don't see auras, but something about that vanity caught my eye, perhaps it was the photos.

I can't remember the last time I'd seen a Polaroid, but Elicia Ford had cornered the remaining market. There where photos along the top of the mirror, scattered on the tabletop, and puddled on the floor in little piles. I snagged one from the tabletop. It was a picture of Elicia. They were all photos of Elicia, each with a different date written on it in black marker. Photo after photo after photo and each was as blank-faced as the next.

I peered at one dated two days ago, the day Elicia killed herself. The writing on the photograph was shaky, and difficult to read. The corner was bent. I stared into her eyes for a long moment. I could still feel the eyes of that thing I had seen inside of her. Suddenly, her eyes became its eyes and its teeth snapped at me. I dropped the photo and jumped back.

"Are you okay?" asked Jordan.

I shook my head and took a deep breath.

"I'm fine. Second guessing my decision right now, I think."

"Will you be all right if I go? I've got more appointments today."

"I have to be alone in here at some point," I said.

"Okay, well, if you have any questions, be sure to call."

"Thank you, Jordan," I said.

"You're welcome. Good luck, Sibilant."

He left and I picked up the photo I had dropped. I looked at it again. It seemed like a normal photograph. I picked up another one, dated one week ago: normal. I picked up one dated three weeks ago and it was the same.

Something was weird here. I grabbed all the photos from the tabletop, the mirror and the floor. There were thirty-eight pictures in all. I stacked them in piles according to date and laid them across the vanity's top. Then I opened the drawers of her dressing table.

The top one was filled with everything you'd expect in a woman's toilette: makeup, brush, perfume, fingernail file. There were three stray Polaroid pictures in it, but nothing else of significance. The second drawer had fifty-three Polaroids in it, all of them dated over the past couple months. Realizing I would need more room for this, I picked up the pictures I had sorted earlier and pulled out the drawer full of photos. I had seen a large dining room table downstairs that would be perfect for a photo comparison space.

As I walked back towards the bedroom, something struck me as odd, making me pause and back up a couple steps. In Elicia's dressing room were the usual wall lined closets of hanging clothes and several shelves of expensive shoes. From there my eyes wandered upward to the many shoe boxes over them. *That's funny*, I thought, *why would she need all those shoe boxes if her shoes were already sorted and in the closet?*

I set down my armload of photos and stood on my tiptoes to reach on of the boxes. It's no fun being short. I manage to grasp the corner of the box in one hand and slid it down without bringing the rest of them tumbling down on me. I laughed to myself at the vision of piles and piles of shoes falling around me.

I pulled up the lid of the shoe box and was not surprised to see more Polaroid photos inside. I groaned and looked up at rows above me. Might as well get started, I thought.

Hours later and it was dusk. There were 573 photos spread across the massive walnut table in front of me. Over a year's worth of photos: one for every day and all of them the same, as far as I could see. I looked at the first photo. It seemed normal enough on its own. I laid it next to the last photo, the one taken two days ago. Side by side, they still seemed the same. Her hair length was the same. Her makeup was the same. Each outfit was different, but that seemed to be the only difference.

I glared at them in the darkening room. There was something… I couldn't put my finger on it. I felt like there was something I should be seeing in the two photos.

Nevertheless, it remained outside my grasp. I took the two photos, put them in my purse and locked up the house. Whatever it was, it could wait until morning. I shuddered. Something told me that I didn't want to be in this house after dark. There were too many unresolved mysteries hanging about.

## Chapter 2

I woke from a sleep of fragmented dreams. I stretched and snuggled for a second into the warm comfort of my flannel sheets. Mmmm... Nothing better on a crisp fall day than flannel sheets.

Cursing my curls, I yanked my hair into a rubber band wishing for the hundredth time that my hair was straight with its brown. I slipped into some sweats and grabbed my keys, phone and mp3 player.

As I jogged my way to a slim body, I thought about the events of the past few days. First was my reading of Elicia: the woman with the black soul. I remembered the feeling of emptiness I'd gotten from her.

Then there were the letters, and Jordan, his request, and the gigantic estate on the edge of town. Finally, there were the photographs, all 573 of them. What was Elicia hoping to accomplish with all the picture taking? What was it she wanted to know about herself? What strange form of record-keeping involves Polaroids?

On my way into the house, I took down my little home psychic sign. If I was going to be working on Elicia's problem, I wouldn't have time to do my readings. I hung my keys up on the hook and went into the kitchen to make myself a cup of green tea. I stirred it, staring out the window at nothing in particular, thinking about the past few days. Something else must be going on here.

I sat down at my table in my little breakfast nook, and took out the two photos of Elicia, laying them out in front of me. I looked at the first photo, comparing it with the photo next to it, the woman I had seen in person, day

573, silent and apathetic.

I tried to imagine what it must have felt like to feel so empty inside. She would get up every morning and shower. Then she'd get dressed and sit down at her vanity to put on her makeup. After putting the finishing touches on her face, and brushing her long, pale blonde hair she would reach into the top drawer of her dresser and take out the Polaroid camera. Looking at her reflection in the mirror, she would then point the viewfinder toward her face. She would have good aim after 573 photos, so the photo would come out centered and as perfect as the one before it.

What did she think she would see? Then I knew what it was I had noticed before but couldn't quite identify. I knew what the difference was between the two photos.

It could be seen in Elicia's face. The first photo had a glow that the second one was missing. The second Elicia seemed more pale, blank, empty, like part of her was missing. It wasn't an obvious difference, but it was enough to peak my interest in Elicia's plight again. Did she have a clue that she was changing in some way? I needed to go back to her house and search for clues.

~~~~~

"Hi, Sibilant, this is Jordan. I was calling to get your social security number and your bank's routing number so I can do a direct deposit on your account. Also, how is the investigation going? I don't want to be a pushy client, but if you could keep me updated, I'd appreciate it. You have my card."

"Hello, baby. This is your mother. We never finished our conversation, but I wanted to say that you're right. It is your gift to do with as you please. I know you would only use it to help people. Your father says, 'hi!' by the way. I love you. Call me!"

~~~~~

I felt like something was wrong as I approached the house. It's amazing how much you can tell from the feel of an inanimate object. I unlocked the door, turned off the alarm, and set my purse down on the table in the entryway and when I walked into the dining room, I saw that my neat piles of arranged photos were scattered all over the dining room and out into the hall.

*Get out, get out now*, my brain started yelling at me. I ignored the silly thing and started picking up the photos. Placing them on the tabletop, my attention was diverted by the photo sitting centered on it.

I leaned over and felt the world zoom in on me, rushing like it does right before you pass out. There was another photo of Elicia, dated yesterday, yet it looked like a gruesome shadow or a zombie. The same blank face, it was true, but this time, she looked more like the creature I'd seen hunting her down during the reading. There were thick black circles under her eyes and her skin was the color of a 4 day corpse, pale gray and cold. Her jaw sagged low, swinging as though unhinged. The worst part was her eyes. No longer cornflower blue, they were black - like the creature's- and they stared at me. I shuddered. The writing on it was nothing more than chicken scratching.

*Oh my God, oh my God, oh my God*. This was not happening, was not possible.

"Two days after? How could it be two days after she died?" I said.

This was a message of some sort, that was obvious. What the message was, I could not pretend to know. I slipped into one of the dining chairs and slid the photo across the table till it was directly in front of me. I opened my purse and took out the other 2 photos, laying them next to the one that had been left for me. The last photo was indeed the same woman, but she was changed almost beyond recognition. This was not the Elicia of the previous photos.

The Elicia of the previous photos had the flushed skin of a living person. She had mortality written in the planes of her face. The photo that had been left for me seemed like a warped clone or photo copy. And now that I looked at it, I could see that the Elicia pictured in the new photo was translucent, and without substance. It was hard to tell, because the visage with its dead eyes was so disturbing. But now that I had the three photos side-to-side, I could see that the new picture was more like a specter than a person.

I dialed Jordan's number. No answer, just voicemail.

"Jordan, hi, this is Sibilant. I'm at the house and I had a couple of questions. You have my number. Thanks. Bye."

Okay, no help there. My next step was to go back to the dressing room to get my hands on that Polaroid camera. After that, a general search of the house was in order. And for that, I would just start from the bottom and work my way up. I didn't know what I was looking for, but a search where you're looking for anything is always better than a search where you're looking for something specific. Trying to find a needle in a haystack is much harder than trying to find straw.

~~~~~

Back at the vanity again, I could find no camera. It had been in the top drawer yesterday, but today it was nowhere to be found. In other words, someone had moved it. There were a few possibilities: a person with access to the house had come in, ruined my stacks of photos, taken the camera, gotten a hold of Elicia Ford's body and photographed it, then come back to the house and place it on the table; Elicia herself could have come back from the grave in ghost form and taken a picture of herself; or something else from the spirit realm, something with an unknown grudge against me had done this.

I had no desire to contend with possibility number one. Possibility number two would be a pain because, as I've mentioned before, I'm no medium. The dead are as silent as
~~~~~

the grave for me, no pun intended. And the third possibility scared the hell out of me. I've heard horror stories through the grapevine about people who were targeted at random by evil spirits they had angered by accident and the idea that I might have pissed something off in the ether world did not sit well with me.

My cell phone rang, interrupting my train of thought; it was Jordan.

"Hello," I said.

"Hi," he said. "You said you had some questions for me?"

"Do you know if anyone was out here at the house yesterday?"

"Elicia had a housekeeper and groundskeeper, but both of them were dismissed upon discovery of her death three days ago. It was at that point that I put her wishes in to action. I had the locks and the alarm code changed. To my knowledge you and I are the only ones who have keys. And you and I and the alarm company are the only ones with the code. Sibilant, is anything wrong? Did someone break in to the house?" he sounded concerned and considering the way I must have sounded, I didn't blame him.

"Remember the photos I found yesterday?"

"Yes."

"Well, I found a bunch more of them in boxes in her closet. Five hundred and seventy-three of them, to be exact," I said.

"Five hundred and -are you kidding?" he asked. "Why would she take all those pictures?"

"I'm still trying to figure that out. In any case, I arranged them all on the table last night before I left and this morning when I got here, they were scattered all over the floor."

"Hmmm… that doesn't sound good, does it?" he said.

"That's the least of it. In the center of what had been a bunch of neat piles was one photograph. It was dated yesterday and had a very disturbing picture of Elicia in it. Now, either someone got to her body, took a picture, dated it, and left it here after I left or something very strange is going on. And I looked everywhere for the camera this morning, but I can't find it."

"That's just bizarre," Jordan said, "Bizarre and sick. Who would do something like that?"

"I don't know, this is going to take more digging. Is there any way someone could have taken a picture of her body?"

"It's possible, if they did it a few days ago. It's not possible if they did it yesterday, because she was cremated, as per her instructions," he said.

"I find it hard to believe that someone would have taken a picture of her a few days ago, since you and I didn't even know I'd be here looking at these until yesterday afternoon. Just in case, I'd appreciate it if you could have the locks and alarm changed."

"I'll get right on that. I have a meeting in a few minutes, but I promise I'll call someone as soon as it's over."

"Thanks, Jordan, I appreciate it."

"No problem. And to be safe, you might want to consider leaving the house for now," he said before we ended the conversation.

He meant well, but I wasn't going anywhere. If I left, all evidence of mayhem would disappear behind me. So it was back to square one for me. Time to do an investigative tour of the house.

I started in the dining room, retrieving all the photos scattered about and stacking them, yet again, by date along the top of the dining table. I looked at the pictures on the walls. Elicia or her decorator had been fond of old family portraits.

Six framed family groupings were featured on the dining room walls. None were labeled and I wondered if any were even related to Elicia or her husband. I pulled them all off the wall, and pried off the backings. Nothing interesting there, just the Ford family and their photos through the years.

I checked the sideboard, and the china cabinet, but there was nothing worth noting. The same went for the professional grade kitchen. It was modern in every sense of the word, but still echoed the Edwardian theme of the house with its beautifully painted tiles lining the walls above the granite counter tops. There was a casual dining area off of the kitchen which also had a modern feel, despite the intricate wallpaper and the matching parquet flooring.

There was a comfortable modern family room off of the other side of the kitchen, hidden at the back of the house. I noticed there weren't many photos of Elicia and her husband, and none of her family. It was like she'd sprung from thin air. There were a few bookcases in the family room filled with self-help books and murder mysteries and even the occasional romance novel. I moved into the formal sitting room which was connected through an open archway to the music room.

The sitting room was another boring formal room -no bookcases, no nooks, no crannies. The music room looked out onto the garden and beyond that I could see the lake and the boat house with its dock. There was a soft glow around the grand piano from the sunlight that filtered in through the window shade.

I could find no basement or lower story entrance so for now I would assume there wasn't one. Which meant that I was now ready to move to the upper stories. The next floor housed Elicia's room, which I hadn't even begun to touch, but since it was at the end of the hallway, I decided to leave it for last.

The first room seemed to be a guest room. It was decorated in yellow: yellow rose wallpaper tangling and writhing up to the ceiling, yellow duvet cover, yellow canopy across the top of the four poster bed, yellow oriental runner across the foot of the bed. There was a small, empty closet, and dresser, empty night stand and a desk with blank stationary and a pen holder missing the pen. A door connected the guest bedroom with a bathroom. I moved through the bathroom to another room, an office.

I searched through the papers on the desk, but found only receipts and other tax-related paraphernalia. While sitting in the desk chair, I looked through the other drawers in the desk. One was filled with stationary, one with the usual desk things: paper clips, stapler, pens, white out pen, etc. and the final drawer held a battery charger and several batteries, some CDs in jeweled cases and nothing much else.

I was starting to think I'd hit a blank spot when I reached the expensive wooden filing cabinets against the wall near the closet. Inside was a veritable gold mine of research. The top drawer research seemed to be all about the Wakefield family and right away I noticed a special file labeled genealogies. I popped that one right inside my bag, along with as many of the others as I could cram into it.

The second file drawer was dedicated to the Ford family and again I made sure to grab the file labeled genealogies. There was more tax stuff in the third drawer. There was paperwork on a Ford Family Trust that I might decide to take a look at later, but for now I left it in the drawer. The last file drawer was locked and none of the keys I had fit into it. Maybe Jordan would know. I'd have to ask him later.

It was then I noticed the waning light. I hadn't seen hide or hair of the locksmith. Was it possible that he'd come without me even noticing? It was and he had. He'd left a note with my keys on the entrance table. I grabbed them as I left and locked the door on my way out. I felt something move out of the corner of my eye, but I chose to ignore it as I walked down the steps to my car. I hoped I had enough with me in my bag to keep me away from this place for a few days.

~~~~~

"I did a reading for you today, just to see how my only child was faring in the eyes of the cosmos," my mother said.

I was eating a sandwich at my favorite café downtown and talking to her via cell phone. The place is close to where I live and has a flower filled terrace area that shimmers with a pleasant light, even in the fall. It's more enjoyable to look at the flowers from in the inside, when it's so cold, however.

"Sibilant? Are you listening?" she asked.

I sighed and put down my food.

"Go ahead, Mom," I said. My mom is a strong believer in the power we have over our cards and she insists that I have the same gift for Tarot-reading as she does. "You choose not to use cards anymore, dear, but the gift doesn't go away," she often tells me.

"It was a one card draw -simpler is better over great distances. Even with our blood to connect us, my power is too limited for a complex reading from so far away. The card that I drew for you was the The Hanged Man."

I drew in my breath, reciting the words I'd memorized before kindergarten: *three triangles representing the Sacred Trinity, man with a face of anticipated surrender, submission to and acceptance of knowledge, sacrifice for a noble cause, surrender to the higher self so destiny can proceed along its intended course*.

"Of course it was," I said, and once again wondered what would become of me.

"You don't sound surprised by this. What have you been up to, Sibby?"

I sketched out the events of the past few days, which didn't do much to allay my instinctual worries about where this investigation might take me. My mother was a smart woman
~~~~~

and I valued her insights.

"What do you think about the photo I found today?" I asked, curious to know her answer.

"I'd say it was a message for sure. If I were you, I'd focus on where your skills are. You know you're all thumbs with dead people, unlike your great aunt Encilla. Your best chance at getting at the truth is to get whatever it is to communicate with you. I'll help you however I can, but everything will have more power if you do it for yourself," she said.

I knew she was right. For years she and I have been working to expand our knowledge of the deep magic, the kind that people didn't have books for or memory of. Deep magic had connections to everything, and it most always related back to the practitioner who called it out. My problem needed to be solved by me. It made sense, but it made my job more difficult, for sure.

"I'm sure we'll be talking about this again, Mom," I replied. "I'll keep you updated."

~~~~~

Upon returning home, I retrieved my mail -bills, junk mail, more bills- and wandered down the creaky little hall to the door that was the portal to my personal domain. Except that there was someone sitting in front of it. Male or female, I couldn't really tell, but he or she was snoring like a snuffling pig. I nudged the being with my foot, but there was no answer.

"'Scuse me," I said, prodding at the lump again.

The figure, a teenage girl with a mop of carroty curls framing her perfect heart face, sat up, gasping like a dying fish.

"Oh, oh, God, I'm sorry," she looked up, then stood to her feet. "I came for a reading, but you never showed up. I thought you did walk-ins."

I laughed at her aggrieved look. Ah, the angst of the young.
~~~~~

"I do walk-ins. But in case you didn't notice, my sign up front is down. I'm taking a hiatus, you might say."

"But, why?" She wailed. "I need a reading really bad. I need some guidance and I know you're not a fake. My friend told me your reading changed her life. Pleeeease? Can't you do just one for me? I'll pay whatever."

Trying not to laugh again, I opened the door and waved her in. She was short, like me, but more slender -I range toward the curvy end of the scale. I assumed her bright hair was hers from birth, and her pert little nose was just snub enough to make it seem like she was sniffing out secrets. Her lips were plump, generous in fashion and pale pink. Her clothes ranged on the conservative side, but she had on the most outrageous blue-beaded necklace.

She sat with a loud thump in the chair, sending a puff of dust motes swirling around her like a dirty halo.

"My name is Sophie and I hate it," she said. "I wanted a name like Kate or Anne -something classic that doesn't make people think of old maids. But no."

"Okay, Sophie, is there something in particular you want to know? A question you want answered?" I made myself, by force of will, keep a straight face.

"Um, yeah. I want to know what I should do with my life. My parents want me to be a teacher, but that's so gross. I want to be a movie star," she said, with a toss of her curly head.

I held out my hands and said, "Here, place your hands in mine and try to relax."

She placed her hands in mine and the answer rocked me back in my chair and made me wonder at the design of destiny. It was one of those rare readings where the person in question is touched by the universe in a way that many aren't. This girl had a calling in life.

I slid my hands out from under hers. She looked up at me, surprised.

"That's it?"

"That's it," I said.

"I thought it would take longer, but whatever. So, what's my answer?"

I started to speak, then stopped. I tried again. Nothing would come out of my mouth.

"Oh my God, what is it? Is something wrong? Am I, like, going to die?" Her eyes widened and she bit her lower lip.

"Someday, dear, you will die, everyone does. But that is not what your reading told me. You're to be my apprentice," I said, wondering how this would further complicate my already crazy life. I'd never taken on an apprentice before. It was not an uncommon circumstance among practitioners, but it was something that wasn't entered into with carelessness.

"You mean I'm going to be a psychic, too?" she asked. "Will I be able to tell the future? Will I be able to see if anyone is going to ask me to prom?"

Talk about someone who had no grasp of the responsibility of using ones' gifts. I guess that's what I was supposed to teach her.

"First of all, I'm not a psychic. I'm a *Reader.* As you just saw, I read palms. Secondly, I don't know what your gift is yet. It's strong, but you might be a medium or a palm reader, you might work with horoscopes or tarot cards.

"You might not be a *Reader* at all. I don't know yet. For now, you should come over a few afternoons a week so we can work together on figuring out what your gift is. Have you noticed any unusual abilities?"

"Nope, not one. Unless you count my ability to fall all over myself. I'm a total klutz. Other than that, I don't think so. I'll think about it, though," she said, which sounded sensible.

"I have other things I need to finish tonight, so why don't you come over day after tomorrow, when you've finished with school? Then we can try some exercises to work out your particular gift is," I said.

Still gabbling about all the things she would soon know about her friends, she took herself out the door and presumably home to parents. I slumped in my chair and wondered what I had done to piss off the universe. Had I done something in a past life that I needed to pay penance for?

~~~~~

"Sibilant, hi, this is Jordan."

"Hi."

"I was wondering if you were going to the memorial service for Elicia tomorrow?"

"I hadn't planned on it, no," though I was curious about who might attend and if it could be pertinent to my puzzle.

"I could come get you and we could drive over together. We should talk about some of the details surrounding Elicia's death," he said.

"Okay, fine with me."

"Great, I'll come for you at 10AM. We'll probably have lunch after, if that's okay. I have a meeting at 2, so I need to get lunch in before that."

"See you tomorrow then," I said, wondering what new information about Elicia would be revealed.

"See you tomorrow."
~~~~~

# Chapter 3

I got my sweatshirt, brushed my tangled chestnut hair back into a ponytail and went for my morning jog. The crisp fall air was refreshing and gave me a clear head, which was good because I'd been feeling foggy for days. As I ran down to the path overlooking the creek, I listened to the morning birds singing.

My breath frosted before me and I started daydreaming about having a normal life. What must it be like to be an ordinary person out walking my dog, having my morning exercise before I went off to my ordinary job? Instead I was exercising before I went to the funeral of the woman who had died mere days after meeting me. What a world.

"Badger! Badger! Come!" I heard, followed by a piercing whistle. I saw a large chocolate lab headed straight for me.

"Oof!" was all I could manage as it ran right into my legs. I had the presence of mind to grab the dangling leash before it could take off again but, it seemed Badger was a jumper by nature.

"I am so sorry! Badger, sit down!" I handed the leash right over to the tall -very tall, although every guy over 5'8" is tall to me- man in jogging shoes approaching me.

"Admit it. You've trained him to help you pick up girls," I said, laughing and looking way up to see his dark blue eyes.

"Well, aren't you smart. Usually, the ladies just fall for my charms and forget all about my suspicious looking runaway dog scenario," he said, showing what must be a gazillion white teeth.

"You mean, they fall over," I said.

We both laughed. It was nice. We were having a moment. Is it a moment when you call it a moment?

"Poor Badger is just a pawn in your sick little games." Was I flirting? I believe I was, indeed.

"Seeing as how Badger and I just moved into this neighborhood, you seemed a likely first catch," he said, and ran his hands behind Badger's ears, giving them a hardy scratching.

"I'm Paul," he said holding out a hand, which I took.

"Hi, I'm Sibilant."

"Sibilant," he said, taste-testing it.

"What brings you to our neck of the woods, Paul?"

"Nothing exciting, just my job."

"What do you do?"

"Don't laugh," he said, looking embarrassed.

"I can't make any promises," I said.

"I'm an accountant."

I giggled a little but then gave him my most charming of smiles. People often told me I had a nice mouth -if a bit on the small side- and at least my teeth were straight. "That's a perfectly legitimate form of employment, if a tad boring. You should try being me."

"Why? What do you do?" he asked.

"Don't laugh," I said.

"I can't make any promises," he said.

"I'm a palm reader," I said.

Pause, and then, "Like what, exactly? Life lines and love lines and all that?"

"I do personal readings, but most of the time they're just messages that a person needs to hear. Sometimes it's that they need to go on a trip. Sometimes it's that they need to change careers. I've weirded you out, haven't I?"

"That depends," he said. "Do you do readings for animals? Badger's been acting strange. Can you find out if he needs to change careers, say like instead of laying on my couch all day long, he'd rather be a telemarketer or something?"

I smiled. "Let's take a look, shall we?"

I squatted down, took the dog's head in my hands and stared into his eyes for a second.

"Oh dear," I said with a serious expression on my face. "This is disturbing."

"What is it?" he asked, his blue eyes lit with concern. It was adorable.

"He wants to be an IRS agent," I said, with a sad look.

"Oh, man. Badger, how could you? Talk about sleeping with the enemy," he said to me.

"Listen, maybe we could set up some counseling or something? I'm going to need a lot of help to cope with this news," he grinned.

"It seems like the only sensible course of action," I said, after which I stood up, leaned in, and kissed him, locking my arms around his neck. After a few delicious lusty moments, I pulled away, smiling. "Why didn't you tell me you were back from your office retreat?" I asked.

"We were hoping to surprise you. I know where and when you jog, so that made it easier."

Paul was my boyfriend of two years. We'd met through a friend of his, who'd come to see me after a bad break-up, poor thing. Afterward, she'd met a great guy and gotten married a few months later. I attended as Paul's date and we've been together ever since.

"You're such a goofball," he whispered, nuzzling my neck.

"Hey, you played along with it," I laughed. "Oh! You'll never guess what's happened. I mean, I would have told you sooner, but your office had to pick a resort that banned all electronics."

"Well, correct me if I'm wrong, but I think that's why it's called a retreat," he said. I rolled my eyes and looked down at my watch.

"Eep! I'm going to be late. Listen, come over for dinner so I can tell you all about it."

"Okay, love you."

"You too," I said, waving good-bye as I jogged away.

~~~~~

I was sitting on the stoop playing with the little good luck charm I always wear. It's a simple pendant, circular, with my birth date and birthstone embedded in it. I held it up, watching it twirl back and forth in different directions, while the sun caught the small emerald and flashed it around like a beacon. That was what I was doing when Jordan drove up.

I must have looked like a little girl sitting there in my hippie-like black straw dress with the black and silver shawl I wore flung over my shoulders. I was leaning back, braced on one arm while the other, as I said, held up the pendant in front of me.

His car pulled up and I got up and into it. I don't pay much attention to car types -as long as it gets me from point A to point B, I'm satisfied- but this one was expensive. The interior was the soft cushy leather that some people tend to brag about and there were a variety of flashy looking accessories to be admired by the eye.

He turned down the easy-listening station that was on the radio and asked me if the temperature in the car was comfortable.

"Yes, it's just fine," I said and that was all the conversation we had until we reached the memorial service. I let the music wash over me as I did some meditative thinking.

The service was like every funeral I'd ever seen on television. People were wearing black. There was a priest
~~~~~

reading scripture. Everyone was silent as the ashes were interred, except for a few quiet sniffles.

It was surreal for me to be here in this place, mourning the death of a woman I didn't know. I looked at the people around me -about twenty-five or so total- and wondered who they were and how they knew Elicia. Was she a stranger to them as she was to me? Most of them were somber, with blank expressions on their faces. The only person that caught my attention was a woman standing near the priest holding a handkerchief to her dry eyes, as though wishing she had tears to fill it. Her suit looked expensive even to my novice eyes -it was tailored to fit like a glove. Jordan looked at me and followed my gaze to the woman sitting near the center of the other grouping of chairs. His jaw clenched.

At the close of the ceremony, Jordan and I rose in unison. He steadied my arm as I stumbled over a crack in the marble floor. I straightened myself and looked into the eyes of the woman I'd noticed before, only this time she was mere inches away from me.

"You've been avoiding my calls," she said to Jordan.

"You might have noticed, I've been busy handling the details of the estate,"Jordan said.

"I just want what is mine by right," she said, her mouth twisted into a puckered frown.

"Jordan?" I said, looking at him, confused.

"Not now, Sibilant," he said in my ear.

The woman heard it and turned toward me, hissing through her teeth.

"This is between Mr. Long and myself. I'd appreciate it if you would give us some privacy."

"By all means," I said, starting to step back. Jordan grabbed my arm.

"Excuse us, please, Mrs. Ford. We have business to attend to. I will get back to you during normal office hours."

"I have every right to those things! They were my son's!" she said, spittle flecking at the edges of her mouth.

Jordan shook his head, then turned and walked away, with my short legs running to catch up.

She followed, screaming obscenities at him. I ignored her and stepped into the car as soon as Jordan unlocked it.

"You'll be sorry!" she screamed as we drove off.

I wasn't afraid of her. She was an angry old woman. Yet her reflection bouncing back at me in the side mirror reminded me of the creature I'd seen at Elicia's reading: full of malice and absent of reason.

~~~~~

We were silent on the drive to the small diner Jordan had suggested for lunch. Nothing was going the way I thought it was going to. I was still curious about the woman. Jordan had called her Mrs. Ford and she'd spoken of her son. She must have been Elicia's mother-in-law. Why was she so angry?

When we were seated and had place our orders, Jordan said, "I'm sure the funeral was more of a trial then either of us were expecting. I'm sorry. I had no idea that woman would be there. She never made it a point to be involved in Elicia's life, so why would she bother with her after death?"

"It's fine," I said. "I mean, I'm sorry she made such a scene at the funeral. That must have hurt you."

He took a sip of water.

"It did. I was hoping that the funeral would help me feel better -give me a last chance to say good-bye. I feel more confused now," he said, and his eyes gazed out the window and seemed to observe the people and cars hurrying by.

"I've lost a few people in my life, my grandparents when I was still a child. I've never lost someone as an adult. It must be hard on the soul," I said.

"I loved her the minute I met her. It sounds so silly. I'm a lawyer, a being of reason and logic. But regardless of my
~~~~~

years of training in the art of rhetoric, when Elicia walked through my door seven years ago and looked at me with those sad blue eyes, I was lost," He said with a gentle smile.

I understood then. His sadness was a deep longing for the woman he loved.

"Did you ever tell her how you felt?" I asked.

"No, I couldn't add to her burdens. You don't understand. This is a woman who was haunted all her life by a darkness that I can't put a name to. I thought maybe she was abused as a child or that she'd suffered some great loss, but now I realize it was more than that. In any case, I could see that she had enough to worry about. I gave her what I could. I gave her my support and my help. I eased her burdens, but I kept my feelings to myself."

"Tell me about her. Tell me what you know and how it was you came to be her lawyer," I said.

"As I said, she came to me seven years ago, after the death of her husband. She had loved him a great deal, but because of difficulties with his mother, she didn't feel like she could trust the Ford family's law firm. So she came to me, to write out the details of her will, to plan for the future and to get legal advice.

"She told me nothing about her past. I didn't ask. It wasn't relative to her life at that point. She mentioned that her husband had died in a plane crash a few months before, leaving her everything in his will. She told me that his mother had taken the trust money away from her, but that was a drop in the bucket compared to everything he had earned in his lifetime. He was quite a bit older than her, but she was no gold digger. She loved him, I could tell.

"Over the years I've seen her at every opportunity that could present itself. The last few years have been hard ones for her. I could see that something was eating away at her spirit, but she never said what. She went on many trips across the country and around the world. I knew she was searching for someone who could help her, but I didn't know it was you. It seems so ironic now, she looked everywhere for someone like you, and you were here in her hometown."

His eyes searched mine with surprising intensity.

"I know she didn't kill herself. It doesn't make any sense. What did you tell her?"

"How did she do it, supposedly?" I asked, sidestepping the question.

"Like you'd figure a rich, depressed woman would: she swallowed a bottle full of sleeping pills. She took them at night, after her housekeeper had gone to bed and by the time the poor woman came to work the next day, she was gone. Gone forever," he said, his voice becoming harsh. I could see his eyes watering as he attempted to compose himself.

"She never said anything about what she was looking for?" I asked.

"Not in specifics. I always figured she was suffering from something that had happened in her past. Who knows, maybe she was soul sick and hoping to find a cure for it. Is that what you do? Are you some kind of spiritual healer?"

I shook my head.

"I'm the furthest thing from a healer that there is. I deliver messages, that's all."

He looked angry and grabbed my wrist in metal-hard fingers. "And just what message did you deliver to her? Did you tell her to kill herself?" he asked.

"Of course not! Jordan, I know that you're looking for answers. So am I. I'm on your side, remember? Or do I have to remind you that you came to *me*?" His grip loosened. "Not that I'm sure I want to help. Those photos..." I said, and shuddered, thinking about the photos.

"Speaking of which, not to change the subject or anything, but I don't suppose you have the pictures on you?"

"Actually, I've been afraid to leave it anywhere, for fear it will disappear. I couldn't handle being crazy on top of everything," I said, smiling.

I reached into my large bag and pulled out the three photos I'd saved from the stash I'd found at the house. I had attached them together with a rubber band, which I popped off and over my wrist. I then laid them out in order and face up for Jordan's perusal. First the one that was dated over a year ago. Then, the one dated the day Elicia killed herself. Finally, I laid out the picture I had found on the dining table, the picture dated 2 days after Elicia died. When I laid it in front of Jordan, he drew back eyes popping, mouth gulping breaths of air.

"Oh my God," he said, then leaned over for a better look.

"This is not Elicia," he said. "There is no way. First of all, look at this thing's eyes, this is not a dead body. The eyes are looking at you. Whatever it is, it is sentient, it is alive -in a manner of speaking- and it is malevolent. Elicia is dead. I identified her body myself. I touched her hair," his voice rose in a half sob. "This thing, this spirit or monster or whatever it is, is not Elicia. She's dead and cremated and in a vault right now."

He was vehement, he was certain, and I believed him. The truth was, I knew it couldn't have been Elicia in the physical sense. She was dead, after all. But being dead didn't erase her from existence; there was still her spirit. The question was: had it moved on or was it still somewhere on earth? This photo seemed to indicate otherwise.

I put the photos back in my gigantic bag.

"Well, I think we've established what this picture is *not*," I said.

"Please tell me if any other photos show up?" he said.

"I will," I said, privately thinking I would rather spare him the grief. "The weird thing is, I couldn't find the camera anywhere. And I'm sure that I saw it in Elicia's dressing room that first day."

"It'll probably turn up. Listen, I hate to cut this short, but if I'm going to get you home before my meeting, we should go now."

He drove me home and I went back into my house full of more questions, if that was possible.

~~~~~

"Hey, it's Paul. I'm on my way over with the dog and some nachos from La Comida. See you in a few."
~~~~~

# Chapter 4

"So let me summarize: a woman came to have a reading done, got what she came for, left, died three days later, and put a letter to you in her will." Paul brushed his charcoal hair out of his eyes, putting on his best pensive look. He was the hottest accountant around, in my opinion. I leaned down to pet Badger, who was curled up at my feet, as usual. It's like he thought he was my personal foot warmer.

"Don't forget the part where I'm supposed to figure out who or what killed her, despite the fact that the coroner says she swallowed a bunch of pills. This is pretty much an impossible task."

"Yeah, remind me again... when did you turn into Nancy Drew?"

I sighed and leaned back against couch, closing my eyes. "I don't know. I just don't know. I couldn't walk away from helping her. After that reading, I could believe almost anything. I mean, I know what I saw. I saw that she was being haunted or maybe hunted is a more appropriate description. To get that letter from her, from days before she died, saying that she was going to die. I don't know. I just think there's something there."

"So, what's the plan from here on out?" Paul asked, feet out, enjoying the cozy fire.

"You're really taking an interest in my little mystery, aren't you?" I said.

"You've been to my house. My bookshelves are lined with murder mysteries and this surprises you?" He laughed.

"Point taken," I said. "My list thus far is short: search the house, read all the research, and contact anyone I can to verify the information and tell me more about Elicia's life. So far I don't know anything about her except that she married a really rich guy whose family hates her."

Paul rubbed his hands together -a gleeful child at Christmas couldn't as excited as he was about digging into a bunch of old files.

“Let's get started!” he said.

~~~~~

I went back to the bag and took out the files of both the Wakefields and the Fords. After my conversation with the elder Mrs. Ford, I was interested in what was going on with the Ford family. I slid the folder onto the table in front of us and flipped it open. Instead of the family tree I was expecting, there were a series of letters. Three of them were from Ford family members and the last was from a man who signed his name only as Struthers.

The first was dated ten years ago and was marked with the number one. It read:

*Mrs. Ford,*

*I understand your passion for the family that you've become a part of, but I really can't tell you what you want to know. My knowledge of the Ford family ancestors is spotty at best, despite the years of research I've done for them. I can give you a few medical records dating back as far as the late 1900's, but I'm afraid they won't tell you much.*

*Also, the information you wanted about their location of origin is currently unavailable. I can tell you where they ended up when they immigrated to the United States in the early 1820's. But whether they were originally English, French, or Turkish, I could not tell you.*

*I'll be sure to send you a copy of the family tree that I*
~~~~~

*am in possession of, along with some of the letters I have from various family ancestors. I have to warn you, though. Some of the other members of our family would not hold well with you researching this particular branch of the family tree. I don't know what your husband told you, but some of the Fords act as though they are part of a cult or secret society. Things that I've heard, stories from when I was a child, would make your hair curl.*

*I'll tell you what I can, believe me. But what I can tell you isn't much. You could also try asking my cousin, Wilmer Ford Astonia.*

*Thank you for your interest and your letter.*

*Sincerely,*
*Clara Ford Hawkins*

The next letter was labeled with a circled four and was again from Clara.

*Mrs. Ford,*

*I know it's been some length of time since my last letter, but I recently came across some information that I think would aid your quest. I met a man by the name of Lyle Struthers whose specialty is genealogies. He has a number of sources that would be quite at the disposal of someone willing to pay enough money for them.*

*I hope this helps. Please let me know how your research is progressing.*

*Sincerely,*
*Clara Ford Hawkins*

At the close of the letter, there was a name and number for Lyle Struthers. I took that letter and laid it on top of the one I'd already read.

"Look at this one, Sib," said Paul, sliding another sheet of paper across the table.

The next page was a hand drawn family tree. At the bottom of the tree was Elicia and the tie she had with her husband, Jackson Ford. It traced up to his mother, Phyllis and his father Magnus. It passed over his mother's background, but gave his father's parents. In fact, without tracing any women in the family at all, it seemed like an endless line of Ford men, reaching past six generations.

Paul also had the next paper, which was a letter from Wilmer Astonia.

*Mrs. Ford,*

*I agree, it does seem strange that you can only put together a partial family tree for your husband's family. You say that you have your husbands brother's birth certificate? To my knowledge, your husband never had a brother. Is there a possibility that he died as an infant? Did you try to find a death certificate?*

*No one in my family is keeping any secrets, that I am aware of. It's true that there have been a few family feuds over the years, but nothing that would cause anyone to hide the existence of a baby.*

*I'm sorry that I couldn't be of more help.*

*Sincerely,*

*Wilmer Astonia*

The last papers were not letters, at all -they were more like reports. They were from the man mentioned Clara Hawkins' letter, Lyle Struthers. The first seemed to be a list of seven names, all of them were Fords that weren't located on the family tree that was sketched out on the previous page. Next to each of the names was a date, which I assumed was a birth date. And next to each of the birth dates was a word:

confirmed or unconfirmed. At the close of the first letter from Lyle Struthers was a short message:

*As you can see from what I've found in the Ford family tree, there was indeed a brother born two years after your husband. I have not yet found out what happened to him, but there are six others like him, with little or no record of birth that I've discovered in the family. I don't know what it means yet, but I will keep in communication with you.*

*-Struthers*

"Wow," said Paul. "What is going on in the Ford family?"

"It looks like a creepy skeleton in the closet scenario to me."

The second letter from Struthers was a photocopy of a book on mythology. The entry was titled *Doppelganger: The One With No Shadow.*

*The doppelganger has long been a creature of folklore, said to cast no shadow, and have no reflection. A doppelganger might follow a person through their life, providing misleading or malicious advice. They might also plant ideas in a victim's mind. Some legends purport that a doppelganger is an evil image of its victim: a ghostly counterpart. Others believe it is a demon, sent to torture innocent mortals. There are also folktales of doppelgangers being harbingers of death.*

*Whatever the circumstances surrounding a doppelgangers appearance, it is considered to be an evil, malicious being. It is also understood that doppelgangers bring about the most primitive beliefs of the magic of twins, whether reflection or shadow.*

Under the photocopy was a short note: *This may help you to understand what it is you're looking for.*

I reread the photocopy and couldn't help the shiver that paced down my spine. What did doppelgangers have to do with Elicia's dead husband? With each piece of information I absorbed, I found myself more confused and dismayed. I had no desire to unleash a doppelganger, whatever I might do. We had heard of them in practitioner circles, too.

Doppelgangers were the thing of scary bed time tales. A doppelganger picked its victim at random, most of the time, but if a hapless person stumbled into one, it would become the brunt of a systematic destruction. A doppelganger was a relentless killer, driving its victim mad.

I was having problems relating the information about the unknown relatives to an evil, shadowless creature. I laid the page on top of the others. The last letter from Struthers was another photocopy. This one was a receipt for a hotel outside of some town in Virginia. And that was it -no note, no doppelganger reference, and no obvious connection with the Ford family. Once again, I was standing in front of a big dead end.

~~~~~

Hours later, I sat in the chair by my window, soothing mint tea warming my hands as I stared without purpose into the darkening world outside. I had slipped into a trance-like state, breathing in and out, slow and deep. I had given up my hold on my surroundings and became a being of thought alone, minus my physical body or a purpose. It was calming, but when the sun finally made its way over the foothills in the distance, I was brought back to myself with a start as Paul leaned in to kiss my neck.

"You seem lost," he said.

"That's a good way of putting it," I said.

"You'll figure it out, Sib. You have a way of cutting to
~~~~~

the heart of things," said Paul.

"If I could just get everything we've learned so far to line up, I think I'd feel better, but there doesn't seem to be an order or a plan in all this research that Elicia dug up.

"Who's to say if the Fords or the Wakefields have anything to do with what happened to her?"

"You think there's a third possibility?" asked Paul.

"I'm not sure yet, but when I have an inkling I'll let you know," I said.

~~~~~

I was walking along the bike path, cooling down after a long jog. Feeling a little disappointed that Paul and Badger couldn't join me, I was still looking forward to seeing them later. It was one of those gray cloudy days in fall, which always indicate a weather switch into winter. There was a cool breeze whipping through the nearby trees, calming down my rapid heartbeat and bathing my flushed cheeks. I love fall.

A prickle on the back of my neck started my feeling of unease and I turned to see a man walking toward me. He was tall and lean, dressed in a long brown coat that reached his calves and black military boots. His blond hair fell to his shoulders, long bangs sweeping across his cheeks with Raphael-like curls. His stare must have been what I felt from behind, they were filled with the knowledge of a power that was not of this earth, steel gray and leering with malice. This was in direct contrast to his beautiful countenance.

He approached and I felt my tension mount, as I backed up a few paces and wrapped my arms around myself. I examined him, glancing at his feet as he strode in large steps toward me -I knew what had made me uneasy- and there was no shadow beneath his feet, like he was a projection of a real person.

He stopped until he was speaking into my face. I couldn't move, petrified and rooted to the spot.
~~~~~

"You think you will find it, but you won't. You have no idea what forces you are dealing with. We are as old as time itself, immortal and perfect. We rule the world and will not to give that up for some silly little girl who thinks she's gifted. Stop your search or you will end up like her."

His hand closed around my throat, blocking off my air. I clawed at his hands, nails scraping deep into the skin of his wrists, but soon the world went gray, purple, and finally black.

~~~~~

I woke from the dream, panting, and felt my throat, but there was not a trace of soreness. I've had vivid dreams before, but this was past the dark realm of sleep. It had felt so real, like it was happening or was going to happen. Trying to tell myself that it was side effect of the reading I had done last night, I dwelt on the images fading from my mind. They were hard to dismiss.

I tried to put order to the information I'd come across thus far. Ten years ago, Elicia had gone searching for information on her husband's background and family tree. She found some information, but also a lot of brick walls. It seemed there were a few family members, all male, who went missing after birth, without any trace of their whereabouts. She communicated with a few family members who weren't able to give her much. Then finally she got some information from Lyle Struthers. A few years later, her husband died.

She hired Jordan Long, and then, later on, traveled around the world searching for something -it is unknown what that was. At some point, she started taking photos of herself on a daily basis. Then she met me, killed herself, and left everything, including her research for potential cure behind her. Piece after piece of puzzle, and yet I still felt like I was on number 3 of a 1,000 piece jigsaw.

After a jog, a shower, and a quick breakfast, I pulled out the folder labeled Wakefield. This was a long and more
~~~~~

detailed family tree. When opened, it stretched across the table, naming ancestors from as long ago as the 1600's. I studied it carefully for a long time, noting the names of Elicia's parents: Victor and Lydia Wakefield. It seemed that Elicia was an only child.

Her family came from Germany, and migrated to the United States around the same time as the Ford family, settling in New England. The original family name, Wagner, was changed around the time of the first World War. This made sense, and I had read about how common it was for immigrated families to do this sort of thing before moving to another town to face persecution. It was a large family tree, but I was able to trace down to Elicia's branch with little trouble, as the way had been marked with little penciled arrows.

If only the way to solve this mystery was as clearly marked.

# Chapter 5

A hesitant tapping at my door indicated that my new apprentice was outside waiting to be ushered in to the spirit realm. I took a long breath and reminded myself to have patience before going to the door.

"Ummm… hi," Sophie said and fiddled with her scarf.

"We're going out," I said, grabbing my purse and keys.

"Out where?" she asked, shifting from one foot to the other.

"To a place that's just filled with atmosphere," I said. I was taking her to the Ford mansion. I wanted to see what she would detect from the house of death. If she didn't sense anything, then I would know that much more about her gift.

She jabbered at me the entire trip, telling me about her friends' reactions to her newly discovered powers.

"They were all jealous, of course. No one understands the burden I bear as one of the gifted," she sniffed and glanced at me out of the corner of her eye.

I, on the other hand, was wondering what in the world was I going to do with a teenager following me around everywhere.

All the words popped out of her head as soon as she saw the house in front of us. Her head fell back as we walked up the driveway, taking in the height and beauty of the house. I had to admit, it was quite a sight with the fall sunlight filtering through the trees against the brick. I took a deep breath of the cool air and enjoyed the smell of dying leaves. The fall colors were out in full, orange, red, yellow, and brown.

"This is amazing. Whose is it?" she asked.

"It belongs to a former client of mine. She wanted me to find out if there were any spiritual forces at play on her property. I think that she sensed something was off. In any case, she's dead now, and I'm here to try and figure out why," I said.

"So, you're like a psychic detective? Like that TV show?" she asked, excited.

"No, no. Not at all, dead people are not my forte, so please stop throwing around the word psychic, okay?" I said.

"So why did you want to bring me here?" she asked, hands on hips.

"Well, as I told you before, I'm not sure what your spiritual gift is yet. There must be some reason that I'm supposed to guide you. I've been here before and there are forces at play in this house, but I'm not sure what they are. I thought this might be a good opportunity to test you out, so to speak.

"What I want you to do is just relax and tell me if you see anything interesting while we're digging through the house. If you see any other people besides the two of us, tell me. If you sense anything, like emotions or a presence or you hear or touch or taste anything strange, tell me. Whatever you come across that seems strange, consider it something I need to know."

"Okay, but I have to be home by 9. That's what my mom said," Sophie said.

"Not a problem. So first off, just looking at the house, do you sense anything about it, good or evil? Do you see a halo of color surrounding it, like an aura?"

"No, it pretty much looks like a house to me," she said, squinting her eyes and squishing up her face.

I laughed. "You don't have to concentrate quite so hard," I said, "Come on, let's go inside."

I unlocked the door, turned off the alarm, and this time made a bee-line for the dining room. There were no photos scattered all over the floor. Instead, they were neatly laid in a circle in the center of the long table, concentric ring after concentric ring, piled over and on top of each other. In the center of the photos were two new photos of Elicia. Both photos looked identical to the one that I had found the day before yesterday. The first one was dated yesterday.

The second one said simply, "Stop looking" in chicken scratch handwriting.

"Oh my God," said Sophie. "What is that, oh my god, oh my god."

I looked at her, she was stumbling over the leg of one of the dining chairs, staring at the photo I was holding in my hand, the one with "Stop Looking" written on it and pointing. Her face was even more pale than her pale skin usually allowed for. She was shaking and as I turned, she jumped back, away from me.

"What's wrong? Are you okay, Sophie? What do you see?"

"That thing, that thing is wrong. There's something very, very wrong with it. And it wants to kill," she gasped and then started retching. I slipped the photos into the pocket of my jacket. I touched her arm.

"Sophie, it's okay, there's nothing there. It's just a photo. I'm not even sure if it's real," I said and squeezed her shoulder.

Her eyes were wild and wide, she shook her curly head. "It's not okay. It's very real. You take my word for it. I've never felt as sure about anything as I do about that thing."

"Okay," I said, in my most soothing voice. "So, you said it wants to kill. Who does it want to kill?"

Her eyes were cold and distant as she said, simple and direct, "It wants to kill everyone."

~~~~~

I went upstairs after this, leaving her sitting down in the kitchen with a glass of cold water. I figured I would give her a little break before asking her to call upon her gift again. This was all very interesting to the practitioner in me, because I felt nothing at all from the photos and I didn't feel like Elicia's spirit was out to get me or anyone else.

I found myself, once again, wondering what Sophie's gift would turn out to be. Maybe she was some kind of barometer for evil, sensing as it waxed and waned. It would take more experimentation for me to pin it down. The extra senses were not a perfected science.

I gathered up the rest of the Ford files I'd left in the filing cabinet. Pondering over the stack of papers in my purse, I was just on my way back down the stairs, when I heard the distinctive sound of a key in a lock and watched, from my position at the bottom of the stairs, as the door opened and Phyllis Ford walked into the house, talking over her shoulder to a man she was with. She sputtered to a halt when she saw me standing at the foot of the stairs.

"What are you doing here?" she asked.

"What are *you* doing here?" I repeated.

"I am here to gather up my son's things and take them home with me," she said, drawing up to her full height, chin lifted. "You have not answered my question. What conceivable reason could you have for being in this house, which has been in the Ford family for generations? Until *she* left it all to charity."

"I'm here at Jordan Long's request. He asked me to go through some of the papers and other things of Elicia's," I said.

"Are you a lawyer from Mr. Long's firm?" she asked.

"I'm more like an employee for Jordan," I said. I left
~~~~~

the steps. She was glancing around the room and her eyes took in the empty spots on the wall where I had taken down many of the family photos. I moved over to the table, and she got a glance at the rings of photos on the table. She got distracted, which is what I was hoping for.

"What are these?" she asked. I got the feeling she was used to having all her questions answered.

"These are photos that Elicia took of herself," I said.

"Why?" she said.

"That's what I'm trying to figure out," I said.

She came over to the table and held one of the photos in her manicured hand.

"That poor woman was out of her mind," she said. "I had suspected, but this is more than anything I could have imagined."

"Did you know Elicia well?" I asked.

"Only as well as any mother-in-law knows her daughter-in-law. My son didn't feel the need to consult me before marrying her. I didn't even get to meet her before they got married. He just came home from a business trip one day and there she was, his wife," she sniffed. "If you'll excuse me, I have some photos to retrieve that don't have the face of this dead woman on them."

~~~~~

Sophie whimpered like a beaten puppy in the car all the way home.

"I'm sorry, I had no idea you would react like that," I said. "If you want, we can hold off on your apprenticeship until after I'm done with my work over at the house."

"No. Seriously, I'm really enjoying it. I just don't like those gross photos. Maybe you could lock them up in silver or something."

"Silver?" I asked.

"Sure, isn't that a metal that evil hates? You know, the
~~~~~

whole silver bullet thing?"

"Oh, uh, I could do that, I guess," I said, wondering what in the heck this girl was talking about. "I'll call you about our next appointment, but right now I'm thinking early on next week would work for me."

"Can't we do it on a Saturday?" She asked, "Then we could spend the whole day together!"

I shuddered. "My Saturdays are pretty busy around here." I said.

"Well, whatever. You call me and we'll pick something. Byiiie!" She said and slammed the door, running up to her house.

~~~~~

Folder Label: Francis Johnson Ford

Folder Contents: Birth Certificate, Biography, and Short Explanation

Birth Certificate: Born June 6, 1954;

Father: Magnus Wade Ford;

Mother: Phyllis Anne Ford;

Time: 2051;

Attending Physician: Daniel W. Blake, M.D.

Biography: Francis Ford was born at the family's home where he lived for the first 6 months of his life. For unknown reasons, he and his wet nurse were then removed to an undisclosed location for the next 3 years. The nurse was let go at that time, and moved across the country to a small town in Idaho. From what I pieced together, she was given a monthly allowance from the Ford Family Trust till she died 35 years later. It was after she left that the trust began to pay a man named Bay Willard.

Willard was born in Texas, worked on a ranch for 10 years and ended up in prison for beating a man to death in a bar. The Fords hired him right out of prison,
~~~~~

with a special dispensation to let him work out of state. It is uncertain what he was hired for or where he went, but my guess is that he ended up finishing the job that the nurse started.

In this same time period there were several unusual purchases made by the Ford Family Trust: a surplus of iron bars, state of the art security equipment for the time period, several libraries worth of books, laboratory equipment, medical supplies and bolt upon bolt of white cotton cloth. I could find nothing more, though I hired many people and spent much money.

Short Explanation: When I asked my husband about his brother, he had no idea what I was talking about. I showed him the birth certificate that I'd run across in my casual attempt at a genealogy and he dismissed it, saying it was probably a stillborn. He wasn't about to ask his mother about it; he's always been a mama's boy. I didn't feel right about pushing it while he was alive, so I let the whole thing go until his death. What is here in this folder represents the very first part of that investigation.

~~~~~

"What happened to you, Sibby? Usually you call me every day and I haven't heard from you in days! What's going on?"

"Mom, I'm fine. I've just been busy, is all." I explained the events of the last few days while she listened in silence. One thing I can say about my mother is that she knows when to talk your ear off and when to shut up.

"And this girl, Sophie, she has some sort of untapped gift that sensed evil emanating from the photo?" she asked.

"Yes, it was weird. When we were outside the house everything was fine, she felt nothing weird. Even in the house was fine. Until she saw those two photos. She flipped out,
~~~~~

screaming and gagging like she was going to throw up. I've never seen anything like it."

"You know, it sounds like what used to happen to Aunt Lucy before she died, God rest her soul. I remember this one time we were in a five and dime store trying to decide on what candy to buy with our allowance. A man came up to us, looked perfectly nice and normal to me, but Lu just up and started screaming in the middle of the store. She cried and cried and pointed at the man and said, 'You're such a bad man, I'm gonna tell my momma. You hurt the little girl, you bad, bad man! Go away before I tell my daddy on you!' And when she got to the part about the little girl, he turned tail and ran. Next thing we knew he was in the paper, saying he'd been arrested. He was wanted in three states for kidnapping.

"She was like that for many years. Had a haunted life, Lu did. A hard life. At the end, she wouldn't leave her house at all, became a complete agoraphobic. We were never sure if it was because of her gift or because of her husbands' death in that construction accident."

"Well, I'll be sure to keep that in mind. Maybe that's why Sophie was sent to me, so I could help her deal with her gift. She's probably felt things about people all her life, an uneasiness when she met a person, that she couldn't put a finger on. I'm going to need more time to get to know her, but when I do, hopefully I'll be able to figure it out."

"Well, whatever Sophie's gift is, it's certain to be a valuable asset to your mystery surrounding Elicia Ford. From what you've told me, there are forces at work here more powerful than we can comprehend. You be careful honey, and wear your charms."

~~~~~

Folder Label: Phyllis Anne Ford
Folder Contents: Biography, and Short Explanation
Biography: Phyllis Anne Burrows was born in a
~~~~~

small Kentucky town to a poor family. She lived in a shack on the edge of town, worked at a local mom & pop grocery store for four years saving up the money to go to college, after which she attended Kentucky State and graduated with a degree in Contemporary Design. At the age of 25, she met her future husband, Magnus Ford at a party held by one of her rich clients.

Their marriage caused quite a scandal, because it was well-known that she was not from a rich background. They were married a year later and had Jackson a year after that. Two years later, they had another boy, Francis, who is not known by any record. Their marriage continued without incident until his death 37 years after their marriage.

Phyllis inherited a fortune, and her son Jackson was also given access to a trust fund set up for him. He never touched the money, which he intended to save for his future children. Phyllis donated a significant amount of money to various charities and formed a foundation for foundling children.

~~~~~

Folder Label: Jackson Alton Ford

Folder Contents: Birth Certificate, Biography, and Short Explanation

Birth Certificate: Born November 3, 1948;

Father: Magnus Wade Ford;

Mother: Phyllis Anne Ford;

Time: 0943;

Attending Physician: Daniel W. Blake, M.D.

Biography: Jackson Ford was born at his parents' vacation home in Maine in the middle of a winter storm. After his birth they relocated to Virginia to the family's home. He went to various expensive private schools as a child and had an unremarkable existence. He excelled
~~~~~

at sports and academics; he was a well-rounded student. He graduated at the top of his class and went on to Harvard, where his father was an alumni. He dated a few girls while in college, and was even engaged to a woman named Lucille Black at one point. It fell through when she met an artist and ran off to France with him.

After graduation, he worked at his father's company for a few years before going on to found his own company: Burrows Technologies, under an assumed name, which though slow to catch on at first, eventually garnered him millions of dollars. He led a bright and rich life, attending parties and various attempts at matchmaking on the part of his mother.

By the time his father died, some years later, he had given up all hope of meeting anyone to spend his life with. That was when he met me. When we flew off to an undisclosed tropical location to be married, we came back to a mother who was understandably upset. She'd forgotten her own experience of love -it will do as it pleases and bring the strangest of lives together. We had many wonderful years together before he died in a random plane crash. And my life has been empty since then.

~~~~~

Folder Label: Magnus Alton Ford

Folder Contents: Biography, Letter, and Short Explanation

Biography: Magnus Ford has had many biographies written of him over the years: magazines, newspapers, and even books on astute businessmen. If you want the pertinent details on his life, I point you to them. I never met my father-in-law; he was dead when Jack and I met. But his hand was on everything in Jacks' life. His demeanor, talents, dreams, beliefs, successes:
~~~~~

all of these had been influenced in one way or another by Magnus.

When I asked my husband about his father, his eyes became distant and he was so wistful it almost broke my heart.

"I wish you could have met him, Leesy. He was such a good man. He loved my mother and I more than any one ever could. He was a busy man, but he always made time for me. I remember when I was a little boy, he set up a little desk for me in his office, so that I could play and be with him. When he went on business trips, he always took us with him. He taught me so much about what it means to be a husband and father."

"So he was happy, with you and your mom?" I asked this question after I had done some research regarding his younger brother.

"Of course he was. He couldn't ask for anything more," he said and seemed content with that answer.
I hesitated to say anything more.

"And yet..." he began after a few moments of silence, "There was something sad about him. You reminded me of him, that first time I met you. Even when you were smiling you had the saddest eyes I'd ever seen. He was like that, happy outside and sad inside. Not all the time, but sometimes, when everything was quiet or during summer days. I'd ask him what was wrong, but he'd always say, 'Nothing.' I never really thought about it until now."

When I asked my mother-in-law, one day when Jack and I were at her house, about Magnus, she was suspicious. Maybe she thinks I am out to get her somehow: kill her off, take her money, and make her son hate her. I don't know if she thinks those things, or if they are hidden fears, but I can feel them scratching at her sense of peace when I am near.

I explained to her what I was doing: researching the family history to construct some sort of genealogy. She clammed up, of course. She told me that their family was none of my business and that I would never find anything to blemish the pristine family name that is Ford. I tried to explain that finding scum in the family pond was not my intent, but there was no convincing her.

~~~~~

Letter:

*Phillips-*

*I don't want to hear any more of your complaining. You knew what you were getting into when we first approached you. I know it can't be easy to deal with, but this is my son you're talking about. This is something that has to be handled with care, for all of our sakes. If there is any way to help him, or reverse this, we need to find it. And you can rest assured that I will pay full measure for it.*

*-Magnus Ford*

~~~~~

Folder Label: Bay Blaine Willard

Folder Contents: Biography and Short Explanation

Biography: Bay Willard was born in Texas in 1940. His father died overseas in WWII, leaving him the only son of the widow Willard. He dropped out of school at 14 to help pay the family expenses by working at a local oil magnate's hobby ranch. He worked as a ranch hand for several years, before finally being promoted to ranch manager. After ten years, he was arrested for involuntary manslaughter and assault, before being imprisoned. As I mentioned before, he was approached by the Fords upon his parole and they arranged for it to be permissible for him to work out of state.

Short Explanation:

When I managed to track down Mr. Willard, to my surprise, he was open about his time working for the Fords, which ended after eight years or so.

"I'm afraid I can't tell you what it was I was doing; I signed a non-disclosure document. I can tell you that I was well-treated by the Ford family. I don't know what it was about me that attracted them, but they offered me a lot of money and I couldn't get a job when I was released from prison. I needed to support my mom, to get her into a good nursing home," he said.

"Can you tell me where it was, that you worked?" I asked.

"Sure thing. Worked at a compound in Virginia, can't be more specific. Best eight years of my life, though pretty queer, I gotta say," he said.

"What about Francis?"

The other line was silent at the question.

"Now Mrs. Ford, you know as sure as you're born I'm not gonna be able to talk about that."

"But he exists, doesn't he? You can at tell me that, at least."

"Yes, I can. He is as alive as you or me or God," he said, and hung up on me.

According to Mr. Willard, he was now living on a ranch, purchased by himself, outside San Antonio. It was a tourist ranch, for small parties. His business came from company trips. He bought it with the leftover money he got from the Fords and has lived a quiet life since then.

# Chapter 6

The thing in the photo was standing over me, as I lay in bed staring up at it. I was terrified, trembling and shaking under the covers.

"What do you want from me?" I managed to ask. My heart felt ready to come out of my chest.

Other-Elicia didn't answer -only stood there looking at me. I sat up, but it clutched at me with its hands, pinching the skin of my shoulders and twisting my nightshirt around my neck.

"Stop! Let go of me," I said, pushing at the hands. I heard its dreadful wheezing breath and smelled the rank stench of death in the air.

I gave a great shove and managed to get Other-Elicia off of me. I sprang from my bed and ran out of the room with it following, drifting like a feather in the air, behind me. I ran straight into the man of my earlier dream, the beautiful, terrible shadowless man.

"Who are you?" I asked, again, as terrified as I had ever been.

"Thcy call me Thadius. You however, shall call me Death," he said and grabbed my throat, cutting off my air supply. I struggled for longer this time, fighting him with all my might. I could feel the wheezing of Other-Elicia getting closer and closer and the world crashed down on me and again I saw black.

~~~~~

I sat up on the couch, trying without success to draw air into my lungs. My second nightmare in a week and I was still uncertain what the dreams meant. It had
~~~~~

featured the same character from my other dream, with a new addition. Why was this happening to me? What sort of forces was I dealing with? My death was so vivid that I could still feel his fingers around my neck. I could still hear the sound of his low, compelling voice, ushering me to my life's end. I shivered and fingered the blanket covering my lap.

The fire was down to coals, that shimmered listlessly in the late evening. I yawned and despite my nightmare, realized the best place for me was my bed. Still, something was nagging at me. He'd said a name… what was it… Thadius. Now why did that sound so familiar?

I stood up and went to my bag. I pulled out the papers and folders that I'd read through over the past few days. I was searching for something, I wasn't sure where it was, but I was certain I'd find it.

I opened the genealogy folder and searched through the papers on the Ford family. There. There it was. A chill ran through me. This could not be a coincidence, there was no way in hell it was a coincidence. The list of seven names that were given to Elicia, and right at the top was Thadius Ford.

~~~~~

I now had a stack of photos featuring Other-Elicia and a pile of folders sitting on my kitchen table. What I needed was a fresh set of eyes. And considering how poor Sophie had reacted at the mere sight of the Polaroids, she wasn't going to be much of a source of information. All this information, all this mystery surrounding the poor woman's death and a week of reading and poking and prodding, and still I felt like I wasn't making any headway.

I gave up, slumping in my chair, with my eyes closed. Thinking, thinking, thinking about who could help me find some answers. I ran through a list in my head, but no one that I knew could help me with anything like this. The truth was, I had no experience solving complicated mysteries. I took the
~~~~~

messages the universe gave me and relayed them to the people who needed to hear them. I couldn't even begin to guess where I should go from here.

I could read more of the files, but if I did, I would have even more facts and stories and summaries swimming through my head, and I wasn't sure that I could handle anything else pulsing through my brain at the moment.

And then, sitting up with a yelp, I knew what to do. I got up and went to my bag -which I'd set down on a table near the door. I looked through the Ford folders until I found the address and phone number of Lyle Struthers. It had only been six or so years ago. The chances were, he could still exist. Of course, he could also have moved or changed numbers or died, but I wasn't about to let that get me discouraged.

I took my cell out of my pocket and dialed the number on the paper. The phone rang a few times and a low, growling voice answered.

"Hello," it said.

"Hello, is this Lyle Struthers?" I asked.

"I don't want anything and take me off your damned list."

There was a click and then a beep as my phone indicated a loss of connection. Well, at least I knew he was there. I tried again.

"Please, Mr. Struthers, I'm not a telemarketer," I said.

"Oh, I'm sorry. I get those calls all the time. What can I do for you?"

"My name is Sibilant and I'm calling about some letters that you exchanged with Elicia Ford," I said.

A sigh on the other end, and then he replied, "I thought I'd be getting a phone call some day. What happened to her?"

"She died," I said.

"That doesn't surprise me. The way she was digging at things no human being should mess with."

"What do you mean?" I asked. "You mean the information you found for her?"

"I can't talk about this over the phone. We should meet in person," he said.

As soon as he hung up, I called Paul.

"How would you like to take a trip with me tomorrow?" I asked.

~~~~~

I was up early the next morning; we had a three hour drive ahead of us. I'd slept fine for the first time in days, a sleep unmarred by nightmares, visions, or uneasy feelings -probably because of Paul's presence. I was early to bed, after a day spent doing more reading than I'd ever done in such a short space of time. I was pushing my way through the stack, with no more success than I'd been having. I did know more about the Ford family than probably anyone alive today, I would wager.

I was hoping that with our meeting today, I would not only shed light on the Ford family, I'd also dissect some of Elicia's family as well. As we left our small town behind us, I felt nervous about what the day would bring. I could be that much closer to solving the mystery Elicia had set before me.

Three hours later, with Paul's expert navigation and there we were, at the beginning of a long windy driveway. As we traversed it, driving smooth and slow, I wondered what kind of person would want to meet us so far out in the boonies. The thought made me nervous. I wasn't sure what to expect from this Lyle Struthers.

"The original mountain cabin," said Paul staring up at the pine planks criss-crossing above the double doors.

Looking at the smoke curling from the chimney, I said, "I want to curl up inside it."

When Paul knocked on the door, we were greeted by a stocky, wool sweater clad man in his late 50's. He had a thatch
~~~~~

of thick white hair and piercing blue eyes. His hawk-like nose hung over his thin lips, which curved into a smile as he held out his hand to me.

"Sibilant?" he said, as a question.

"That's me," I said, "This is Paul. And you must be Lyle."

"Please, come in," he said, and opened the door wide to let us in.

He led us through a beautiful, rustic style lodge, complete with high ceilings, a fireplace and old fashioned rag rugs. The cloudy morning light filtered through the large windows that looked out on the pond across the way. He seated us in a couple of chairs near the fire and asked if we wanted any refreshments. We settled on two cups of hot coffee and he disappeared into the kitchen. I was mesmerized by the flames licking up into the chimney and started suddenly when he came near, holding the mug out for me.

"Thank you," I said, and smiled. Paul did the same.

"You're welcome. It's good to some new faces around here, don't get much company and I can only force myself to go down into town every couple of weeks these days. So you knew Mrs. Ford?"

"It's becoming a complicated story," I said, looking at Paul, who shrugged.

"I'm game," he replied.

"I met Elicia a little over a week ago. She came to me for a reading -I'm a palm reader. During the reading I saw some really disturbing things, not the least of which was that evil forces have been circling around Elicia for some time. After I gave her a description of what I saw, I thought I'd never see her again. I was right. She killed herself three days later.

"It was then that I was contacted by her lawyer, who hired me to look into the events surrounding her death. He gave me access to her personal research and when I ran across her files on the Ford family, your name came up. Which is why I'm here. I'm hoping you can tell me about her search into the past," I said, fluttering my hands in the silence.

He leaned back in his chair, deep in thought, for a few minutes.

"The first time I heard from her, I was doing some research for a professor friend of mine, Clara Hawkins. She'd gotten a letter from Elicia and asked if I'd be willing to take on her project. It seemed she was up against a brick wall with her husband's relatives. All of them shut up like raw oysters whenever she asked a question. I read over the letters that she'd sent, did a bit of shallow digging, and decided that I could do some research on the side.

"She gave me a lot of money -helped me buy this land out here. I gave her little in return, at first. It took me a long time to get anything of substance. Once I finally got past that hurdle, I found things you would not believe. It finally got to the point that I was afraid to send her things through the mail or tell her over the phone. I was even afraid to do more research.

"I'm not a timid man. I was in the army, you know. But there was just something about that family just twisted my innards. The mother, the father, the brother -hidden away in the mountains -it was all too weird. In the end, I had to stop. I couldn't take it anymore. I left her with the pieces. I showed her where to look and sent her off to finish.

"I don't feel good about that, but I couldn't ignore the fact that we were brushing against something evil. I could feel it and so could she. I had no desire to keep nosing around somewhere that I wasn't supposed to. So I left her alone and something happened to her."

"What do you mean?" Paul asked.

"She called me a few years later. Said she was feeling off. Didn't feel right inside anymore. She had her answers, at least, the closest she'd ever come to them, but it was at the expense of her sanity, I guess.

"She told me that she kept seeing herself doing the most terrible things. She felt like some evil part of her had gotten loose into the world and she was afraid of what it might do."

"What was it that you found out for her, before you convinced yourself to give it up?" I asked.

"The Fords stretch all the way back to the beginning of this nation. But despite what they tell everyone about their Mayflower arrival, they were really just part of a slave ship: criminals from Ireland. When they came over, they disappeared into the wilds of Virginia, violating the terms of their contract. There were the usual searches for them, but no one ever found them. It was said that they were a family of dark warlocks, who lived in hovels scattered throughout the Blue Mountains.

"I don't know how they survived up there, but they did it for years. They lived in absolute secrecy, until the early 1920's. It was then that Jackson Ford's ancestors came down from the mountains, filthy and ragged, bearing strange tales about "the coven" that they'd escaped from.

"The family -mother, father, two daughters- thought their life would be peaceful away from what they'd left behind, but the horror was just beginning. The daughter grew older and got married and that was when the trouble started. The oldest girl, Lila, had a son, who they could tell from the start was more like their kinfolk than themselves. He was a strange little boy, who from what the tales tell had even stranger powers.

"There are many different accounts: that he could kill small animals even as a toddler, that he never spoke, that he could fly, there were many and they were imaginative. Whatever the child was capable of, it was enough to scare his parents into hiding for a while. They went back into those hills and when they returned, he was not with them.

"For a while things were better, but then their next child, a girl, grew up and had a child. He was the same. Whatever it was, it only seemed to affect certain male children. Some were born normal, like Jackson, and others were born different, like Francis. I don't know how they knew or where they took them, but I do know it was up into the hills like those crazy people before then."

"So the files that Elicia made, they're full of your research," Paul said, taking the words right out of my mouth.

"Some of them are mine, and some of them are her continuation of my research. The more recent research was what I gave up on. There are things in this world that you don't fool around with."

I was confused. It was becoming a regular state of affairs for me.

"Francis is still alive?" I asked.

"As alive as I am. What that means, I don't know. But that's the truth."

"Well, where is he?" said Paul, excited.

"I have no idea, and I really don't want to know."

"It's just that, well, he might be able to answer some questions for me," I said.

"Let me give you a piece of advice, Miss. You don't want to go messing with Elicia or any of her people. Pure evil runs in that blood, make no mistake. What do you think happened to Elicia? Think she just keeled over one day?"

"No, she committed suicide," I said.

"Piffle. I don't believe that for a minute. Is that what the autopsy said? Never mind, it doesn't matter. When she contacted me a couple of years ago, and I started digging around for her, finding information on both sides of the family, I started hearing about stuff that I knew I shouldn't be messing with. Hexes and evil and disappearances that no one could account for. There were things I'd never heard of before, grotesque rituals and midnight chanting, spirit summoning of the darkest kind. But I'm sure you've already heard of all that."

"No, not a bit. The most I read about was the doppelganger article that you sent. I haven't found any files that seem sinister at all."

"Yeah, believe me, there's not much there," agreed Paul.

"Well, don't expect *me* to tell you about that stuff. Even now, I feel eyes that watch me. I have no interest in pissing anyone off. I gave her all I found."

After an exchanged glance, Paul and I stood to leave. It was clear that Struthers had no interest in continuing the conversation. I couldn't say I blamed him.

He walked us to the door.

"Thank you again, for all your help. I apprcciated your candor," I said "Please call me if you remember anything else."

I handed him one of my business cards -yes I have them.

"I don't know about you, but I'm feeling more confused than when we started," said Paul as we walked down the driveway toward the car.

"I hope something else comes up soon," I said.

It was a long drive home, and I full of anxiousness for most of the miles I traveled.

~~~~~

"Sibilant, hi, this is Jordan. I'm so sorry about this. Mrs. Ford is threatening to have me fired or even disbarred. Her money has a lot of influence in this town and frankly, I'm afraid she could do either of those. She is worried about you taking her son's things or any of the information that Elicia has on the Ford family.

"I assured her that you wouldn't be out to the house any more, so if there is more that you need, then I'm afraid you're going to have to go through me. Just to keep all of this above
~~~~~

board and official. Don't worry. We'll figure it out. For now though, you're going to have to work with what you already have. Again, I'm so sorry. Call me as soon as you get this, okay?"

~~~~~

I was mulling over Jordan's message. I'd tried calling him back, but he was in a meeting. This couldn't have come at a more inconvenient time. I was itching to get back to that file cabinet and break into that last drawer. If they existed, I wanted to find the dark and scary files Struthers had mentioned.

I was just unlocking the door to my apartment, after Paul had dropped me off, when my cell rang.

"Hello?"

"Sibilant, hi. Sorry I missed you earlier." It was Jordan and he sounded tired.

"Are you okay?" I asked.

"Not really. I just talked to Phyllis' lawyer and it's pretty obvious to me that she isn't going to compromise at all. She doesn't want you anywhere near that house."

"But I'm not going to tell anyone anything about her precious son and her family," I said.

"She doesn't know that and she doesn't know you. I don't think she cares, either. You have to remember, she and Elicia had a complicated relationship. She was angry when Elicia started nosing around in the family closet for skeletons."

"That's unfortunate. I wonder what Elicia could have done to make her feel that way?"

"Married her son, I guess."

"I guess. So what is our plan of action?" I asked.

"I think we can offer to make you sign a non-disclosure agreement. It's the only thing I can think of to make this all go away as soon as possible. How are you feeling?"

"Well, this is quite a setback as you can imagine. How
~~~~~

am I going to figure this out without access to the house?"

Silence.

"You still have the other keys, don't you?" he asked.

"Yes, but I don't know what they're for."

"What if I help you find out what they're for? I can look through her papers and see what I can find about them. I feel really bad about this. I know you thought you'd have unlimited access to all of her things. Let's meet up tomorrow and see what we can find out."

"Okay," I said.

We settled on a time and place and then I hung up.

## Chapter 7

Jordan met me at his office late the next day, and seated me in the chair across from him.

"Okay, you brought the keys?" I held them up, jangling them with irritating musicality.

"Here on my desk, I have an itemized list of Elicia's belongings. We can look at the key labels and try to figure out what they belong to."

I laid the keys on the desk between us.

"Let's see what there is of note in here," Jordan said. I saw several sheets of paper in front of him and he also dug out a file to his right from a tall filing cabinet. Jordan took no more than a few seconds to pluck all the information on Elicia that he was in possession of -every bit of it seemed to be right at his fingertips. This was impressive to someone like me; I could barely find my keys, much less a bunch of important papers.

"Here is the list of Elicia's properties and copies of all her deeds of ownership, her receipts of purchase, and the taxes and or registrations related to the properties in question," Jordan said. "Let me just give you this summary I made, so that you don't have to dig through everything."

"Thanks," I said, thinking that it was a joy not to be a lawyer and have to have endless details at the ready. The sheet of paper contained two houses: a vacation house on the coast of California -which neither of them had been to since her husband was still alive, Jordan told me- and the tall Edwardian monster house on the edge of town. She owned only one car, a luxury car that her husband had purchased for her upon their marriage. There was a boat, which also hadn't been used since before her husband's death. I was starting to notice a pattern here.

"So her life basically shut down when he died, didn't it?" I asked.

"Pretty much," said Jordan, "She didn't buy anything new, that I could tell. A computer, as you can see here, and a blender. But that was it."

"How sad," I said.

"But to love someone that much," said Jordan, a bit wistful. I thought of his love for Elicia and gave him a sympathetic smile.

"And here," He said after a few moments of silence, "are the bank accounts, stocks and bonds, all the money stuff." He was trying to put things in easy to understand terms and I appreciated it.

"What's this one?" I asked, pointing to a small local bank in a little town an hour or so away.

"I'm not sure. I always assumed it was an account that she had open before she married Jackson. Let me see if I can find out." He shuffled through some papers for a few minutes, while I considered whether or not it could be related to my keys.

"Oh, look, I think this may be what you're looking for," he said, and handed me a receipt for the opening of a safe deposit box with the former bank in letterhead at the top.

"Perfect," I said. "Now I just have to go and see what's in it."

~~~~~

I was sitting with Sophie in my little apartment. We were doing exercises to help her hone her talents as a new practitioner. They were not going well.

She'd come over to my place very eager to begin her next phase in her "psychic journey" as she put it. Her
~~~~~

enthusiasm bowled me over. We started with a few traditional exercises- things that my mother had done with me, back when I was even younger than Sophie.

The first exercise was for her to close her eyes and let go of all her thoughts. This must have been difficult for her to do, because she scrunched up her eyes and puckered her mouth; she looked like she was trying to pass a kidney stone.

"Uh, Sophie?" I said.

Her eyes popped open and she looked at me like a trained puppy looking for a treat. "Yes?"

"Why don't you relax a little more? That's what this exercise is all about. When you relax the mind and let go of all outer distractions, inner power can come forward. So take a deep breath, then let it out slowly, and try it one more time."

She took a deep breath, closed her eyes, and this time managed to have a relaxed look on her face. After a couple of minutes, she dispelled an angry grunt. And those big gray eyes popped right open again.

"I can't do it. My brain's all full of clutter. It's too hard to clear up."

"You can do it, Sophie. It just takes lots and lots of practice. You want to be a practitioner like me, right? You want to use the gift you've been given? "-an eager nod-"Then you have to do this step first. Trust me, after a while, it will be second nature for you, like it is for me."

We worked on this for quite a while, until it was obvious that we weren't getting anywhere. I tried something different.

"Okay, so, since the last exercise was hard, in the fact that you had to empty your mind, now we're going to work *with* all the clutter. Close your eyes. This time, instead of emptying your mind, I want you to follow its currents, follow its lines, go wherever it leads you. Okay?" She nodded.

"Now, when you feel comfortable with that, when you

have a feel for it, I want to you leave behind your thoughts and start searching for things that might be out beyond your regular, everyday thoughts. Things that may stick in your mind and seem unusual." I waited for a few minutes, practicing my own relaxation techniques. After some time she opened her eyes again.

"So, tell me what you saw."

"Um… I saw my friend Tara, and she was wearing a black dress."

"Okay."

"And I think she was going somewhere special with her boyfriend."

"Uh huh."

She hesitated. "Maybe they were going to the prom?" She was uncertain. It was kind of heartbreaking.

"How does that seem unusual, Sophie? Didn't you mention to me that there was a winter formal coming up? Hasn't your mind been on it, lately?"

"Yes, but Tara told me that she wanted to wear blue, like ice. So that's unusual right?"

I sighed. "Sure. That's fine."

She wilted, a thirsty flower. "I'm sorry. I just don't know what it is that I'm supposed to be looking for. I don't know what it is that will pop out at me and make me think I'm special."

"No, that's understandable. With me, I always had my ability, but my mother has always been there to guide me. It looks like we're going to have to dig around a little bit to find your gift, that's all." I had a sudden thought. The photos -why hadn't I thought of them before? She'd had such a strong reaction when I showed them to her the first time. Maybe that was the right direction to head in.

I dug the bag out of my closet and got the pictures I had. I put them behind my back so she couldn't see them.

"Okay, now close your eyes," I said. She complied and I laid the photos out in front of her face down.

"Now, do the same thing that I asked you to do before. Let your thoughts go wherever they might wander. And tell me if you feel different this time." She was silent for a few minutes, but after awhile she opened her eyes, shaking her head.

I flipped over a photo and her reaction was immediate. She pulled back from the table, shuddering and heaving.

"Please," she whispered, "get it away from me."

I turned the photo back over.

"I don't understand," I said. "When I look at that photo, I'm intrigued, and disgusted, but it doesn't make me react like you. What do you see when you look at it?" I flipped the photo over again and she leaned away from it.

"I-I don't know. It just scares me on some level that I can't explain. It feels so very wrong, like it's the opposite of what should be. It feels unnatural. I see a woman, but it's not her. It's like, it's an echo of her, a shadow or something. And it just feels wrong to me, inside. Looking at it makes me sick. It makes me so sick." She whimpered. I flipped the photo over, giving her a respite. Meanwhile, my brain was racing.

"Sophie, have you ever gotten a feeling about someone, when you first meet them, that won't go away. You know like 'this person is a flake' or 'this guy is a total jerk'?"

"Sometimes," she said.

"Have you ever noticed that you're usually right, when you have feelings like this?"

She seemed in deep teenage thought -if there was such a thing.

"Well… my friends always ask my opinions about boys, even though I don't have a boyfriend myself, because I can tell if the guy is a nice guy or a jerk."

I nodded encouragement.

"Oh! And one time, I met this guy that my aunt was dating and I couldn't stand to be around him. My mother was always yelling at me for being rude. But it turned out that he was a horrible guy. He beat her and everything. My mom told me that I'd hit the nail on the head."

Thoughts were pouring through my head like water through a sieve. It was entirely possible that Sophie was a *Detector* much in the same way that I had seen that Elicia was an *Attractor.* The question was, how could one even begin to practice and hone such a talent? I'd never met one in person, although I remembered what my mom had told me about Aunt Lucy -who had made it her calling in life to save women from bad relationships. This made me wonder, how strong her gift was. She could see it in a photo. Could she read it?

"Okay, let me try something else," I said. I scooped the photos up and slipped them into my pocket. She relaxed visibly.

I grabbed the files that Elicia had made of Jackson Ford and his brother. I laid Jackson's in front of her and asked her to read it. It took a few short minutes for her to finish then she looked up at me questioningly.

"What are your impressions of him?"

"I'd say, he seems like a nice man, but he's kind of close-minded though. His wife is, I think, a lot more open to weird things than he is."

"Okay. Now try this one." I handed the folder containing the bio on Francis Ford to her. She opened it and read it silently for a few minutes. She set it down. She picked it up and read again. She went to set it down, seemed unsure, then decisively set it down.

"Yes?" I asked.

"This one was harder to read. He was so young and she knew practically nothing about him. I couldn't get a read on what type of person he was or is? But I can tell you one thing… bad things like him."

"What do you mean?" My heart started pounding. This was sounding too familiar for my comfort.

"Bad things happen when he is around. Strange things. Not to him, bad things don't happen to him, but they happen when he is around."

I nodded, and felt a tinge of excitement.

"So what does this mean?" She asked me.

"Well, I'm not exactly sure. We'll need to do some more experimentation before I can guess for sure. But I think you are one of those unique people detect good or evil around them. It is a rare talent, but also a very difficult one.

"You will feel strongly about a person without knowing why. It's hard to prove a feeling or impression. Many of the most evil people in the world keep such things hidden so deeply that most of the world would be hard pressed to tell otherwise."

"So what do I do with my gift?"

"Well, for now, the universe tells me that I must make you my apprentice. You are young for it, especially considering the sorts of things I'm dabbling in at the moment."

"I'm 16!" she objected, with a teenager's typical belief in her own adulthood.

"Really? So you think you're ready to face this on a regular basis?" I held the photo in front of her face. She lost all color.

"This thing is wandering around somewhere close, and I might come in contact with it. You're telling me that you feel able to deal with that?" I asked.

She hunched over, chin to chest. "I c-can't. Please, put that thing away."

"Usually an apprenticeship would entail you following me through my readings and observe my day-to-day journeys as a psychic. But there are some gruesome things going on right now. I'm dealing with forces that make me shake in my own boots.

"I promise you, I will do my best to involve you in my life, but I feel like I have to protect you, too. Your talent is new and shiny. I want to polish it up, not tarnish it. I'm responsible for what you become from here on out; I am in charge of directing your schooling in the practitioner's arts. That's nothing to take lightly."

She took the photo from my hand, swallowed, and looked at it for several seconds. It was one of the bravest things I've ever seen -I could sense her will tackling the sight of Elicia and see how she forced herself to stand firm against the fear she was feeling.

"You know this is looking for you, right?" she asked, handing the picture back to me.

"What do you mean?"

"Somehow or another, this thing has gotten ahold of your scent and it's only a matter of time until it finds you."

~~~~~

That afternoon, I made my way to a small bank, in a small town about an hour south of where I lived. It didn't look big enough to hold money, much less a safety deposit box. *How strange,* I thought. The street was lined with old brick buildings that had seen better days. There weren't many cars out either. I saw a pickup that was parked in front of an old hardware store and a few cars in front of the mini-mart and gas station at the end of the road. Other than that, it was pretty quiet.

I walked into the empty bank. There was one teller, over by the old-fashioned teller counter in the middle of the room. An elderly man, he was, and looked to be more in his grave than in his booth. He was reading the local paper, from the look of it.

Glancing up when the bell over the door rang, he set
~~~~~

aside his paper.

"Can I help you, young lady?" He asked, as his droopy white mustache quivered. His dusty voice reminded me of shuffling papers.

I held up my key. "I have a safety deposit box that I'd like to open," I said.

"Alright, let's see it."

I handed it over and he looked at the number. He took it behind the counter and compared it to a sheaf of papers at a desk.

"Oh, yes, I remember this one. Where's the woman who opened it originally?" he asked, looking at me with squinty-eyed suspicion.

"She's dead, I'm sorry to say," I said. I showed him the death certificate that Jordan had given me.

"Hmm… sure was a strange one. Came in here about… oh… 11 years ago? Wanted to put away some papers. Nothing much of interest in my opinion. We're not supposed to notice what people are puttin' in their boxes, but it's not like she hid it away or anything. Brought in a stack of papers with her and didn't bring it out again. Made me wonder what was on those papers that would want to make her hide them away in a place like this."

I said nothing, but I was wondering the same thing.

Inside the tiny private room, he slipped my key into the slot, slid the long drawer out, and set it on the table in the middle of the room. Then he nodded and ambled out.

I hesitated for a breath, then pulled up the top of the box. Inside were three things: a stack of paper, bound with twine, a small, battered, oval gold locket, and a doll -wooden and hand carved- about the size of my fist. *Curiouser and curiouser*, I said to myself.

The locket was damaged and took some effort to open. When I did, I saw a picture of a man and a woman on opposite sides of the locket. Didn't mean anything to me, as I had no idea who either of them were.

The little wooden doll was as long as my middle finger, carved with a fat round belly, arms that stood erect at the sides. It was made from dark wood, and slick with age and oils. It smelled like an old house. The face was crude and rough, and looked odd.

I unbound the papers, looking through them. They appeared to be financial papers of some sort: bank statements, invoices and the like. They were photocopies, some of them were gray and hard to read. I tried to make any sense out of them, but it was beyond me. I would need a professional understand them.

I pocketed the locket, rebound the papers, and set the doll on top of them. Then I closed the lid of the box.

I walked through the door with my burdens, and nodded to the old teller on my way out.

"Hope you found what you were looking for!" he said, as I walked through the door.

## Chapter 8

"Hmmm... You say you got these from her safe deposit box?" Paul asked.

I'd invited him over with the bribery of some potato soup and homemade bread, if he agreed to help me out with the papers I'd found in the box.

I nodded. I was seated across from him at my kitchen table, trying my best to pay attention to the work at hand, and not that stray lock of dark hair that kept dangling in his stormy cloud eyes.

"They date back several years… twenty-five at least. Most of them deal with Magnus Ford. That name rings a bell, doesn't it?"

"As a matter of fact it does. Are they bank statements or something else? I couldn't tell. I mean, I can barely do my taxes, much less try to figure out someone else's money."

"All the papers here center around one central account that was in Magnus Ford's name. Over the years, quite a lot of money went into the account from a trust fund, and then went out again to several regular sources.

"Then, about, oh, 15 years ago Jackson Ford took over for Magnus. The payments went out for a few more years and then it looks like they stopped a couple of years later."

"Does it tell who the payments were made to?"

Paul shook his head. "They're all just check numbers and dollar amounts. Then there were some interesting papers here near the end." He handed me a letter that was dated a few years after Elicia married

Jackson.

*To whom it may concern:*

*This is outside of enough. I've made every payment without question since my father died, but these new claims for money are just ridiculous. You're talking about thousands of dollars here, for a person that I haven't even seen, and don't know anything about. I don't know why my father was paying this man, Barrows, but from here on out, it's going to stop. Until I see proof that he actually exists, how do I know that I'm not sending money to some con-artist? Let me know if you have any evidence you want to submit to my lawyer. The address is enclosed.*

*-Jackson Ford*

"What do you think it means?" he asked me.

"I think it means that Jackson didn't know about his brother at the time of his father's death. He thought he was just paying out money to a random guy -this Barrows guy. This letter is the last of the payments toward caring for his brother. I wonder what happened to him," I said.

"So, do you have any idea what happened to Elicia?" he asked.

"Not yet. I think I'm putting it together, though. Those dark stories in her husband's family history might indicate a blood curse."

"Blood curse? That sounds like something out of a horror novel."

"Well, most mythology holds a grain of truth. A blood curse can be explained in a less scary way. Most people consider blood curses to be as simple as a bad genetic marker. A disease that passes down through a family line. That's what I think happened in this case.

“There must be a supernatural blood curse on the Ford

family. I don't know what it is yet, but it was bad enough that they've had to put the tainted children in seclusion somewhere."

"Tainted? That seems like pretty strong language to describe a young kid," said Paul.

"Maybe. I'm not the one who sent my infant child to live in seclusion. I don't know how they perceived him. I can only speculate from the evidence I've been able to gather. What I don't understand is how Elicia is connected to all of this."

"I bet he got all pissed off when they stopped sending him money and came after her."

"It could be," I said. "But that seems so easy. Why is this adult man, who has got to be in his late 40's, needing or wanting money from the father he never knew?"

"Why does anyone want money? It buys stuff." He grinned. "It can't be easy to have everything provided for you all of your life, and then to just be cut off from your only source of income."

"I wonder if they tried to contact Elicia before her death. She must have known about Francis or at least suspected something. Were there any other papers worth looking at?"

"Yeah, look at this one. It doesn't look like it has anything to do with the other papers."

It was a receipt from a Virginia Ozark Foundation donation.

"Holy cow!" I said, "Thirty thousand dollars!"

"Yeah, but look who the donation is from."

I looked down at the name on the receipt: Elicia Ford.

"What do you suppose that means?"

"I have no idea, but at least it's a place to start next."

~~~~~

There was no address or phone number on the receipt,
~~~~~

so we did what everyone does in such situations; we looked it up on the internet. A few websites came up.

"Look, that one is for the organization's site," Paul pointed to a spot on the screen.

I clicked on it and a main page loaded up. In the corner were an address and phone number.

"Oh, go to their mission statement," he said, pointing at the screen.

The page loaded up and we read the blurb.

*VOF is committed to bringing education, specifically literacy, to the blue mountains. Our preferred method of outreach is to offer college scholarships to former residents in return for a year long commitment to go back and teach the local children themselves. We are entirely funded by donations and over 80% of our money goes to our outreach.*

"This is too weird," I said. "Why would she save the receipt? There must have been a reason she put it in that box, but I'll be damned if I know what it was."

"Yeah, I have to agree with you on this one. Maybe we should make a trip out there and find out. Someone had to have talked to her."

"We?" I asked, eyebrows raised.

"Well, yes, of course. I mean, this could be dangerous. You might need an accountant to get you out of a difficult numerical bind."

I snuggled my head onto his shoulder. "That sounds nice. I could use a big strong accountant for work like this."

"Good, we'll go bright and early tomorrow morning."

~~~~~

The next morning we pulled into the parking lot of the small gray building that was the Virginia Ozark Foundation. I was feeling good, for the first time in a week, and felt curious
~~~~~

to learn how these people were connected to Elicia's mystery.

We walked in and a young woman looked up from her desk.

"Hi, welcome to Virginia Ozark Foundation. What can I help you with?" Her smile was welcoming and I returned it.

"I'm checking on some of the financial contributions of a woman named Elicia Ford. She donated quite a bit of money to your organization and I'd like to talk to someone about it."

She bit her lip and frowned. "I better get Nell. She handles all the donations."

She dialed an extension on her phone and lowered her voice, turning around in her swivel chair. I could just make out a few key words: "She wants to know about Elicia's money." Pause. "Well, I can't tell her that. No, no, no. It's your job. Okay. Thank you."

She turned back to me, with an apologetic smile. I had the feeling I was about to be denied.

"Nell can fit you in for a few minutes," she said to my surprise. "Head down this hallway, and it's the third door to your left."

"Thank you." I said.

"That was pretty close, wasn't it?" Paul muttered to me on our way down the hall.

"Yes, I thought for sure they'd send us away. There is something weird going on here."

"You're starting to sound like a broken record," he said and laughed a little.

"Yes, well, if everything wasn't so weird, I wouldn't have to say it all the time."

We arrived at our destination and I tapped on the door. It was opened by a slender, gray-haired woman wearing a lovely cream suit and a small VOF pin on her front.

"Hello, I'm Nell Black. Please, come in and have a seat."

"Now, what can I do for you?" she asked, polite and to the point, after we had taken our seats.

"My name is Sibilant, and this is my friend Paul. We're here about Elicia Ford's donation." I pulled out the receipt and laid it in front of her on the desk. "She died a week ago, you see and we're trying to sort out all her financial doings."

"Oh my!" She exclaimed. "What happened?"

"She committed suicide."

"Oh, how terrible. Although, I can't say I'm surprised. I've never met a woman who seemed as sad as she did."

"The reason I'm here," I began, "is because I'm interested in donating to the same charities as Elicia did. I think that's how I would like to honor her memory. When I found that receipt, I thought I'd come here and talk to you about her donation."

Her eyes widened. Money always had the same effect on people, didn't it?

"Of course. That would be wonderful. Just tell me what it is you need to know."

"Well, first, I was wondering if you could tell me a little bit more about what you do." We already knew the answer to that question, but Paul and I had discussed this ahead of time. It would be the best way to make our interest seem more general than it actually was. And it could help to add some details that we might miss otherwise.

"VOF is an organization that believes in the power of education. We want to see everyone, no matter what their background have the tools they need to survive in a world where you need a college education. We also believe in working one-on-one with people. We don't just throw money at a problem, we help others to give back to their communities with volunteer work and a one year commitment.

"Our mission is a simple one: to reach the poor citizens of the Ozarks, who have no money to help themselves. These people, who live right here in the United States, have little if any shelter, food, or teaching. The county is required to make schooling available, but because of extreme poverty and addiction to prescription drugs, many of the parents give up trying to make a better life for their children. Many of them grow up illiterate and suffering.

"We send teachers to them, their own people, so the trust is already there. We sponsor the best and brightest of the children, send them to college, and bring them back to take education to their families and friends.

"We've been doing it for the past 10 years and it's working. I can show you our information and statistics if you want -our success rate. We have an information packet. Here, let me just dig that out for you."

She turned to a file cabinet behind her. When she opened it, I spied several folders with names and dates labeled on them. She ignored these for a stack of packets at the front of the drawer. I looked at Paul, and he nodded. He'd seen the folder bearing Elicia's name, as well.

"Thank you," I said, when she handed it to me. "Can you tell me why Elicia was so interested in your foundation?"

"Oh, because she came from Appalachian mountains, of course." My surprise must have shown.

"You didn't know that?" she asked.

"No. I didn't know her when she was younger. She never talked about her past."

"Well, I don't think she'd mind you knowing now. I mean, it can't matter, her being dead and all. Her father and mother died one night in some sort of hunting accident, I'm still not sure on the details. She never forgot her roots, however.

"She came to us and offered us the money. We were astonished. Her only request was that we take her on a ride-along of sorts -up into the hills with one of our teachers, so that she could see our work firsthand. I think she just wanted to make sure that her money would be well spent. We were happy to comply. It was the least we could do."

"Is that something that you do normally for your endorsers?"

"Most of them don't care. We get a lot of contributions from large companies just looking for a write off. In fact, that's where most of our biggest donations come from, but Elicia wasn't like the others. She went on several ride-along trips and even gave of her time to help the children personally. Like I said, she had a history in those mountains."

"Would it be possible for me to do a ride-along? So I can see what she did before I decide that this is right choice for me?"

"Sure. Let me go check the teachers' schedules and see what we can come up with. Okay?"

I smiled. "Sounds good." As soon as she left the room, I turned to Paul and whispered, "Can you distract her for a minute or two so I can get a look at that folder? I want to see if there's any information about where she went when she was up here. I think she used the organization to explore the area and investigate ."

"Investigate what?" he asked.

"We'll talk about it in a minute, just quick, go distract her before she comes back."

He got up and left the room, heading down the hallway toward where Ms. Black had gone. I prayed he was good at dissembling and knelt down by the cabinet that was still ajar. I reached in and grabbed the folder labeled with Elicia's name. At first all I could see were a multitude of disappointing tax forms, but finally I noticed a log containing the different routes she'd gone on with the different teachers. I was looking it over when I heard a noise in the hallway, and so I succumbed to the inevitable and pulled the page out, stuffing it in my purse, and placed the folder back in the drawer, before sitting back in my chair.

"Well it's all settled," Ms. Black said, a smile on her face. "Paul told me about your availability in the next week and I think we can fit you in on Tuesday. How would that be?"

"Great," I said and hoped I didn't look too suspicious.

~~~~~

"That went well," I said, as we got back in the car.

"That's what I was thinking," Paul replied.

"So Elicia came from a really poor background -or did she? If I were her, it is just the type of story I'd use to gain the trust of an organization like the VOF."

"You make an interesting point," Paul agreed. "Want to get some lunch and talk about it?"

"You just want to eat," I teased.

"Can I help it if sitting around listening to two people talk really works up my appetite? I saw a burger place down the road that looks good."

"Works for me."

An hour later, as we were finishing up the meal, we were discussing again how various pieces of the Elicia puzzle fit together.

"I really don't understand why you feel the need to follow this lead." Paul commented and ate one of his remaining fries. "Elicia just felt attached to the people she came from. She wanted to give back to her community, help some of those other poor kids out."

"I think it was more than that," I said. "She went back so many times… why?"

"To work with the kids firsthand," Paul said. "That's what that lady told us."

"Yes, but I don't think that's really what she was up there for. I think she was looking for Francis."

"What makes you think that?"

"Lyle Struthers told us that the Ford family went up into
~~~~~

those mountains to escape their indenture. Remember, he said that in the early 1900's the family came back down from the mountains and tried to live a normal life. I think Elicia was up there to see if it would lead her to Francis."

"It's also possible she was trying to build on her knowledge of the Ford family tree."

"Well, considering the photos and the files I've read so far, I think she knew that something bad was happening to her and she was trying to figure out why."

"So, tell me what happened when I distracted good ol' Nell for you. You find anything good?"

"Not at first. First it was just boring tax stuff. Then I found this." I reached into my purse and pulled out a crumpled piece of paper. "Oops, I guess it's kind of worse for the wear."

I laid it flat on the table and tried my best to straighten it.

"Whoa, look at that!" Paul said, leaning over for a better look. "Elicia gave them a lot more than $30,000. What are these numbers here? And what is this?" He pointed to a list of locations.

"Hmmm... " I said, "It almost looks like they coincide with her donations. Do you still have that map we brought?"

"Yeah, it's in the car. I'll go get it."

When Paul brought it back, we spread it out on the table and put the paper on top.

"Okay, this one," I said, pointing to the map, "What *is* that? See here, on the list it says, 'Jericho Ridge,' but I don't see it on the map. Do you? Or this one here, 'Harken Meadow,' or that one, 'Echo Creek.' How are all these on the list, yet not on the map?"

He leaned in and I smelled his soap and his clean skin.

"That is strange. So she paid money and they took her somewhere, but wherever they took her, well, it's not listed on the map. You checked all of them?"

"Just doing that now. Nope. None of them is on the map. She did say she went to local places, right?" I asked.

"Yeah, I think so."

"Well, what if these are local names? What if she was searching for something and these were the specific places she wanted to visit?" I was starting to form a picture of her strategy. "So she offered them this money each time she requested a location? Where did she get this list?" I wondered.

"That is a good question."

I sighed. "Why do I feel like I'm asking lots of questions and getting no answers?"

~~~~~

"Where are we off to next?" He asked, when we had paid our bill and gotten back in the car.

"Well, since I can't check who the people are in the locket's photos against the files from Elicia's file cabinet, then that's out -until we can convince Mrs. Ford to drop her threats. Spiteful woman. Why does she have to hate Elicia so very much?"

"Don't ask me. I'm still catching up on the whole 'Elicia didn't kill herself' part of this story."

"I think I'm going to make an appointment with an anthropologist at the university to see what I can find out about that doll. It looks tribal."
~~~~~

# Chapter 9

It was still early, not quite 4PM, by the time Paul dropped me off at home, so I called my friend at the University to see if there was anyone in the anthropology or even the art department who specialized in hand crafted figure sculpture.

"I think I'm going to need more context than that," Susan said. "Where did you say you found this figurine? Did you buy it in a garage sale or something?"

"No, Sue," I said, smiling. "I'm working on my own little mystery over here and I'm trying to get as much information as I can to figure everything out."

"What kind of mystery?" Sue and I went way back, to college days. I studied American History with an emphasis on Folklore and American Myth Culture. I know, big surprise, right? Susan and I had a lot of classes together, and she was an anthropology major, specializing in cultures of the Early Americas, so you can see how our interests would overlap.

"Well, Sue, let's just say I'm looking to put some of your schooling to use. I'm not sure how relevant it is to my investigation, but I need to know how old this thing is, what culture created it, and what it symbolizes. This may be a long shot, but just looking at it, I think it may be religious and not artistic. But that's why I need an expert."

"Since when are you an investigator? Don't you still have that hokey little business out of your home?"

I would just like to point out, my business is not hokey, but instead of snapping at her, I held back. I wanted to be nice, so I could get some information.

"I still do that. This is more like a side project for a friend of mine. Call it a spiritual investigation."

"Well, do you think it might be Native American? I might be able to help you out, if so. If you want anything African, etc. I can refer you, but I'm probably not going to be able to tell you anything myself."

"Somehow I don't think this is Native American. And I don't necessarily think it's African, either. I get the feeling it's from around here, just old."

"Well, I remember from experience that your hunches have a way of panning out, so bring it and I'll look at it."

"Thanks, Sue! I really appreciate it."

"Sure, but you know you're going to have to fill me in on the whole story once you get here."

"Well, I don't know what there is to tell you, but I'll let you in on what I've figured out so far."

"Sounds intriguing. I can't wait! Come over tomorrow and we'll chat."

~~~~~

After we had settled on a time to meet up, I cleared my dining room table and spread out everything I'd gotten so far from Elicia's house. I had all the Ford files I'd gotten previously, the files on Elicia's family, the pictures, and the research she'd done.

I shook the thoughts from my head, and went to my kitchen to put on the kettle for a cup of tea. There was a lot of reading to be done and I was not going to get to all of it today, but I needed organize everything to figure out where to start. I set out the cup and reached into my tea cupboard -yes, I have a tea cupboard-for a packet of apple spice.

I took the stack of files on the Ford family and I sorted them into a pile and put them on the high left corner of the table. In the center, I put the photos of Elicia that she'd taken herself. I had the first Polaroid she'd taken, the last she'd taken,
~~~~~

and the three that had been left at the house, warning me to go away.

I was overwhelmed by all the information I had in front of me, and yet still, I had so much more: a stack of transcripts from faith healers, psychics, gurus, religious leaders, and such, several research letters received from her many inquiries into the Ford family past, and findings on various paranormal phenomena that Lyle Struthers had done for her. There was also a stack of research that she'd done herself and what looked like a journal she'd kept near the end of her life. Glancing at the copyright on the back of it, the book was printed in 2002.

The histories, transcripts, the journals and paranormal research went on the right hand side of the table. My tea water was done, brewed and growing cold, and I was just now done sorting. I went back into the living room and got the locket I'd found, with the pictures in it, and the small figurine and set them on the table as well. Finally, it was all there, everything that I'd found or been given regarding the mystery of Elicia Wakefield Ford.

I closed my eyes for a moment, clearing my mind like I did before a session or before I worked the Tarot. Centering was a good way to open up the mind to new ideas or different modes of thinking. I opened my eyes and felt a distinctive tug toward the left side of the table. At this point in time, I knew there was one thing I wanted to focus on and that was Francis Ford. I went over to where my purse was and pulled out the paper with the different locations on it. I stared at it until my eyes crossed, but I still couldn't make any more sense of it than before.

After a few moments, I gave up. I decided to start with Elicia's words themselves, and taking the journal and my tea, I sat on my couch and started to read.

~~~~~

*Entry 1: I lay awake at night, shivering and alone in my*
~~~~~

*bed. I feel its presence. If you were to ask me what it is, I couldn't tell you. I only know it is stalking me. It has been following me around for years, this darkness, but until now I was unaware that my simple bad luck was a thinking, breathing malevolence. Even now, as I sit in my room -which used to be my haven- I force myself not to look in the corners. Here in the dark, anything could be lurking.*

*Entry 2: I looked at the photos today. It's subtle, this little bit of death I feel. When I look in the mirror, I almost see it, peering back at me. It's a smudging around the corners, the reason I add more blush and concealer. I try to disguise it, but there's nothing I can do. I know this. So why am I trying so hard to fight it?*

*Entry 3: I hate this house. I hate its loneliness. Life was so different when Jack was alive. Our giant, formal house was filled with life and love. We were so happy together. I guess I should be thankful for that. You'd think that after all these years, more than 50, I'd be reconciled to losing everything. I lost Nanny, my brother, Mama, Daddy, my baby, and Jackson. And each time I lose someone it hurts as though it was the first time. There is good news. I have no love left to give and I have no one left to love. I never have to feel that pain again.*

*Entry 4: The first time I noticed that something was wrong was about a year after Jack died. I was walking out on the grounds at dusk and I heard someone say my name. It was clear as the lake water on our property and I turned, surprised, to see who was calling me. No one was there. In that moment I felt the cold, a bitter, biting wind, spill over my body, grabbed at myself and stumbled back into the house. It was like nothing I'd felt before. No, that's not true. There was one other time I felt this way. It was so long ago I'd almost forgotten it.*

*Entry 5: I've tried cleansing the house. I've hired gurus and shamans and faith healers. I am diseased, I accept that. I do not accept that I am without a cure. I've earned peace in my life. I've earned the right to sleep without dreams or nightmares. I refuse to accept that my life will always be haunted.*

*Entry 6: There was a time when I thought I'd made it. I'd met Jackson and we were married. He never seemed upset about the fact that I couldn't give him children. For once in my life I didn't have to worry about where the next meal was coming from. I didn't have to count every penny. I was so naive. What made me think I could ever have a life without pain? What a silly child I was.*

*Entry 7: Something Jackson once said to me has been bothering me. He said, "Sometimes, without even a breath of life, we are already cursed." I wonder what made him say it.*

*Entry 8: It was the shaman who told me that I was doomed. I did not believe her at first, but her words convinced me.*

*"I can't cleanse you of this evil. It is beyond any power on earth that I was given." She wouldn't take my money either. I have lots of money.*

*"What is wrong with me?" I asked her.*

*"I know not," she told me, "but I know it is killing you, as you say. It is sucking the marrow from your bones. It eats at you like a child gorges on candies."*

*"If I can't be cleansed, what can I do? Surely not just sit and wait for it to take me?"*

*"I know not," she said again. "Perhaps if you find someone who sees with the third eye, they might be able to see deeper into your problem."*

*"The third eye?"*

*"Someone who uses the third eye sees things most people can not. Sometimes they see the dead, sometimes they see the heart, sometimes the future. Find one such as these and perhaps you will have the answers you seek."*

*So, I have searched out every psychic, gyspy and palm reader, with no success. They are all frauds. I don't think the third eye exists.*

*Entry 9: My time grows short. I know this with the certainty that the sun rose this morning and will rise every morning after I leave. I'm going to die. The shadows that I sensed for so long in the corners of my room have, in their wafting way, drifted out into my room, touching me and whispering hateful things in my ear. I don't jump at every little sound anymore. I am resigned. My doom approaches.*

*Entry 10: Last night I had a horrible dream about myself. I'm still not sure if it was me or some evil clone. I could see myself doing such horrible things: torture, mayhem, savagery. Even in my dream, I was appalled at my behavior. Dr. Jekyll watching Mr. Hyde from another body.*

*When I woke up this morning and looked at myself in the mirror, I could still see the evil lurking there, deep in my eyes. I ran to the bathroom and threw up. It's horrible, feeling like your soul is being twisted and stabbed by a darkness you can't name. I wish I could find someone who could help me. I'm dying. I feel that every breath I take will be my last, and yet I can't tell you why I feel that way.*

*I went to the doctor's last week and requested a full work up, but there was nothing wrong. I am, according to my doctor, a perfectly healthy woman in her mid-fifties. He looked at me like I was crazy and recommended a few psychiatrists that he works with. Am I going crazy? Do I need help from a professional? Sometimes I think so, but other times, I realize THIS IS NOT MY IMAGINATION. I have seen and felt things in my lifetime that would have sent most people over the brink. Yet until now, I had no fear that I was moving toward insanity. I still feel as though I am in my right mind.*

*Entry 11: Jackson was my salvation, there is no question in my mind about that. He was my reward for a life filled with pain and terror. He was my light at the end of the tunnel. Except for Mama and Nanny and Bridget, I don't think there was another person in my life that loved me just because I existed.*

*I never believed in soul mates until I met Jack. I never believed in happy endings. When we met, when I looked in his eyes that night in the restaurant, I felt a connection between us. I didn't know what it was then, just that I was drawn to him. Now, so many years later, I think I know what it was. We both went through so much pain in our lives that there was a longing in each of us for understanding. He and I understood each other. We could feel sympathy for one another without pity.*

*I didn't know anything about his past or his family when we met. I didn't know about his family until after he died, and I wasn't surprised. His past, though he was more distant from it than I was from mine, was dark enough to scare the most normal person. I wasn't afraid. I've seen past the edges of darkness.*

*Entry 12: I feel like I'm being followed. Everywhere I go now, I feel the urge to turn and look over my shoulder. That darkness around me is starting to take shape and I'm afraid, deeply afraid that I won't be able to face it when it catches up to me. Even when I was being abused, I didn't feel fear like this. On that first night so long ago, when I didn't know, I was still innocent as to why he was in my room after I had gone to bed. I was confused and sick when I realized that he wasn't coming to say goodnight, but it was nothing compared to what I feel these days.*

*I feel like something has attached itself onto my skin. Unable to see it, I feel it on me, leeching the life out of me. The phone rings, but there is no one there. A light is on in the house, but I didn't turn it on. Objects are misplaced and sometimes in bed at night I hear the whispers of a hundred dead men crying out to me in some garbled language. Once, I thought I heard my name, but the room was empty.*

*It follows me wherever I go. When I leave to find another failed attempt at a psychic or clairvoyant, I huddle in the bed of whatever luxury hotel I sleep in, pretending not to feel the darkness that lurks nearby. I've been turning on the 24 hours news stations on, because then I feel like I'm alone, lost in the noise of someone's voice.*

*Entry 13: I've found someone here in town who does readings. She's not a psychic, but her ad says she helps people find their purpose, what ever that means. She works out of her apartment and her name is Sibilant. It is a strange name, that is a word, not a name. Sibilant: a consonant characterized by a hissing sound (like s or sh).*

*I have nothing left to lose at this point. I would love to feel like I have control of my own life again. I'm not sure if that's possible. Maybe I'm at a point where there is no respite or rescue and as I've been been feeling for months now, my life is headed toward its end. I can feel that sinking sensation in my body, telling me that time is ticking down -subtracting the hours and minutes to my death.*

*I don't know why I even try any more.*

# Chapter 10

This time, I was walking through the woods, on a cloudy fall day, leaves falling in soft piles around me brushed by the gentle breeze. I could smell the damp soil -that distinctive scent of the earth after a short rainfall. Each of my steps crackled and crunched over dried branches, heralding my presence to any interested parties -animal or human- nearby. I have always been hopeless at stealth. I don't know why I was trying to be quiet, since there was no one around for me to sneak up on -I was in the middle of an Appalachian wilderness. My breath came in fast white puffs as my pace increased.

I still don't know what it is I was looking for, but whatever it was, I wasn't seeing it. I looked past tree trunks and sappy pine branches. I stumbled over bushes and logs and small rodent holes. I am not a woodsman. I kept my balance, but it became more difficult as my steps quickened.

I heard a sound to my left, a faint crackle. I jerked to try and see what it was, but there was nothing but empty woods. Not even a bird call to warm my bones in the loneliness. There -I heard it again, a dragging sound, like something creeping along the ground towards me. That was all it took. Like a frightened doe, I scattered, dazed and frightened, forgetting my original quest. I thought being alone in the woods had been frightening, but being in the woods, with an unknown someone is much more terrifying.

I ran without heed of my surroundings at this point. I ran without thought of where I was going or where I was coming from. I didn't think about what I was running from, either. I just had a sense of danger, the merest scent of evil, and the thought of a predator kept me going. I ran on, keeping ahead of it, trying to avoid the blackness I felt reaching toward me and stumbled into a clearing.

In the center of it, there was a ramshackle old house. It stood, single story, in front of me, halting me from my escape. The wind was more wild here and I now knew the rain to be imminent. The house shuddered and creaked under the force of the wind. The roof shingles flapped in a giddy danced as though they were ready to fly off the house and into the woods. With each moment the house seemed ready to rise up and take to the wind, but instead it stayed there, taunting me.

I heard a sound behind me and turned to see nothing, but I wasn't fooled. I knew something was there, waiting for me, hunting my trail with ruthless intent. I took a step toward the house and hesitated. It didn't seem to be any safer in there than it was outside, but any moment that thing would be upon me, or the sky would open up and drench me without mercy. I took another step, and another, and then made it to the first porch step of the house.

The door slammed open and the black entrance of it loomed in front of me. Something was coming out through the door.

~~~~~

I drove out to the campus on Monday for my 9:30am appointment with Sue. I pulled in to the visitor parking lot, paid for a parking pass, and parked in an open spot next to a luminous red maple. I've always loved fall foliage, and the University was a picture-perfect example with its tall brick buildings and sweeping pathways lined with bright orange, yellow, and rust colored trees.

I sighed as I walked, mulling over the journal that I'd stayed up reading last night, disappointed to find nothing about
~~~~~

Francis in the entire thing. Still, it was an interesting read and a clearer picture of what Elicia was experiencing toward the end of her life.

Her life had been filled with anxiety and nameless terror. It was no wonder she looked like she did in those last photos. The question was, what was haunting her? What nameless ghoul had made her life its personal pastime? I thought about the dreams I'd been having and the pictures of Elicia that had been left for me as a warning and shuddered.

I was starting to understand what it felt like to be in her shoes; those moments made me wish I'd done what the messages suggested and left her mystery unsolved. Not that I'd solved it yet, but every day I was getting closer. I knew that I was deep enough now that I didn't care if a year came and went, I would keep searching until I figured out what had happened. I owed her that much, at least.

I had looked online last night, right before bed, at a map of the campus to be sure where I was going, and now I could see that I had arrived at the Anthropology Department's building. I waited for the student exiting to finish before I went through the door, then stopped, letting my eyes adjust to the dim florescent lighting. Sue's office was down the hall, number 146.

"Come in," she said, to my knock. Sue hadn't changed much since the last time I saw her, a few months ago when we met for coffee, and not a lot since college, either. She'd always been long and lean with sandy brown hair. It was shorter now, and it looked like she'd gotten new glasses frames in a pretty gold color, but other than that she was the same. We hugged and she invited me to sit down.

"Now, show me what all the fuss is about," she said.

I dug in my purse for the bag I'd put it in.

She laughed. "Really?" she said, "Only you would have put it in a ziploc bag. Oh!" Her attention moved from the bag to the figure inside.

"Where did you find this?" she asked, eyebrows raised.

"So you know what it is then?"

"Know what it is, of course I do. Do you have any idea how rare these are? The idea that you stumbled across one, is just *crazy.* I have to call Dr. Carter, he'll be so excited."

"So, can you tell me what it is?" I asked.

"This, my dear Sib, is an *All-Inside*. I'll give you a bit of background, first, so you understand. High in the Appalachians, there formed a practice called Sin Eating, in which each village would choose a beggar or orphan or even someone who was mentally handicapped- to bear the sins of the recently passed. The custom was that this person would be a living vessel filled with the sins of the deceased person; they would eat food and drink ale passed over the body of the person whose sins they were accepting and voila, the deceased was then blemish free in the eyes of God.

"Don't ask me how this got started. Maybe it was a twisted version of communion for the dead. In any case, in some villages, another practice entered in, which scholars think was based on another practice popular in the deepest and most remote of the Appalachian peoples -witchcraft.

"Have you ever seen that witch movie with those three lost students? Remember those doll things hanging everywhere? Those are poppets, which are a lot like "Voodoo" dolls you always see on TV. Poppets are bound to a certain person and used by witches for spell work and such. Well, somewhere along the way, the idea of the Sin Eater and poppets merged, and it is called an All-Inside.

"This little figure was something that got passed down through a family for generations, passed from the death of one person to the birth of another. The idea is that it is bound to a person and carries their sins for them. It's very like a Sin Eater you see. The practice is that the person would hold it and whisper some kind of chant or spell and their sins or evil deeds would be pulled from them and lodged into their All-Inside.

"The reason I was excited to see this little fellow, is because it is so rare to come across one of these. They are kept in secret by the family or owner. It is considered tantamount to blasphemy to show one to an outsider.

When someone dies and there is no one left to give one too, it is buried or burned. The only one I've ever seen was in a picture Dr. Carter showed me. He's written a paper on many archaic Appalachian practices, made it his pet project. In fact, I think I can get a copy for you and email it to you, if you're interested in learning more. But please, please, you have to let me show him. He would be crushed if he found out we had one in the office and he missed it."

She looked at the clock. "He should be finished with his first class of the morning in about 20 minutes. In the meantime, tell me about it and where you found it. Why is it so important?"

I had to be careful here. I wasn't going to go around spreading the story of the Ford family or Elicia. I didn't know who it would get back to, so I settled for a more general story.

"I had a client come to me after suffering a string of bad luck. She told me that she'd been experiencing some out of the ordinary events. She told me about them and then I took a tour of her home. She collected a lot of interesting statues and figurines, but this was the only one she was unable to explain. Said she'd picked it up awhile ago, felt drawn to it, but couldn't tell me where or when she'd purchased it. The carving was interesting, so I decided to investigate it myself. If you remember, I'm always interested in the history behind an artifact, especially if it may have connections to a particular mythical or religious group."

"And you say she couldn't tell you where she got it?"

"Well, she had a lot of stuff. I bet she couldn't tell me

where she got half of those things. Most of them were recognizable, however. I saw some Hummel and Royal Dalton figurines -easy to label for anyone who loves antiques."

"Wow. And she had this little guy buried in with all that junk? Amazing." Sue sat back, examining the All-Inside once more. Then she glanced at the clock, exclaiming, "Dr. Carter should be in now. Can we go see him?"

I assented, after all, he might be able to tell me something that Sue could not. We walked down the dim corridor till we reached a door about four doors south of Sue's office. She knocked and we heard a deep voice say, "Come in."

We walked in and there sat a man as dark as his mahogany desk, reading glasses perched on the end of his nose, olive green threadbare cardigan and brown corduroy pants on, pouring over an academic journal. He looked up, smiling at Sue, and then looked at me.

"Dr. Carter, hi," said Sue. "Sorry to interrupt, but my friend Sib brought in a carving that I knew you would want to see. Sibilant, this is my fellow professor, Dr. Tempo Carter. Dr. Carter, this is my friend Sibilant Bedgood."

"Very pleased to meet you. Please, sit down." We did and I noticed that his office was more spacious than Sue's with larger windows and a collection of books that was at least three times as large, featuring several books on the Appalachian people. The room was dusty and cluttered, a cliché of office descriptions, but it was homey all the same.

"Now, what have you brought to me?" I held out my bag and he took it, peering at it through his glasses.

"Oh, my," was all he said for several moments, twisting and turning it. "May I?" I nodded and he opened the bag and pulled out the figure, again staring at it for several moments.

"Thank you, Sue, for bringing Miss Bedgood in today. What a delightful piece of early Appalachian folklore. Did Dr.

Simons tell you what this is?" he asked.

"Yes, she also told me a bit about the origins. I'm afraid I don't know where it came from or who owned it. In fact, I have no information about it at all."

"How intriguing. There are many stories about the use of the All-Inside. One of my favorites, which I mentioned in my paper on Appalachian objects and the lore surrounding them is about an All-Inside that comes alive."

"What is the story?" I asked, leaning forward.

"Well, according to legend, a man owned one of these figures that had been in his family for generations, except one day it went missing. He couldn't find it anywhere, hunted all around the house for it. Later that day, his wife and daughters asked him if he'd caught anything when he was out hunting.

"'I never went hunting,' he said. 'I was chopping wood and then I repaired the fence for the livestock.'

"'We saw you earlier, walking around in the woods. We thought you were hunting,' said his wife.

"Later that night, he found his All-Inside sitting on the front porch, though he was sure that he'd kept it in a small chest near his bed. Again a few days later, it went missing and this time it was the man himself who saw his mirror image stalking near him in the woods. He was struck with a deep fear, as he realized what had happened. He'd put every evil and worthless thought into his All-Inside and now it had become a living breathing thing, filled with all the ugliness he'd given it. When he found it, once again on the front porch, he burned it. It was too late, however. The next week, the man was discovered dead from unknown causes, no mark on him, but with a horrible silent scream upon his face.

"It was said that when an All-Inside was used for too long, the evil filled it to the brim and gave it powers. Some of them were said to come to life, mirroring the features of the owner, except more like an evil twin. Still others were said to infect their owners with evil, causing them to do horrible things. There are even stories about the All-Insides communing with the devil himself. Overall, however, they were an enduring and much revered part of the Appalachian culture."

I thought about Elicia's entry -where she dreamed that she was another person, an evil part of herself , and couldn't suppress a feeling of dread that washed over me. It could be a simple story, as Dr. Carter said, but maybe it was also too coincidental, considering where Jackson's ancestor's came from. It was possible it had been passed down from generation to generation. And maybe this little carving wasn't evil or didn't cause evil, but it lent credibility to my suspicions that the Ford family weren't as pristine as they would like others to believe. Maybe that was why they didn't want anyone looking at their family background.

"Thank you so much for sharing that with me. I had no idea a simple carving like this could have such a rich and interesting history."

I stood and took back my bag. Dr. Carter and Sue stood as well.

"Indeed, all of the Appalachian folklore is fascinating, which is why I wrote a paper on it. Would you like a copy? I think I have one here somewhere."

"Yes, please," I said and waited for him to finish digging around in his desk for it. He handed it to me.

"Here you are. I knew I had some copies. I always make my students read them. They enjoy it, so I hope you will too. And if you find anything else interesting or have any questions, please call me. Here's my card." I took it and shook his hand. Sue and I said our good-byes after leaving his office and I stared at the little figure for a moment before heading back to my car.

Why had Elicia put it in the safety deposit box with a

locket and some receipts? Where had she gotten it from? It was important to her, but why? Was it hers? Did she find it on one of her trips up into the hills? That seemed the most plausible. Maybe she had found it buried somewhere. If so, why did she think it important enough to save like she did?

On my drive home, I made some plans for the rest of the day. I would write up a report on the All-Inside, and call Paul to come over when he got off work. Oh, and next time Sophie came over, I would have her look at the carving and see if she had any impressions to give me. I didn't really believe the story was true, it seemed too easy, but there was no harm in investigating further.

# Chapter 11

When I got home, I pulled out the paper Dr. Carter had given me. I reread the entry on the All-Inside, then moved on to some of the other entries. It was an interesting article.

~~~~~~

Poppet: In folk-magic and witchcraft, a poppet is a doll made to represent a person, for casting spells on that person. These dolls may be fashioned from such materials as a carved root, grain or corn shafts, a fruit, paper, wax, a potato, clay, branches, or cloth stuffed with herbs. The intention is that whatever actions are performed upon the effigy will be transferred to the subject based in sympathetic magic. It was from these European dolls that the myth of Voodoo arose. Poppets were also used as kitchen witch figures.

*Tinsey, Tansey, Toppet, I've got myself a Poppet, I've got myself a Poppet. Poke it with a needle, yank its little arm, cut it with a carving knife, twist it up with yarn.*

Witch Ball: A hollow sphere of plain or stained glass hung in cottage windows in 18th century England to ward off evil spirits, witch's spells or ill fortune, though the Witch's Ball actually originated among cultures where witches were considered a blessing and these witches would usually "enchant" the balls to enhance their potency against evils.

In the Ozark Mountains, a witch ball was made from black hair that was rolled with beeswax
~~~~~~

into a hard round pellet about the size of a marble and is used in curses. In Ozark folklore, a witch that wanted to kill someone would take this hair ball and throw it at the intended victim; it was said that when someone in the Ozarks is killed by a witch's curse, this witch ball is found near the body.

*There was once a witch living close by the local village. The villagers were used to having her around, and went to her for various magical remedies, such as a failing crop, a colicky babe, or a lure of love.*

*One day, however, Mistress Livey started telling tales about her around town. She accused the witch of using her powers to turn the love of her suitor from her. Soon, all the women could remember were times when the witch had thwarted them or cursed them. Doing what women do best, they convinced their husbands and lovers that the witch woman, who up until that day had done none of them harm, was evil of the highest order.*

*The men gathered together and snuck up on her in the dead of night, and burned her house down around her. When one of the women went to check the next day, the house was gone, not even a pile of ashes left to show it had been there.*

*That night, there was a witch ball sitting on Mistress Livey's pillow when she went to bed. She asked everyone in the house, but none of them had put it there. Soon all the women were finding them, on their pillows, in their best baking dishes, in their sewing baskets, and in with their clothes. And one by one, those women who had told lies about the witch woman died, though no one could figure out why.*

Salt: In the Ozarks, women that complained of food being too salty were suspected of being witches. A method of detecting a witch, according to Ozark legend, was to sprinkle salt on the seat of a chair. When a woman sat in the chair, if she was a witch, the salt would melt and cause her dress to stick to the chair.

Angel Wreath (also known as Feather Crown): When a relative was close to dying, the members of this person's family started talking about the feather crown. The verdict was split as to whether a feather crown boded well or not for the dead family member, but every one still checked to see if there was a ball or tangled wreath of feathers nestled in the pillow where a dying relative rested their head. Some people might say that it meant the person went to heaven, others are just as convinced that they went to hell.

Buckeye: The inedible nut-like seed of the horse chestnut. In this context, a buckeye was carried in the pocket of the person, and used as a method of protection against evil. In some cases, it was also considered a good luck charm.

*A boy was walking home from Sunday school one winter morning when he saw a blazing fire in a snow covered field in front of him. He approached cautiously, for every boy in the hills knows to beware of the strange things that go on when you find yourself alone in the woods. He finally got near enough to see that it was a beautiful woman, glowing like a house afire, sitting on the rock in front of him.*

*Her hair fell to the ground and was tangled through with diamonds and pearls. Her hands held a harp, and she strummed it with great skill, matching each note with an even more beautiful voice. She suddenly seemed to see him, and she smiled, putting down her instrument and beckoning with a pale hand.*

*"Come, boy, let me show you how to play this fine harp," she said and waved him near again.*

*The boy was caught up in her glance like one hypnotized, and he walked closer to her, almost within the circle of her flaming light.*

*"Please, little one, come closer," she said again, and again he stepped toward her.*

*He was now so close that she could reach out and touch him, and she did, with an even greater smile on her face. But when her hand sought to grasp his arm, she drew back like she'd been burnt, and gasped.*

*"What did you do?" she screamed, putting off all pretense of beauty and kindness. It was an old hag, seeking a little boy for her supper, but for some reason she couldn't touch him.*

*The boy, shaking in his boots, ran all the way home and didn't stop till he had thrown himself through the door of his very own house. It wasn't until he told his granny the whole story that he remembered he'd been carrying a buckeye in his pocket for protection.*

Caul (or veil): A caul is the afterbirth, or bag of waters that most times breaks during labor, but in this instance is intact around the baby as it is born. When the baby came out, the midwife cut the caul from around the child before passing it to its mother. A family member, usually the mother of the woman in labor, saved it, preserving it in salt to dry, and presented it to the baby upon maturity. It was said that if this was not done, the child would have nothing but misfortune all its life.

*Once a baby was born in the veil, and very properly her nanny took it and hung it out on the line to dry. But in the excitement of the child's birth, the woman forgot it was hanging there, and great wind came up, blowing the veil out into the hills, where it fell into the hands of a hated enemy of the family. Forever after, the poor girl was without a will of her own, for she had to follow all the orders of the man who held her veil. Much evil did he perpetrate with her as his slave, and much was her sorrow upon her death.*

Charm String: A charm string is a simple sort of spell that any young girl can make for herself, without the help of a witch. All a girl would need is a string and some buttons collected from various places. If she collected a button from the dress of a married woman, it was said that she would find true love. If she gained a button from the clothing of a person who had become well after a long sickness, it was said that she would never be sick. If she collected buttons from a baby, she would have one for each button collected. A girl was never to collect bad luck buttons: from sick, sad, or mean people and she was never to put a black button on her charm string.

~~~~~

"Wow, look at you, all organized," Paul said.

"Be nice," I said, wrinkling my nose at him.

"Well, I'm sorry, you're just not normally organized."

"What? I am so organized! I-" I broke off, looking around the room at the piles of books, papers, knickknacks and other assorted sundries.

"Yeah, honey, I hate to break it to you, but the only other thing I've seen this organized is your tea cupboard. And let me just say, that is freakishly organized. How many different kinds of tea do you have? I think my last count was twenty-seven, but you've probably added a few dozen since then."

"I like tea, okay? There's nothing wrong with that."

"I think we both know you have a tea obsession. Sometimes I'm even jealous of the attention you give your tea cupboard."

I laughed, and then, just to show him, I put the kettle on.
~~~~~

"Oh no, she's serious now," he said. "Now the question is will it be mint or lemon jasmine?"

"Okay, okay, you've made your point. Let's get down to business."

"Explain to me your system. What have you got going on here?"

I quickly went over the layout, and then told him about the journal I'd read and about the All-Inside.

"Wow, you've been busy in the past day and a half. So what's the plan now?"

"I really think our next course of action is to try and decipher the map locations or find some other way to track down Francis. You took tomorrow off, right? I really want you up there with me when we scout out some of these locations."

"Yes, I got tomorrow off -like I'm going to let you drive around in the mountains without me. I think your best bet on these locations is to ask the person we go with. Let's just hope it's not Sue. Boy, did she have her panties in a bunch." He leaned over the receipts we'd looked at the day before. "You know, you could try tracking down the bank these checks were deposited at."

"How can I do that?"

"Well, usually the bank that deposits it stamps it and then it goes from there back to the issuing bank. So you get your check back. Unless you tell them otherwise, your bank holds on to that canceled check for you."

"But there's no way of finding out if Elicia had the canceled checks sent to her or if the bank held onto them."

"I think you could ask Jordan about that. I know he'd be happy enough to help you, since he feels bad about giving in to Mrs. Ford and her demands."

I laid my head down on his shoulder, looking up at him. We sat like that, in our chairs in front of the table for a minute, before he leaned in and kissed me. The whistle on the kettle blew, interrupting us, but I decided I wasn't all that interested in Elicia or her checks at the moment.

"Stay over?" I asked, nuzzling into his neck.

"Already planning on it," he whispered, and pulled me closer.

~~~~~

Early the next morning we rolled out of bed, showered, ate and said our goodbyes to Badger, before heading back to the mountains. I made sure to grab the map we'd taken on our last trip along with the list of odd locations that we wanted clarifying on. The office was closed upon our arrival, but there was a young woman waiting at the entrance for us. Paul whistled, a long low note of amazement, and I elbowed him, but I couldn't blame him. She was everything I wasn't and by that I mean tall and willowy, with the most gorgeous buttercup hair.

"That can't be real," I muttered and took in her straight cut gray pants and white blouse topped off by a shiny moss colored blazer.

She approached us, looking at me.

"Sibilant?" she asked.

I held out my hand and smiled. "That's me," I said as she took my hand, and I thought, "Oh!" There was something there, hard to identify at first, something familiar. I cocked my head.

"Have we met before?" I said. She laughed.

"No, but I get that all the time. There's something about me," she shrugged. "My name is Kinsey, by the way."

"No, I don't mean it like..." My voice trailed off and she stood there, considering me.

"Oh, that," she said. "It's interesting you picked that up. I'm what the locals up here call an 'herb woman' or maybe you'd be more familiar with the term medicine woman? What
~~~~~

are you?"

"Someone that looks for truth wherever she can find it. Is there a name for that?"

"You're not here for a simple tour." Her face became flat and her voice was not reassuring. "I think maybe I should cancel our trip today."

"No, please. We're not here to make trouble for you or anyone else up here in the hills." I could sense that she was serious about her role as protector. Paul just stood there looking between the both of us, probably wondering what was going on.

"Why are you here? And don't lie to me, because I'm not going to stand for it."

I rummaged through my purse for the sheet of paper I'd taken from the file they had on Elicia. I held it out for her to peruse. She snatched it from my hand and looked it over.

"Where did you get this?" she demanded.

"I got it here, of course. I took it right out of the file." I took her word for it on the lying. "We're here because something bad happened to Elicia before she died and I'm trying to figure out what. Did you meet her?"

"Yes, I was the one that drove her around to all the places on that list."

"So you know that there was something wrong with her."

"Well, I suspected. I don't make it my business to inject myself into other people's lives. I mean, it was obvious she was under some kind of curse, but she never talked about it, so I figured she must have had a good idea what she was doing."

"Why do you think she was under a curse?"

"I've seen it before. Back when I was apprenticing we ran across a woman who was under a minor curse -lack of fertility- and so I knew what one looked like. Elicia's was no minor curse. If I didn't know better I'd think, well..."

"You'd think it was a blood curse," I said. Her eyes widened and she nodded. "Yes, that's what I suspect, as well. And what's even more disturbing is that she doesn't seem to have survived it, does she?" She shook her head, eyes still wide. "Yes, I haven't ever dealt with a blood curse, period,"I said, "much less after the person involved is dead. I've heard there are some really nasty forces involved when you try to clear one up. But that is my task."

"If you want, I can show you these places. I have to warn you, it took us weeks to get to all of them, though."

"Is there any place on this list that she showed particular interest in or excitement for when you took her there?" She thought for a moment.

"Actually, there were a couple. Do you want to see those first?"

"Yes, please," I said and we all piled into her car.

It was good to know that this area had a shaman. As crazy as it seemed, knowing the spiritual health of a community told me a lot about what I might be facing in regards to Francis and his relationship with these hills.

"How far does your community extend?" I asked. Medicine women or men, as the case may be, practiced in local areas called communities. It was their job to maintain the health of their citizens. They could deal with minor curses, feuds, some of the lesser witches -not including hags or demons, which were above normal powers- had the skills to enact some weather charms, and anything that could affect their local economy in positive ways. They were like the kitchen witches of old, who made it their job to protect the hearth and home of the women in their villages.

"Oh, from here up to Jericho Ridge. Right here," she said, pointing to the map. "It's pretty quiet around here. None of the crazy stuff that went on in my granny's day. She was a pretty famous shaman around these parts. Now, it's just setting deer wards around the gardens and calling the rains down when the need arises. I have a friend who lives down in the city, she's busy night and day. I guess there's no real support for spirit work down there."

We talked shop for the rest of the drive, Paul soaking in the conversation in his quiet way. Since dating me, he'd come into contact with most of what we were discussing. Not first hand or anything, I try to shelter him from that. Heck, I've never done a reading on him. I'm afraid of what I'd have to tell him. I think he is, a bit, too.

"So really, what are you?" she asked again.

"Well, I guessed the closest label would be a Reader, but it's so much different than that."

"No, I know what you mean. When I try to tell someone I'm a medicine woman, they want to know if I can change into an animal." We both laughed at that. Hollywood and the American paperback fantasy market had twisted our craft into something based more on showmanship than substance.

After about an hour, she pulled onto a rough path in the woods.

"I didn't even notice it was here at first," she said. "Elicia found it, she just sat up and said, 'Oh my gosh, I didn't think I'd know where it was, but that has to be it!' Then she jumped out of the car and ran up this road. I got a call right then -can you believe I get cell reception up here -so I stayed down here to finish my conversation.

"She was gone a while, and when she got back she was so quiet. I asked her if everything was okay and she said it was, but she seemed so sad. I wasn't sure what to do, so in the end I suggested that we go home."

We continued up what must have been a road at one time. After what was minutes but seemed longer, we came to the end of it. Sitting there in front of us was an old cabin. It was, in fact, the cabin I'd seen before -in my nightmare, when the door had opened up like a great cavernous maw in front of me. This time, the door was already opened and I sat in shock staring at it.

Paul exited the car, and I stumbled out afterward, calling out, "Paul, no, don't-" while Kinsey cried, "Stop, no!" at the same time. Paul was slow to react, walking in his long-legged way up the first steps of the cabin before he stopped and turned back toward us.

"What is it?" he asked, puzzled by our dramatic reaction to the house.

"Paul, please listen to me. You know how sometimes I get a feeling about something and later on it turns out to be true?" He nodded, turning all the way around to face me, by this point.

"Paul, walk down those steps and come over here, right now. Please."

I kept my voice calm, but it took all of my will to pull it off.

"Sibilant, it's just a house," he said, walking down the steps. He stepped on something and looked down for the first time. He then saw what I had seen after my initial shocked recognition of the house and what Kinsey had seen upon arrival. He leaned down and picked up the small black ball, examining it.

"What are they?" he asked, referring to the witch's ball in his hand and also to the ones scattered in multitude over the front porch and the surrounding ground.

"They're curses," Kinsey told him. "Your best bet at this point is to put that nasty little charm right down and walk back on over here by us."

He listened to her, thank goodness, and dropped the hairy black ball on the ground, before walking with careful steps back to us. I grabbed his arm when he got back and the three of us stared at the ramshackle building. The roof was filled with holes, remnants of wind storms over time, not to mention bowed from water damage. Shingles were blown off and lying about in several places. Sagging, the front porch looked like it was falling into a pocket of quick sand. The front door hung open and half off its hinges. It looked desolate and abandoned, and I wondered how many years it had been since someone lived here.

I could tell from the hundreds of little black balls blocking the entrance of the cabin that someone was going to great lengths to keep people away from the house, and if not that, then at least to instil them with such a sense of unease that they would leave without knowing why. I turned to Kinsey.

"What are you feeling about this place?" I asked.

"Well, I don't know if these witch balls are the worst thing at work here. I'm sensing a deeper rift in the normal balance of good and evil in this place. Look at all of them, Sibilant. Someone with a deep hatred was working here. Each of those balls requires hundreds of hairs, black because that is what the curse requires, and at least a tablespoon of warm beeswax.

"And then there is the incantation said over each one. It could be something as simple as, 'Curse each heart that nears thee with fear and self-loathing,' or it could be as complicated as a curse that acts over an extended period of time.

"I couldn't say for sure, but I'm almost certain that these are about a thousand minor curses, meant to either give the educated person a healthy fear of this place, or give the uneducated person a feeling of edginess strong enough to keep them from remaining around here for long." I nodded. Paul looked confused at first, but as Kinsey talked, I saw his face grow somber and I could feel his body start to tense up, like the prey sensing the predator nearby.

"I have to say, in all my years working with unnamed

and mysterious powers, I have never seen anything like *this*," I said, my skin prickling when I thought of the malice the practitioner must have felt to cast these hundreds of curses.

"Well, I think I already mentioned that I've only dealt with the most minor of curses, and even then I was a mere apprentice," Kinsey said. She walked toward the house chanting The Four Seasons protection canticle. It was a favorite among shaman, because it harnessed the powers of the solstices and equinoxes.

The practitioner would start with winter, calling upon the power of the cold winter moon, then move to spring, calling upon the warm spring rain, next calling upon the summer sun's hot rays, then finally finish up with the autumn and the cool autumn winds. It is thought among shaman, that this canticle has the power to protect and also break minor curses.

As Kinsey walked, however, she seemed to grow less sure and then stopped, right at the top step of the porch, staring into the black hole of the doorway, shivering. I walked up after her, and grabbed her hand in mine. It was cold, which surprised me given that we were both dressed for the fall weather and had been outside the same amount of time. I looked up and saw that her face was white, washed free of all color, and I tugged on her hand.

"Kinsey," I said, "Kinsey, we need to leave this place. It's evil here and it goes beyond those silly curses."

She didn't respond at first, and then she started whispering in a husky voice the ending to the canticle, "Beyond these seasons, and beyond all time, I banish thee to the dark from which thou came."

I dropped her arm and shrank away from her as she pointed towards the house, and for a second I thought I saw a shape moving in the shadows. I shook, whether it was from the Witch Balls, I didn't know and I grabbed her hand, yanking her down the steps behind me, still reciting her that last line, over and over.

"Paul, you drive. Get us out of here, *now*." I hopped in the back seat, and yanked Kinsey in, leaning over her to close the door on her side and then pulled her seat belt on. She was silent now, a stricken look on her face. Paul pushed the limits of safety getting us down the hill, but I knew that we were still better off than staying up there a minute longer.

"I think we should go back to the office," I said. "She's not looking so good."

"Do you want to stop somewhere?"

"I don't know. It depends on whether or not I can get her talking. She looks like a ghost right now."

I touched her hand again, then brushed her blond curls back from her face. She seemed to shake herself awake and she turned to look at me.

"I'm sorry I freaked out back there," she said. "I thought it was as simple as a bunch of silly little curses, but it was deeper than that, and I should have seen it. I got up to that top step and it was like stepping into a whirlpool of hatred, fear, and greed. I became paralyzed by sheer overwhelming power I came in contact with. I don't understand it."

She shook her head, disbelieving. "I thought this area was so small pond now. I thought stuff like this had been weeded out in my granny's day. That was... it was terrifying. I remember the stories Granny used to tell me, ghost stories you'd tell a little girl. They were scary and all true: covens and rituals, hags and power struggles, evil trying to gain ground at every turn. I thought that was gone now. I thought people were too enlightened for that to happen any more. Nothing like this."

I sighed and leaned my head back against the seat. "Well, I don't mind telling you that was pretty scary for me, too. I had a taste of that when I met Elicia the first time, and

I've been coming in contact with an evil presence so large and powerful it terrifies me, too. I don't know what is going on here, but I know it's all related. In the end, it all seems to point back to Elicia.

"This is where she asked to go. She knew where she was going and whatever was up there, she faced it. But we still have no idea why she wanted to come out here, and we don't know what she knew. I wish I could talk to her, just for a couple of minutes. So much of this could be cleared up with a few simple questions, I think."

"I don't know, but I do know that we're safe, for now."

I couldn't argue with that, so I stayed silent the rest of the ride back.

# Chapter 12

By the time we got back to the Foundation's office, there were a few cars in the parking lot. I wasn't sure we were doing the right thing in leaving Kinsey there, but I also knew that I had some major things to deal with, first and foremost, looking at the rest of the places on that list and from there, finding out about Francis. The problem was I didn't feel like doing either. I was a big ball of tension and turmoil and I was not enjoying my quest.

"Are you going to be okay?" I asked Kinsey as we pulled up in to a parking space.

She took a deep breath, exhaling slowly. "Yes, I'll be okay, but that thing is in my territory. I'm going to have to get some advice on that. Granny's gone, but my mentor should be able to help or at least give me an idea of who can help me."

I was relieved to see she looked more determined than frightened. She was concerned about her community and that was giving her the courage to even think about facing that thing.

"Can you do me a favor before you go? Can you mark the rest of these places on an actual map? I think Paul and I will continue to try and check these out, since we didn't find what we were looking for."

"I can do that," she said. She took my red sharpie and made a few other marks on the page. Then she placed a large 'X' on the map and handed the pen back to me.

"That's where we went today."

"Oh, okay. Thank you so much for your time and your insight. I hope we can meet again under better circumstances." I took her hand in mine, intending to shake it, but I glanced into her eyes and I was sucked back into that place I'd been before with Elicia. Except this time, it was like I was viewing it from a distance, instead of being in the middle of it. Suddenly, I knew what she had seen, there at the edge of the cabin. Whatever was up there, it was a piece in all of this. I came out of my mini trance with a shake of my head and Kinsey said goodbye to both of us before heading back inside.

"I need some coffee," I said.

~~~~~

"So how did you know, before you ever left the car, that the cabin was evil? You're no shaman," he said. I nodded.

"No, you're right, I don't have the ability to sense what the earth is feeling around me. I can't tell something is evil by looking at it. But I've seen that house before. I didn't realize it until we got up there, but I had a dream about that cabin a couple of days ago.

"I was wandering around in the woods and I think I met something bad, because then all of a sudden I was running away from it and ran almost smack dab into that shack. I stood there fearing what was chasing me, but I couldn't move forward, because I knew that something even worse was waiting for me in that cabin." I was silent for a moment while I stirred my mocha. The cafe we had stopped at was quiet and dark at this time of the day.

"Oh no," Paul said. "I've seen that look before. I know what it means."

"Hmmm?" I said, half paying attention to him, my mind still on the cabin.

"You're going to go back. I can see it written all over your face."

"Well, maybe. Not right now. I have other priorities right now and the last thing I want to do is walk into some sort of hex situation unprepared -which I am at this point. I can't
~~~~~

help feeling that place is important somehow, but I don't deal with these kind of situations.

“You have to remember, Paul, I'm the lady with the one bedroom Victorian apartment. I have a comfortable green chair and people trust me when they look at me. I tell women about their love lives. I don't deal with the undead or the half-dead. I don't deal with curses and evil and magic. It's not part of my everyday experience. These things are best left to the experts. Elicia, however, couldn't find an expert, for whatever reason and somehow the universe led her to me. The least I can do is try to help."

"Just do me a favor, sweetheart. Don't go up there alone. That place was creepy." His face was serious and I smiled at him.

"Oh, I'm with you. It was seriously creepy. You'd have to pay me a million dollars to go up there by myself. Besides, I think that whatever role that cabin served, it's long over now. There is some lingering part, but I don't think it's important to this story anymore. In fact, I think that might have been where Magnus and his wife had Francis at first, before they moved him and set someone to guard over him. So there is possibly still a connection to this whole Francis and Elicia thing, it's just residual."

"So you're saying, it's an important piece of the overall story, but it's in the past and its usefulness is gone. We're moving upward and onward toward finding Francis."

"Well, through all of this, I've still felt like he was the place where our story ends."

"It will all work out," he said, starting up the car, and backing it out of the parking space.

"I feel like time is running out. Something is moving this story forward, and it's not a good thing."

"Time is running out like, it's almost up?" he asked.

"Not so much that, as this gut feeling I have that

something bad is going to happen. I can't shake it from my bones. I feel it in the marrow and it is scaring the heck out of me."

He frowned. "I'm getting worried here, Sib. I don't want you in danger. I admit I don't understand a lot of this spiritual forces stuff, but I know that you come into contact with a lot of things that can't be explained."

"I think it may be too late. I think these events were set in motion when Elicia walked through my door. I'm playing out a role that I'm being forced to take and right now all I can focus on is trying to end this."

~~~~~

I woke up with Thadius standing over me. I gasped and sat up, backing away at the same time. He stood by my bed, floating there, restrained in a way that made me wonder if he was being held back by something. The last time I'd seen him in a dream he'd tried to kill me by strangulation.

"I warned you," he said. "I tried to keep you away, but you did not listen. You walked right into the middle of it, mocking me." His flowing black robes hung around his arms and shoulders. I was puzzled.

"You tried to kill me. Why are you here?"

"I tried to warn you that your actions would have consequences. You did not listen and and now innocents have paid the price."

I felt a chill at his words and thought of Paul.

"What do you mean?" I asked. He stood there, glowering at me, then reached down and grabbed my arm.

"Come," he said, yanking me to my feet. I had time to slip on shoes, before we were floating through the walls of my house and up above the apartment, into the cold autumn evening air. The night was full of black shadows and I estimated that it must be late, but I was unsure of the time.

"Where are we going?" I asked, but he didn't answer. I
~~~~~

was freezing and my eyes and nose began to water both in reaction to the battering wind and also to the biting cold. We floated past the town where I lived and up, up into the hills we'd come out of just that afternoon when we went home to Badger and our evening run.

As we flew, I felt a growing dread and wished with all my heart that we were moving in the opposite direction.

"Yes, you feel it. You call it instinct and deny your greater powers, but I know you feel that unease. That is death. It has no mercy, which you shall soon know." His fingers tightened on my arm and I flinched, whimpering. His lip curled, I could see he was sneering at my weakness. I felt cold inside and out.

I had thought we would end up going back to the cabin, but instead we moved away from the hills and back down into the valley. We flew for a few minutes longer, then he took an abrupt dive towards a set of steel and concrete apartments that were a short distance from the hills we'd just left. We floated down through the top of the building and deep into its core until we came to a door. I started pulling away from him, fighting against the idea of going into the apartment, but he ignored me, his vise grip forcing me onward.

The inside of the abode was a mess, broken dishes on the floor, cupboards open, papers and food scattered about, books off the shelves, a lamp flipped on its side and blinking off and on. We were no longer floating and now he was pulling my arm, making me stumble over a broken vase and skirt my way around the debris, while he led me down a hallway to the left and to what I knew was the bedroom.

There, lying half on, half off the bed was Kinsey, or what was left of her. She'd been wearing pajamas at the time of her death and they were slashed and torn, her hair was a tangled mess of bloody blond hair. Her arm was bent at a strange angle, her head and neck were stiff and her face was a bloody pulp. Worst of all was the blankness in her eyes. They were blank and empty. I wanted to weep when I thought of how kind and full of life they had been mere hours ago.

I turned my face away, but he made me look at her.

"Look, look upon your handiwork, child of light. You pushed and pushed your way into matters that do not concern thee, and this is the result. Have you not already been told of our immortality? Have you not felt our malice upon your own body? And yet you continue to believe that you are immune to the effects of our power. Look on her body, feel her pain, and know that you will soon follow."

He let go of my arm and back handed me, sending me reeling to the floor, except that somehow I landed in my bed, and lay there, crying, feeling that my life was over.

# Chapter 13

It was afternoon before the police showed up at my door. I'd spent the morning doing laundry, cleaning my kitchen, and trying to convince myself that my dream was not reality. The images from the dream flashed through my brain: the apartment in a shambles, Thadius' cold gaze, and finally Kinsey's beautiful golden hair spread over the bed, covered in her blood.

Sophie was in my living room, having come when I asked her to come over and look at the All-Inside. I'd taken to carrying it around with me; it was the perfect size to fit in my purse. We sat staring at it for a while, admiring its simplicity.

"It's unassuming, isn't it?" I said, handing it to her. She took it, peering at it like she was trying to read all the secrets in the world.

"I don't feel anything. Nothing," she said after a few minutes of hard concentration.

"Just relax," I said. "Then try again."

"No, what I feel is, it's empty. It doesn't have anything in it, no feelings. I don't sensc what I did when you showed me those other things. It feels like it's waiting for something."

"Well, that makes sense, considering its purpose, but I figured it would be holding something, like a vessel. Interesting."

Sophie started to say something and then there was a knock at the door. I knew who it was, even though I had no reason to believe that they would need to talk to me. Somehow, I knew that it was about Kinsey.

I walked to the door, feeling like a wind-up toy, my heart pounding. I reached for the handle and opened it. Two officers stood on my stoop.

"Sibilant Bedgood?"

"Yes, that's me," I said, pasting a look of concerned curiosity on my face.

"We would like to speak to you about Kinsey Holcomb. May we come in?"

"Of course," I said, opening the door wide to admit them. Then I turned to Sophie and said, "These officers need to speak to me now, Sophie. Why don't you leave and I'll call you later?" I ushered her out the door, ignoring her curious looks and eager eyes.

As I shut the door, I willed myself to be calm and turned.

"Sorry for the wait. I'm sure you're busy. Now, how can I help you, officers?"

"You had a meeting schedule with Ms. Holcomb yesterday?"

"Yes, my boyfriend and I met her at 8:00 yesterday morning at the foundation. She was going to take us on a tour of the area that the foundation reaches out to."

"How well did you know her?"

"Not at all. We hadn't met previous to that morning and we didn't see her afterward. She drove around with us for a while and then we dropped her off there around 10 or so."

"Was she acting nervous or frightened? Did she seem distracted by anything?"

I paused at this. *You mean when we ran into the haunted cabin and got scared out of our minds by the Witch Balls and the crazy curse*, I thought.

"No, she seemed normal to me. I have to admit, I don't know her, but looking back, I didn't notice anything out of the ordinary. Has something happened to her?"

They looked at each other for a moment. "Ms. Holcomb had breakfast plans with a good friend this morning and didn't show up. Her friend tried calling several times, but she never answered. Finally she went to the apartment, supposing that she had slept in, and found her body."

"Oh my God," I said, and didn't have to force feelings of my dismay. I couldn't really believe that my dream was true. I sat on my green chair and felt pale and wrong. *Why, oh why,* I thought. She hadn't done anything to anyone. She hadn't done anything. She hadn't. I couldn't even form full sentences anymore.

"Ms. Bedgood? Ms. Bedgood?" I shook myself and stared at them, pulling myself back into the real world.

"I'm sorry," I said, "I'm just, well, shocked. I saw her yesterday. Yesterday."

"Yes, we understand. And you're sure that you didn't notice anything out of the ordinary when you met up with her?"

"I didn't notice her behaving in a way other than normal."

They stood in unison, a move perfected from years of practice, I was sure.

"Thank you for your help, miss. If you remember anything else you think might help, please give me a call." She handed me a card and I glanced at it, but I knew I probably wouldn't be speaking to them again.

What would I say, "Oh, hey, I just remembered, a demon came to me in a dream and he showed me Kinsey's dead body?" Yeah, that's just what I'd do.

So instead of being insane, I said goodbye to the police officers, and let myself absorb the new development.

I reached for the phone, calling Paul. The phone rang and his voice mail picked up.

"Oh my God, Paul. She's dead. Kinsey is dead," my voice broke and tears clogged my throat.

"I can't believe it. I had a dream about this last night, but I hoped, I hoped it wasn't real, but it was. I just got done talking to the police. She's dead, Paul, and I as good as caused it. They told me that I caused it and they were warning me that someone else will die if I keep trying to find out why Elicia died. I can't talk more right now. Call me."

I pressed “end” on my phone and stood staring off at the wall, deep in thought.

There were now two women who were dead and I still hadn't figured out what was going on. I hadn't found even a hint as to where Francis was, and every time I figured out another piece, I got stonewalled. I was just about ready to throw in the towel.

I sank into my chair, slumping forward with my head in my hands. I sat there for about 20 minutes, thinking about the hopelessness of my quest. That is when the phone rang.

~~~~~

"Sibilant?" It was Jordan.

I made some sort of muffled despondent noise from the cushion of my chair, the phone pressed up against my cheek.

"I know where the check was deposited and who signed it." I sat up.

"How did you find that out?" I asked.

"I called the bank. We got to talking and now I pass that on to you."

"I'm listening."

"So the bank is the same bank that the safe deposit box was located. And the person who signed the check is... Bay Willard."

I gasped, remembering the file I'd read from Elicia's research.

"Does that name sound familiar?" Jordan asked.

"Uh, no. I just dropped my glass and splashed water all over the place. I have to go clean this up now, but thanks,
~~~~~

Jordan. I'll follow up on those leads."

"Sure, and good luck, Sibilant."

I hung up the phone and went over to my kitchen table organizational space. I picked up the stack of file folders dedicated to Elicia's research on the family and read through the entry that she'd written on Bay Willard, the former caretaker for Francis Ford. I read the phone call she'd made, but I didn't see a phone number listed anywhere. I guess I would have to do it the internet way and find a good old fashioned search engine.

I typed in Bay Willard and Texas and came up with a couple companies, a ranch and nothing but a bunch of misspellings. I almost gave up, but I remembered that the interview mentioned that Willard was living on a ranch in rural Texas. So I gave the ranch number a try. It picked up on the third ring.

"Willard, here." A gruff voice informed me.

"Is this Bay Willard?" I asked.

"It is. How can I help you?" he said.

"Mr. Willard, my name is Sibilant, and I'm a friend of Elicia Ford's."

"I can't talk about that."

"What?"

"I can't talk about the Ford Family, signed a non-disclosure agreement. And believe me, if there's anyone I don't want to cross, it's that bitch woman, Phyllis. I had enough of her with the constant visiting and checking up on me. Like I was going to steal something or not take proper care of her precious son."

"Wait, Phyllis visited Francis? She came to see him?"

There was silence. "I've already said too much. I should go."

"Wait, can I just ask one question? It's not about Francis, it's about Phyllis."

"I might not answer, but go ahead."

"How often did she visit him? Was it once in a while, like once a year? Or was it more frequent than that?"

"She visited him every Sunday morning for as long as I worked for them, the Fords. Is that all?"

"Yes, and thank you." I hung up the phone, astounded. Elicia had made it seem like Phyllis had cast her child aside and spent her life pretending he didn't exist. Another thought occurred to me. No, it couldn't be that simple, could it? I dialed Jordan's number. His secretary put me through to his line.

"I need Phyllis' address," I said, when he answered the phone.

"Why?" he asked.

"Jordan, do you really want to know? I mean, is it going to get you into some kind of trouble, telling me? If so, I'd rather not involve you if I don't have to."

"Hmmm... better not. No one will know that I gave it to you anyway," he pointed out. "Do you have a pen?"

"Yes," I affirmed. He gave me an address located on one of the older streets in town. It was a grand old neighborhood, filled with three story brick townhouses built in the late 1800's by Northern investors hoping to rake in some cash during the Reformation. Each of those houses was in the several hundred thousands of dollars range. It did not surprise me that Phyllis Ford had a home smack dab in the middle of that vicinity.

"Be careful and don't do anything that will get you arrested," he warned.

"I promise I'll be good," I said, and settled down to make plans for the morning. I wondered if my hunch would pay off, or if I would run into yet another brick wall. If I was right, Mrs. Ford was not only much maligned, but she was more human than I'd given her credit for.

~~~~~

Paul insisted on meeting for dinner. The first thing he did when I walked into the restaurant is give me a tight squeeze. It's nice being short when you can get the perfect hug out of it.

"Sib, honey, I'm so sorry, I got to working late on this project didn't get a chance to check my voicemail. It must have been horrible get the news like that after such a terrible dream."

“Oh, Paul, it was. It was awful,” I said into his chest. He held out my chair, then sat across from me.

“What in the world did you tell the police?” he asked.

“What could I tell them, Paul? That she was killed by a malevolent spirit?”

“So at this point, Elicia and Kinsey have both been murdered by someone who comes to you in your dreams?”

“I don't know, maybe,” I said. “Are my dreams real? There are real elements to them.”

“How many dreams have you had about him?” Paul asked.

“Three so far,” I said.

“Do you think this murder was to warn you away, because I have to say, I'm scared for you right now, Sib,” he said.

“I'm scared for me, too. I'm not sure what to do, here. I feel like I should give this up, for the sake of my sanity. But every time I think about Elicia and Kinsey, I get so angry that I want to keep going.”

“So now you're off to stake out Mrs. Ford's house? Do you think that's a good idea? You told me that she was not the most calm person. If she catches you, you could be in some serious trouble,” said Paul.

“I don't know what else to do. She has been seeing him, Paul. He's the only lead I have. The faster we find him, the faster we figure out how to help Elicia.”
~~~~~

~~~~~

Early the next morning I drove over to Phyllis Ford's house and parked across the street. She lived right across from the park, of course, in one of the most sought after areas of the city. It worked to my advantage, because no one would notice in all the traffic if there was a car parked in front of the park for a longer than usual time. I pulled in to a spot a couple houses down from Phyllis'. I pulled out my breakfast burrito and started in on it, sipping cocoa occasionally.

~~~~~

Four days later, I was still in the car. Vehicles drove by and I was dying a slow death of boredom. Paul had come a couple of the nights to bring me dinner and sit with me. We'd even walked Badger in the park across the way.

Finally, today at around noon, I saw her leave in a mint condition Mercedes, no chauffeur. I pulled out of my spot and followed a discreet distance behind. It was a mistake. We went to the post office, the drug store, the bank, and then back to the house. And that is where I spent the rest of the day, disgusted with myself.

What did I think she was just going to lead me to him? Did I think if I just followed her around long enough we'd end up at a remote mountain cabin? Pathetic.

Just as I was about to pack it in for the day, my cell phone rang. Fumbling for my purse, I grabbed it and pushed the talk button.

"Hello," I said. I didn't recognize the number.

"Sibilant, hello. This is Lyle Struthers. We met a few weeks ago regarding Elicia Ford."

I smiled. "Yes, I remember."

"I went down into town today to buy some supplies and pick up my mail. I drive there every couple weeks or so." He paused and I wondered where this was going. "I'm sitting here in my truck looking at a letter from Elicia. It was postmarked the day before her death, according to what you told me."

I was silent, taking in what he'd just told me. The only word that I could process at this point was, "How?"

"Sibilant?"

"What's in it?" I blurted.

I heard a rustling over the line and could hear the rumble of passing vehicles around him, which the truck did a poor job of muffling.

"It's a key," he said, "It's just a key with a tag."

I couldn't contain my impatience.

"What does the tag say?" I asked.

"File cabinet, bottom drawer," said Lyle.

"File cabinet... oh!" I said.

"I take it you know what this is."

"Yes, yes I do. Is there any way you can mail it to me while you're still in town?"

"Sure I'd be glad to. Why don't you give me your address? Wait, I need to get a pen."

After more shuffling and rustling, he found the pen and I gave him my address.

~~~~~

I must have drifted off, because the next thing I know I was sitting up in my car, wiping my eyes to get the grit from the corners. I sniffed, smelling a the faint scent of dog and looked to my right. There was a white dog sitting on the seat of my dirty cab.

*Wait a minute,* I thought, *I don't have a dog and I don't own a truck.*

I looked down at myself, examining my old flannel shirt, rough leather work boots, and my wrinkled tan hands. I flexed fingers that were weathered with age and speckled with liver spots. I shuddered and panted, wiping my hands on my pants, as though trying to wipe the age off.

I flipped down the visor on the driver's side and stared
~~~~~

into the little mirror. I had piercing blue eyes, a thatch of white hair and a nose that tended toward hawkish. I knew myself, I was a man. I was Lyle Struthers.

My hands were shaking, and I wanted to pick up my phone and dial Sibilant -who was myself and not myself. But my hands moved of their own accord to the ignition, where I started the car, moving my hand down to shift the gears and move my foot slowly off the clutch. I pulled out of my parking spot at the post office and pulled into the line of traffic heading toward the outside of town.

I switched on the radio to the local country station and whistled along with the rowdy tune that was playing over the air waves. My dog howled along with me; we were two souls free and enjoying our long drive towards home.

It wasn't until we hit the highway that I noticed the dog had started whining. I glanced over at him, and almost as though he could sense my eyes on him, he looked at me with his soulful eyes, then turned his head so he was looking out at the front of the cab and growled, low and long.

I looked back at the road, couldn't have had my eyes off it for more than a second, but when my eyeballs flashed their way back, there was a man standing in the road in front of my car.

My immediate response, besides the shout that burst from my lips, was to slam my feet on both the clutch and the brake. I yanked the wheel around to the right and my truck followed suit, swerving around with a horrifying squeal of melting tires and grinding brakes.

The car did a hop forward as it bumbled across the edge of the road. I tried to correct my course, but it was far too late and I plummeted down the steep grade of the hill.

It was a strange moment of clarity for me, my complete inability to rescue myself from my current situation. I was thrown forward against seat belt, feeling the breath pushed from my body with a whooshing sound. I felt -or maybe it was I heard- one of my ribs pop and buckle, sending a spasm of pain through my chest.

The car pitched sideways and rolled over, sending the dog flying against the seat, yelping. The truck continued to roll and then smashed up against a boulder, where it flew up in the air once again spun around 90 degrees and landed upside down, crunched like a child's tin toy.

My dog, who had whined and yipped his way down the hill with me now lay still, half in and half out of the truck's rolled down window, blood dripping from his muzzle. I tried to reach him but I was still held captive by my seat belt. I groaned, more from the situation I found myself in, then from pain. I couldn't feel anything, but I sensed that I was more badly hurt then I could grasp under the circumstances.

I coughed and shuddered. I needed to get out of the car, but it was like my brain couldn't connect itself to my various limbs. My strings had been snipped and I was a lifeless puppet, dangling in the cab of the truck. I gave a halfhearted shove at the driver side door and to my surprise it seemed to fly off, tilting and swaying on its hinge.

There was no way to cushion myself from the pain that would come when I released my seat belt; I had no choice, it had to be done. It took me three hard -or what seemed like hard- presses against the belt buckle to get the latch to release and when it did, I oozed downward like a plate of wet pasta. I aimed my head so my body would end up at least partially out of the cab.

I ended up with my head, left shoulder and part of my arm outside the door. Panting and wheezing, wiping at my bloody eyes with tired hands, I wriggled my body further out of the cab, now my entire torso was hanging over the crunched metal roof that rested against the dusty ground. I smelled rust, metal and gasoline and I knew that I had to move even more, but my legs wouldn't budge.

Like two lead bars they curled across the worn leather seats, taunting me with their silent ineffectualness. I pulled at them until the sweat beaded and ran down my face, mingling with the blood there and staining my shirt. I was losing strength as the enormity of my injuries started to take a toll on my old bones. I breathed loud and fast like a hot dog, but the more minutes that passed drained away my precious energy even more.

I sagged against the ground, staring up at the clear fall sky. The day had started out so well, and now I was dying in a pool of my own blood. My breathing became that classic shallow death rattle, and I felt the peace of ending steal over me.

I thought of the letter and the key.

"Sibilant," I whispered, and closed my eyes.

Then, I died.

## Chapter 14

I was crying again. My dream was no dream. As with all the others, I felt the truth of it, aching inside of me. I mourned Lyle, who at the very least didn't deserve to die that way, by the side of the road and in such pain and confusion.

For a long time, that's all I could focus on, the thought that I had caused another death. I had found another piece to the puzzle and the consequences of headway in this sick game always seemed to be death. I was so sick of the dead and dying. I wanted my old life back. I wanted to feel normal again.

*Normal, what's that*, I wondered to myself. Normal was only a few short weeks in the past, but at this point in time, feeling the blood of the others' lives on me, normal seemed light years away from where I sat in my cheap economy car.

I brushed an errant tear from chin and sat up with new determination.

*That's it,* I thought. *I can't do this any more and I don't want to. I was wasting too much time.* It had been a week and a half since I'd met Elicia and I knew barely anything more than I did when I started. I was going in, God help me.

I got out of my car, took a steadying breath, and walked across the quiet street. I dragged my feet up all twelve of those steps up to the front door. I stood there for a few minutes gathering my courage and wondering why I had thought I could do this. I rapped the ornate bronze knocker against the solid oversized door. A few minutes later an older woman in a uniform opened the door, peering up at me. She was stocky and severe, iron gray hair pulled back in a bun that was tight enough to give her a mini-face lift.

"How may I help you?" she asked.

"I was wondering if I could speak with Mrs. Ford." I said.

"Who may I say is inquiring?"

"My name is Sibilant Bedgood. I believe she knows who I am," I said, hoping that she wouldn't insist that I leave immediately. I waited, clearing my throat, hoping, hoping, hoping that I'd done the right thing, made the right move.

I heard her shuffling steps on the gleaming hardwood inside and knew that I was about to hear the verdict. She opened the door wide.

"Mrs. Ford will see you in the green room," she said, ushering me toward a beautiful room decorated in sea foam green. There were pale, almost white translucent drapes that ran from floor to ceiling. The lamps clear with puffy green shades. The two love seats positioned at right angles from each other were pinstriped green and cream, with scarlet cushions plumped up at the ready and scattered over them. The rug was also green and cream, and the end tables were a pale wood. It was a calming room and I wanted to live in it forever.

She made me wait, but I wouldn't expect anyone with her caliber of snobbery to do anything less. The woman lived across from the park in a three story mansion, for heaven's sakes. I resigned myself to a long wait, but to my surprise she came in about ten minutes after I had been seated.

She was not pleased to see me. How did I know this? Well, her first words after entering the room were, "Why are you here in my home?"

"I'm here to talk to you about Elicia. I know you didn't

approve of her or of the fact that your son chose to marry her."

She flinched, and gazed off towards the window, lost in her own world.

"Jackson was always such a wonderful boy. He deserved better than her. She couldn't even have children. I will never have grandchildren thanks to her."

"Isn't that a good thing, considering what happened to you?" I asked, knowing she would be less than pleased at the bend in our conversation.

"What do you mean?" she asked, squinting at me. She seemed cantankerous, but then, she had no reason to see me as friend rather than foe.

"I mean Francis. Would you rather she had been able to have children? She would have ended up with someone like him, eventually." Her mouth was open like a fish.

"How do you know about Francis? Did she tell you about him? There is nothing wrong with him! There never was."

I mulled over how to be tactful in my accusation that her demon spawn child had done away with Elicia.

"Everyone I've talked to seems to think that Francis has some problems." I said.

She stalked toward me, stomping her tiny feet. "There is nothing wrong with Francis, nothing! I'm so sick of people trying to convince me that he doesn't deserve to be treated as well as anyone else."

"You have to admit he has some... er... peculiarities," I said.

"You sound just like my husband. Just like him," she dropped down on one of the couches, as though she were a wind up down run down. She was pale and forlorn.

"When I married Magnus, I was caught up in the glory of him. He was charismatic and stunningly handsome. He was the sun and I was the flower. I was completely bowled over. I had no idea that there was a horrible curse over his family. I didn't find that out until I was married to him and pregnant with Jackson.

"He was acting strange, distant and brooding. Finally, I got him to tell me about the curse that plagues the sons of his family. No one knows how it started. No one knows why it affects those it does, but in each generation it seems, one of the boys is stricken.

"Jackson was perfect and I think Magnus deluded himself into believing that we had escaped unscathed. Then I got pregnant again, this time with Francis. As soon as he was born I knew something was different, but I hoped that it was all in my head.

“By the time he was six months old both of us could tell that Francis was not like his older brother. He was... different. It was hard to tell at first, the differences were so small and almost undetectable. As time passed, however, we realized we were going to have to make some hard choices."

She leaned forward, hiding her face in her palms. The room was quiet.

"So you sent him away," I said.

"It was Magnus' idea to hide him away from the public, not mine! His company was becoming famous around the world and he was afraid of any blemish on his image. I wanted to keep my baby with me. I told him that I knew Francis would be better off with the love of his mother, than languishing away under the care of some person who was with him simply for a paycheck.

"Magnus put his foot down. Not only was the boy going to be sent away to some desolate and secretive location, but I was not to have any contact with him. It could, in Magnus' words, jeopardize everything. So he hired a string of people to care for my son. And he kept me from him.

"I hated him for it. Jackson was the perfect son, but he

never needed me like Francis did. Eventually, the strength of my desire to see my son overrode my fear of my husband and I figured out a way to go and see him. Neither Magnus or Jackson ever went to church with me. Magnus did not believe in God and insisted that faith was for the weak. He wouldn't let me take Jackson to church, though he never kept me from going.

"Every Sunday I would get up early in the morning, and instead of going to church, I would drive up to where my son was, and for a few wonderful hours, he would be mine again.

"When Magnus died, I knew that Jackson was paying for the care of my boy, but one day I got a call from the man in our employ. He informed me that Jackson had stopped payments and that unless I kept paying him, he would leave. Well, Magnus was dead, and Jackson didn't know his brother existed. So I told Jackson that it was time that he had our big house all to himself and I bought this house here.

"I brought Francis home with me to live. I hired a couple of people to help me around this rambling old place, but Francis is all mine. And no one will ever ask me to leave him again." She folded her hands together as she said this, and I sat across from her, speechless.

"I don't understand," I said, "Francis has been living here all along? Did Elicia know that?"

"What do I know what was going on in that woman's brain or not?"

"So as far as you know, Elicia wasn't trying to find information about Francis? Where he was located? What happened to him after you gave him up as a young child?"

"I never gave him up! Never. It was all Magnus' idea. I never wanted him to be alone. I never..." she trailed off then, looking lost.

"I'm sorry to bring up what must be a sore subject. I don't want to bring up bad feelings for your husband or your son, but I'm just trying to understand. You know there are stories about Francis, don't you? That he's a student of the darker arts? That he can set curses on people?" She came out of her revelry with a jerk of her head, sitting up straight and looking at me.

"About Francis?" she asked, laughing a bark of a laugh. "My Francis? That's absurd."

"Why do you say that?" I asked, confused, thinking of the many files I'd read about the Ford Family and the dark secrets that haunted them.

"Why bother telling you when you can see it with your own eyes," her voice was shrill.

She stood, gesturing for me to follow her. The long flight of stairs to the second floor was covered with a deep cream carpet that my feet sank into as we moved along. The entry at the end of the stairs was well lit by the afternoon light shining through the windows that rose from floor to ceiling.

She led me to a door on our right and stopped briefly in front of it, turning back toward me to murmur, "Please keep your voice low and calm. Francis reacts strongly to the emotions of those around him. If you are calm he is calm. You do not want him to become upset, things become... difficult... when he is upset."

I nodded, curiosity pushing out every other feeling. It was hard to believe that I would finally be meeting the person I'd focused so much attention on investigating.

She opened the door and stepped inside, holding it open for me to walk through, then closed it behind me with a decisive click. When I saw him for the first time, all I could think was the person sitting in the chair in front of me was *not* Francis.

## Chapter 15

I cringed at the stark contrast between Francis and his mother. Phyllis, an older yet still attractive woman, had a shoulder length layered hair cut and snow white hair. Her clothing was tailored and smacked of money. Diamonds gleamed in her ears and from the pendant at her throat. In short, she was the perfect picture of an upper class urban woman.

Francis was short and stocky -overweight, even. He sat in the chair like a potato sack, dark hair messy, but trimmed. He was in his late 50's, and his stubble was salt and peppered. He was lifeless, staring without expression, toward the window.

I knew when I saw him what Phyllis meant. Francis was not responsible for the curse laid on Elicia; neither was he part of a blood curse -at least not a magical one- though it might be genetic. He was not mentally capable of tying his shoes, much less harboring a malignant vengeance for Elicia or anyone else.

Phyllis walked over to Francis and laid a hand on his shoulder, caressing it. She leaned in and kissed him on the cheek, but he gave no sign of acknowledgment or reciprocation. I looked at the devotion in her eyes and felt respect for Phyllis. It couldn't have been easy, feeling torn between her husband and her son all those years. It must have been agonizing for her, having to be cut off from the child that needed her so much.

"Now you see what I meant downstairs," she said, looking at me.

I nodded and took careful treads into the room,

eyeing Francis.

"I don't want to shame your family or dig up skeletons," I said, still looking at Francis, feeling like an utter failure. "I never did. As far as I'm concerned your family is your business."

Her face softened.

"I could tell, downstairs when we were talking, that you're not a bad person. I'm sorry I called Jordan and made trouble for you. I was just so angry at the thought that you'd be in the house going through Jackson's things, even if it was on behalf of Jordan. I thought... I had hoped Elicia and I had reconciled before she died. She was sick and maybe felt like she needed resolution. She was so pale," she said.

"You don't know this, but Jordan hired me to try and find out more about her. She left a bit of a mystery behind her when she died. I thought Francis was the answer to my quest, but I can see now that I was a fool. I'm sorry for wasting your time," I said, feeling bitter.

"It's all right, my dear, how could you know? The Fords kept their curse a secret for generations. That's probably why so many weird stories cropped up."

She led me out the door and down the stairs, then held the door for me. I didn't want to leave without one final statement.

"You know, Mrs. Ford, there is one good thing in all of this," I said.

"What's that?" she asked.

"The curse is over for you. You can finally have peace." I don't know if the truth of this had occurred to her before. She nodded, eyes tearing up.

"You're right. I hadn't thought about it, but you are right. The curse is over, forever."

I left her there, standing in the doorway, watching me leave. Her hand reached up to brush away a tear.

~~~~~

I called Paul. The news was too important not to tell him.

Since it was his cell number, he picked up right away.

"Hey, honey, how are you doing?" he asked.

"I have big news," I said.

"What is it?" he asked.

"I found Francis," I said.

"What?" he said. "When did this happen?"

"Today," I said and explained what happened to lead me to Phyllis Ford's house.

"Oh my gosh," he said. "I can't believe it. I did not see this coming. And you're sure that Francis is, well, incapable of cursing anyone? Could he be faking it?"

"That would be a nice twist, if this was someone's mystery book, but this is real life we're talking about, Paul. Real life is not like a package you can just tie a pretty bow on and call it a present." I sighed.

"So I guess now we're back to the old drawing board," he said.

"Pretty much," I said, then I gasped, falling down against the hood of my car. "Except for the key."

"What key?" Paul asked.

"I got a call from Lyle Struthers today. He received a letter in the mail from Elicia," I said.

"She's been dead for about two weeks now," he said.

"Yes, but he lives up in the boonies and goes down to town every few weeks to check his mail. That's why he didn't see it earlier."

"What do you think the key goes to?"

"I know what it's for -the bottom of that file cabinet. He said he'd pop it in the mail for me, but I'm not sure when I'm going to get it. Honestly, I'm stumped. I was so focused on Francis and the Fords I don't even know where to start next."
~~~~~

"Why don't I come over after work and bring dinner? We can look through the information we've got and try to come up with a plan for where to go next."

"That would be fantastic," I said.

~~~~~

Paul's words echoed through my brain. Back to the old drawing board. I felt sick and exhausted. At the end of my rope and in a fit of frustration and pique, I got out my paper recycle basket and tossed every Ford file into it. The whole left side of the table was empty. All that was left was a few photos, the Polaroids, and everything on Elicia's side of the family. That's where the truth was now. Buried somewhere in Elicia's life. Time to start from the top. This time, I sorted the piles into a "read" and "unread."

After that was done, I resolved to start from the bottom and work my way up. I reached for the other side of the family, the Wakefield files.

~~~~~

File, Biography: Victor Alexander Wakefield III

Like me and Mama, Victor was an only child, but unlike me he grew up in a household with two parents. He was the apple of his parents' eye, spoiled and given everything, taught that life was a ripe fruit for the picking. His father was a successful businessman and he learned those life lessons at his father's knee, becoming twisted and power hungry.

He married Lydia just out of college, she was the socialite debutante of a local and powerful family. She was young, just 17, but he liked them young. I've wondered so often since then what her early married life was like. Did he say the things to her that he said to me? Lydia had never wanted children. As she told me that day she kicked me out, I was his toy, not hers.

His job was difficult. He often felt emasculated at his job, though he held a high ranking position. He had a need to feel powerful in some way and I guess raping a innocent and helpless little girl did that for him.

~~~~~

"Oh, my God, Paul, look at this."

He read the file I handed him. "Does this mean what I think it means?"

"He called her a toy. Her own father."

"It explains why she ran away from home so young," Paul said.

"Who the hell was Lydia? Her stepmother?"

"I don't think she's her mother, because look here she refers to someone as 'Mama' and then there is the woman called 'Lydia'. They can't be the same person," I said.

~~~~~

File, Biography: Lydia Melissande Bellefleur Wakefield

Lydia was born into a wealthy family. She was the middle child in five children. From what I've read of the Bellefleur family, they were a boisterous and happy bunch. They were the talk of the town, with their three beautiful daughters and their handsome sons. She loved Victor and according to her sisters they had a whirlwind courtship, marrying after only six weeks. Their wedding was the most expensive of the year and had over 500 guests.

After Victor died she was devastated and became a raging alcoholic. She spent a few years struggling to stay conscious, but after a while she joined Alcoholics Anonymous and sobered up. She got her realtor's license, sold the house she lived in with Victor, and spent the rest of her life as a swinging single.

I got all the last part after she showed up on my

doorstep while I was still working my way through college. I was one of the apologies in her 12 step program. We never stayed in touch after that, but there was no animosity between us. She was sorry about what she had said that night, and she was sorry for not stepping in when Victor started abusing me, but really we were both victims of Victor's need for power.

~~~~~

"What are you up to now?" Paul asked, when we abandoned our reading hours later to sit on the couch and switch on the television.

"I don't know. I thought I'd watch the news. I just have this feeling..."

The 11 o'clock news was just beginning to air and the headlines were being announced.

"Local man dies in car crash today, stay tuned for more in a moment."

My hands started shaking and I fumbled with the remote for a minute before Paul took it out of my hand and turned up the volume.

"Sibby, what's wrong?" he asked, turning to look at me.

"I-I h-had a dream," I stuttered, putting my hands against my flushed cheeks.

"What happened?"

I was interrupted by the new cast.

"Local retired teacher, Lyle Struthers was killed today in a fatal car crash when he lost control of his Ford pickup truck and drove off the side of a cliff. Mr. Struthers was found dead on the scene along with his dog."

The news continued, but for me it was in the background as I raced to the bathroom and vomited up my dinner, crying and hacking.

I heard Paul's step behind me.

"What did you dream, Sib?" he asked.
~~~~~

"I dreamed that he died, of course," I said. "I don't understand. I've never had dreams like this. Three people I've met in the past few days have died -innocents who deserved better. I feel like everyone who helps me gets hurt. I worry for you, Paul."

"Sibilant, I'm here now and I've been here. I'm not going anywhere."

He helped me clean up and put me to bed, where he climbed in beside me and held me until I fell into a dreamless sleep.

~~~~~

"What about the dreams, Mom? How do you explain those?" I asked her, the next morning, as I waited to see if Lyle had sent the key by overnight delivery.

"That I don't know. I've never heard of anyone in our family having such a gift. Does it seem like you've gained a new ability?" she asked.

"That's a good question," I said, "and one that I've given a lot of thought towards in the past few weeks. But it doesn't seem like a new gift. It feels more like someone is trying to communicate with me.

"I keep seeing that evil man. He talks to me. He tells me horrible things about killing those people and killing other people. I'm scared, Mom. I feel like I'm in over my head."

"So what are you going to do, honey? Are you going to quit this investigation? It seems like someone wants you to."

I thought about that for a long time. I thought about how if I just dropped this whole silly business I could go back to my small and normal existence. I could read palms and eke out a living for myself without putting myself or anyone else in danger.

I shook my head. "No. I want to, I mean, I'm tempted to drop this whole thing and run the opposite direction, but it's almost like I'm compelled to see this through. Elicia deserves
~~~~~

the peace that she couldn't attain in this life. No one has the right to keep her from that."

"Do you want me to do a reading for you?" she asked, when I finished.

"No, I don't think it will have changed much."

"Okay. Please be careful, Sibby. For what it's worth. I know you're doing the right thing."

"Thanks, Mom," I said.

~~~~~

The letter came later that afternoon by next-day air. *God bless Lyle Struthers for rushing this to me,* I thought. I called Jordan as soon as I had the key in my hand.

"I need to get over to the house," I said, "Is that possible?"

"Funny you should call me. I was just getting ready to contact you. I got a phone call from Mrs. Ford's lawyer today. She is releasing her hold over the estate. If you want to head out there to look around, she won't try to stop you."

"Thanks, Jordan, that's great news."

“Anything to advance the mystery solving,” he said.

“I hope to have good news for you, very soon,” I said.

~~~~~

I turned the key in the lock of the bottom file drawer, my breath stopping for an instant as I opened it. It was almost as though I expected an explosion or a loud crashing of symbols announcing, "You've made it. Congratulations! Welcome to the end!"

None of those things happened. Instead, I found myself holding a book and another single file folder in my hand. The file folder contained several more biographies and some photos. The book was a journal set in the 1960's, written by Elicia herself.

*Finally,* I thought, *someplace new to start.* I settled down on the floor and started to read.

# Chapter 16

*February 4th, 1966*

*Mama always said to me, "Leesy, when you grow up, you're gonna meet a nice man and you're gonna get married, and you're gonna have lots of cute chubby babies to love and kiss." And then she'd hold me close and kiss my cheek.*

*I miss her so much that it feels like I'm walking around with a hole where my heart should be. When I was adopted by the Wakefields I was so hopeful. Finally, finally, I would have a family to love again. And they would love me.*

*I'm lying here in bed, listening to the quiet house and I'm waiting. I'm waiting for the creak in the hall, and his soft tread on the carpet. I know that it will be followed by his hand slowly turning my doorknob. Then he will come into my room, pull down his pajama bottoms and slip into my bed. He expects to find me naked or he will find subtle ways to punish me. Then, without preamble, he will climb on top of me and start his nightly routine of whispered obscenities and the raping, of course.*

*He calls me a whore, and a piece of mountain trash. He tells me that I should be grateful someone like me has a roof over my head and a decent meal to eat. Maybe he's right, but I can't help thinking about Mama. Nobody could call her trash. She was so pretty.*

*When I was little, I used to sit in her lap and watch her brush her long, golden hair. I would look at the sunlight lighting it up like fire and wish that some day I could be as pretty as her. She was a mountain princess, and the kindest woman I've ever met. The only person who really loved me, I think. Except maybe for Nana. They all seem so far away from me now. I'm so alone.*

*February 15th, 1966*

*I try to live a normal life. If I'm perfect on the outside, no one will know what happens in the secrecy of night. If I dress like the other girls, those carefree, chattering ninnies, then everyone will think I'm one of them. If I tease the boys and dance at the dances I can pretend to be a regular girl.*

*I've joined the dance team on basketball. I've joined Rainbow Girls of America. I tutor some of the other students in the help room at school. I've been making some of the costumes for the school drama club. I chatter and socialize with some of the most popular girls in school. I'm a pretty girl. Pretty girls are always popular, especially if they're rich, like I am.*

*I keep wondering when my term of service here will be over. When will I finally make my way out of this hell? I wake up in the morning, wishing I was still in our small mountain cabin. When I was a little girl I would wake up with the sun and sing in my heart while the birds sang in their trees. I would run outside, no matter what the weather and drink in the fresh mountain air.*

*When I wake up here, I smell the sweat and cologne of the man who rapes me. I smell the perfumed edge of the professional cleaners who come once a week and clean the house from top to bottom. I smell the death of my innocence and the inevitable escape I will make, when I go off to college in two years, if I can hold out that long.*

*You'd think I'd be busy enough to keep all this from circling in my mind like some kind of endless recording, looping around scratchy and skipping. I miss having a home. I miss having a safe place. I miss Mama.*

*February 27th, 1966*

*He's gone for the week: a business meeting in Tulsa. I'm so happy. For one week I can act and feel like a normal person. I can lie in bed and sleep, just sleep.*

*Last night was the first night he was away and I found myself dreaming strange mixed up dreams about my dad. It's funny, I hardly ever think of him any more. He was always gone when I was little and I spent most of my days with Mama.*

*Last night I dreamed that he and I were walking through the woods near our house and I could feel the forest turning dark and cold around us. There was something watching. I slipped my hand into his, for comfort, but when I looked up, it wasn't him any more. It looked like him, but it was someone else. I tried to pull my hand away, but he held on.*

*March 6th, 1966*

*He comes home today. I was sick all day yesterday, vomiting up everything I tried to eat. I didn't even try to eat today. I can't live like this anymore. Just the idea of seeing me again makes me feel the cold sweat of terror. I need to get away. I need to save my money and get away from here. My allowance isn't very big, though. Lydia doesn't believe in children getting allowances, just because their parents have the money to give to them. I mostly get money for lunch.*

*If I ask for money, say to see a movie with my friends, she'll give it to me, but only on a case by case basis. Which means, I need to get a job. Lydia approves of teenagers working after school. It helps them to feel a sense of responsibility.*

*This morning I asked to see the classifieds and she smiled at me. "I'm glad to see you taking an interest in your future, Elicia." They never changed my first name. The head of the orphanage told them it could have a detrimental effect on my mental development.*

*Lydia refuses to give me a nickname, however. "Your full name is much more dignified and befits a young woman of your social status." I'm relieved. She's never tried to call me Leesy -it was my mama's name for me. He calls me Elicia or Cia in public. In private he calls me "bitch whore." Oh, my god, he comes home today and he will expect to have me. I wish I lived in Alaska during the summer. No night time. I am convinced if it were always light out, he would never feel strong enough to sneak into my room.*

*March 11, 1966*

*I got a job at the Pancake Shack. It has decent breakfast food, great tips for pretty girls, and plenty of waitresses to educate me in the ways of the world. I've met one already. Her name is Bridget, she's 19, and she lives with her boyfriend in a cheap apartment downtown. She calls it "real livin'".*

*The first thing she said when she saw me was, "Honey, we may be able to teach you to waitress, but we are never gonna be able to get rid of that rich girl look in your eyes." I never laughed so hard. I told her where I was born and she was impressed. It's nice to feel like you have more value for the true things about yourself than the things you just put on every day.*

*Bridg is the first person I've ever told about my adopted parents' true selves. She never looked at me with pity, just shrugged and said,"Honey, my dad was a mean drunk who killed my mama when I was 11 years old. We've all got a little darkness in our hearts."*

*She isn't like the girls at school would be. They would shrink away from me or think I was telling lies for attention. Or worst of all, they might blame me and say I was doing something to entice him to my bed. I remember the first time, trembling, I tried to tell Lydia about what he did to me.*

*Her eyes glazed over, her face grew still as stone, and she said to me, "Be careful with what you're about to tell me, Elicia. There are many things a lady does not talk about. I would hate for you to lower yourself in my eyes."*

*I could see then that she knew. How could she not? She slept in the same room as her husband. She must have heard him leave every night, rise from his bed only to return minutes or hours later out of breath, sweaty, and smelling of my room.*

*Ever since the moment I realized she knew that, I've hated her as much as him. He hurts me, but she condones it or ignores it. Either one is unforgivable. I would never allow a child to be treated the way I have been for the past four years. My breath catches as I realize that he's been doing this to me for four years. I would like to kill him, but I know that the force of his evil will always be stronger than my ability to fight against it.*

*March 13, 1966*

*Bridg and I have formed an unstoppable duo. Today, during the busy Sunday lunch hour, a couple of God fearing folk wandered in after church toting their Bibles and wearing their Sunday clothes. They sat in Bridg's section, made several changes to their order and then tried to skip out on the check. I caught the wife as she sneaked out of the bathroom and caught Bridg's eye. She'd been delivering food to another table and got distracted. I sidled in front of the door while she grabbed the check and hurried over.*

*"Excuse me, Ma'am," I said, "I think you dropped something on the floor over there."*

*"What?" She turned, just as Bridg pretended to pick something up off the floor. Bridg came over with the check in*

*her hand.*

*"Here you go," she said and smiled her good waitress smile.*

*The woman's face soured, but she mumbled a "Thank you," and paid her bill.*

*We did a little happy dance after she left, though Bridg never got her tip.*

*March 22, 1966*

*I've escaped, if only for a night. Bridg invited me to come stay with her in the "den of iniquity" as she calls the smarmy little apartment she lives in with her boyfriend Stan. Stan is a cool guy who works as a mechanic at the downtown filling station. It wasn't hard to finagle a night from Lydia. I told her one of the popular girls in school had invited a bunch of us for a sleepover.*

*Of course, Lydia will imagine us all dressed up in our modestly becoming nighties, enjoying snacks and singing along with "The Beatles" records. I don't think I've ever met a woman in such denial. Part of me feels sorry for her, but usually I despise her.*

*In any case, the lie worked and I'm here, sitting on her couch listening to her humming "California Dreamin'" under her breath while she browns the meat she's using in her shepherd's pie. She calls it the poor man's meal. I can see why: ground chuck, canned vegetables, and instant mashed potatoes. It smells good though.*

*I've never seen Lydia make anything in her kitchen but toast. The housekeeper, Mrs. Brown, comes in every morning to make breakfast, clean the house, make dinner and then goes home. She's a nice woman, such an air of peace around her. I have to confess I've never tried to get to know her very well. Lydia treats her like another appliance: the trash compactor or the food processor.*

*Bridg looks so domestic, with her hair down and tied with a kerchief, dancing around as she adds ingredients to a casserole dish. Some day, she and Stan will get married and have kids. Some day they will get a little house and they will be so happy as a family.*

*March 24, 1966*

*He was angry with me.*

*"Don't you ever leave without getting my permission first, you little bitch," he said and pinched the skin on my stomach so hard that I whimpered and tears pricked my eyes.*

*It's been so long since he's had the power to make me cry I was surprised by the intensity of the feeling. I didn't take it this time. The pain was like a stone, sharpening my anger to a point.*

*"What do you want to do, tell Lydia I have to stay home so you can fuck me? Should I tell my friends I'm not allowed to stay the night like all the other girls because my 'Daddy' has to have sex with me?"*

*My mouth twisted and I almost choked over the words "Daddy," but I glared right into his eyes and to my surprise he seemed to back down for a moment.*

*"Just try to escape me, just try and I will make your life hell."*

*"More than it is right now?"*

*"Do you want me to answer that question, Cia? Because I can show you right now," he said and climbed on top of me, ignoring my discomfort.*

*He was right, he can make my life more of a hell than it already is. What he doesn't know is, at this point in time, I don't really care anymore.*

*--Later--*

*And in any case, it was worth it. I had such a good time with Bridg. It was so nice to sleep somewhere else, away* *from this horrible place. I've saved up $5.27 so far. It's not nearly enough to get me anywhere. I wish there was a way for me to get the money I need.*

*April 20, 1966*

*I've been so busy with all of my school clubs and working as many hours at the restaurant as I can, that I haven't had much time for anything. He comes every night and I fall asleep immediately afterward. It's a blessing, really, not having to lay awake at night missing Mama.*

*There's a reason I'm writing today. I think I'm pregnant. I've been so sick lately and every time someone orders Salsbury Steak at the restaurant, I have to run to the bathroom to be sick. My body feels different too. I'm bloated and my breasts hurt.*

*I told Bridg today, "I think I'm pregnant."*

*"Oh, honey," she said, "didn't you ever think of getting on the Pill? It's the least that bitch Lydia can do for you, since you're doing her the favor of taking her husband off her hands."*

*"Bridg, I live in upper class suburbia hell. No one talks about sex, much less birth control. I'm so scared. I can't have a baby, period, not to mention his baby. I would hate it on sight."*

*"I wouldn't blame you, kid. Listen, don't freak out. We'll get you an appointment with a doctor I know and confirm the news before we start to worry."*

*Despite my terror, I felt better after telling her. Bridg has this confident demeanor that has a way of inspiring trust. Please, please, God if you exist, please don't let me be pregnant.*

## Chapter 17

I set aside the journal when Paul knocked on the door. He greeted me with a warm kiss, asking, "What took you so long? I've been knocking for five minutes."

"Sorry," I said, taking the bag of Chinese takeout he'd brought from our favorite Peking restaurant, Pauline's. I went to the kitchen to set a couple of plates up at the breakfast bar and then dished out a healthy serving of broccoli beef and pork chow mein for each of us. The potstickers I put on a plate in the between both of our plates with the special sauce on the side -Paul liked them with, but I liked them without.

After I'd started to read the journal, I realized there was more to it than I could read in a few minutes, so I'd packed up my things and come home to wait for Paul.

"I was reading Elicia's journal from when she was a teenager. I wish I'd had this one at the start -fascinating reading. Elicia was adopted by the Wakefields when she was a little girl. Her parents died when she was really young and she got sent to a home. Oh yeah, she *was* from the Ozarks, by the way. Anyway, the Wakefields adopted her and then a few years later the husband started molesting her."

"My God," said Paul, frowning.

"I know, horrible right? That's not all. She got pregnant."

"I thought she couldn't have children." Paul said.

"Well, she did say that in her more recent journal," I said. "But I haven't finished reading the journal, yet. Maybe something happened between then and now."

"Well, fill me in when you find out. I've gotten to the point where I can't figure out where this story is going."

"Paul, for the last time, this isn't a mystery novel," I told him.

"Well, it sounds like one to me. I mean, think about it. Beautiful woman with a dark past dies mysteriously, leaving a smart and sassy team of amateur detectives to follow clues and solve the murder. Consider this: we have already experienced a classic case of misdirection, which is paramount to the mystery novel. Next we'll find a clue that will break the case, and voila, mystery solved!" He was cheerful in his triumphant conclusion.

I shook my head, laughing. "Well, if we're going to find the clue to break this case, we'd better hurry up and eat dinner."

Our meal was a lighthearted affair compared to the events of the past few days. Being near Paul was relaxing, he had such a great sense of humor. It was a balm to my tired and battered senses.

After we finished off our meal, we sat over the table, shuffling the evidence around. It was like playing Scrabble, moving pieces around to form cohesive words, only this time it was us trying to make sense out of the past that was Elicia's.

"So let's do a summary here," I said. "Elicia is the main focus of our investigation. She died under mysterious circumstances. She married a man with a past, but that past turned out to be worthless to our investigation. We got rid of those files. So something relating to her past affected her to the point that she was forever changed. It could have happened before, after or during her marriage to Jackson Ford, but knowing what I do about blood curses, it's doubtful that anything but a hallmark event in her life would set one off."

"What does create a blood curse?" Paul asked.

"Well, you've seen a lot of scary movies. It's the same idea as a cursed house or a cursed object: something horrible happens to a person that is so terrible that it not only affects that person till their death, it also moves through their family like a genetic disease, except it's spiritual. And not only does the curse move through those of "the blood" -hence its name- it hunts them down, one by one, enacting its specific form of vengeance.

"Blood curses are the hardest to break and they require the greatest sacrifice. I don't like the idea that it's what Elicia died from because it means I'm going to have to go to dangerous lengths to free her from it."

"This is no joke, is it, babe?" he asked, putting his arm around me. I laid my head on his shoulder.

"No, it's not. It's a curse that's already killed two people that I know of," I said.

"Well, we can't know for sure that Kinsey was a victim of the blood curse," he said.

"It's true, she wasn't blood related, but that dream I had made it clear to me that the investigation we were conducting had everything to do with her death. Then there is Lyle, as well," I still felt sick thinking about it. "We're all at risk: me, you, Jordan, and anyone these harbingers of death believe are in the way of their master plan."

"So what are some non-dangerous ways to break a blood curse?" Paul asked, pulling up the stack of photos I'd set aside but still hadn't had time to go through yet.

"I'm not sure. I need to talk to Mom about it. She knows a lot of the old ways that I'm still working my way through."

"I thought your mom did the Taro?"

"Oh, it's true, she does the superficial everyday household readings that people use for love, marriage, baby carriage, stuff. But beyond that is the deeper practice. Did you know that she used my cord blood in the paint that she used to create my own personal Taro deck?"

"Wait, those cards are hand made? Really?"

"Given to me on my first birthday. I don't use them much, because I'm not tied into the cards like she is. While I'm more like a traditional palm reader/divinist, Mom is in the branch more closely linked to witchcraft -which is not to say she's a witch. She has practiced the Craft and studied it to understand her own practice better. I'll call her tomorrow to get some more specific ideas that might help to release the curse and still keep me safe. For now, all I have is the basics that I've learned.

"To release a blood curse, the most effective method is the time honored ritual with the four elements: canticle, belonging, binding, and sacrifice. For a minor curse, it can be as simple as a word, an item of clothing, a circle traced with salt around you, and the gift of your time and effort.

“In this case, it will require a lengthy unbinding spell, something that was precious to Elicia, a complicated weaving -string is best, with posts for complexity of pattern- and something of myself. Blood might be enough, but it could also require a life.

"A blood curse needs something of the practitioner to release it. The question will be what this particular curse will require. For that, like I said, I'll go to Mom for help. The last thing I want is to get knee deep into this mess and find out it is going to take human life.

"In order to make the sacrifice minimal, I have to be very specific with my canticle and binding. The object of Elicia's must relate to the curse in some way. That is why we're doing all this investigation -mystery solving as you call it. If we find the cause, we will know how to word the canticle and how to pattern the binding. It will help us choose the belonging and dictate the level of sacrifice."

Paul looked serious. "I don't know if I'm on board with this any more, Sib."

I sighed and shrugged my shoulders, slumping over the table a little more. "I didn't realize what this was at first, Paul. I had no idea what I was getting into. Despite what Thadius, told me, I know this won't be over if I just give up my investigation. Blood curses don't work that way. Now that Elicia is gone, this malevolent force will focus its attention on another victim and work its way through that family. For all I know, it's already centered its attention on me. Even if it hasn't, it's still dangerous.

"I know it's scary and you've never seen me deal with something like this before -well, to be honest, I have never dealt with anything like this at all-, but this is what we commit to when we follow The Way. It means committing to make the world a better place for humanity to live in, even if that means putting ourselves in mortal danger. It's what I believe in, and even though something this difficult has never been asked of me up until now, I can't walk away from that responsibility. I wouldn't respect myself."

"I love you so much, Sibilant. I wouldn't know what to do if something happened to you," he said, pulling me close and nuzzling into my hair.

"That is why I'm trying so hard to make sure I do this the right way. If I can arm myself with the proper information and some major planning before I attempt a release, I might make it out of this unscathed, but it's going to take some major balancing to get everything right. Which is why we need to get back to work. Why don't you go through those photos while I read the rest of this journal?"

~~~~~

*April 25, 1966*

*I'm pregnant. The doctor came in to break the news and I was holding Bridg's hand so tight my knuckles were white. I started crying and Bridg put her arm around me.*
~~~~~

*"Isn't there something we can do, Dr. Armstrong? This baby is not just the product of a silly teenage mess up. This is a product of rape. She can not keep this baby."*

*Basically, I have three options: run away from home, go live at The Pillars home for unwed mothers, or get rid of it. Marriage would normally be an option, but not in this case -no big surprise there. I can't run away. Even though Bridg has offered to help me, she and Stan live in a one bedroom apt. There's no room for a person with a baby.*

*The second option won't work because then Lydia would have to know. She'd know whose baby it was and she would hate me. The third option would normally be against the law, but they make some exceptions, medically. Dr. Armstrong is willing to work with me, given the circumstances. It will mean a lot of paperwork, but it seems like the best option for me.*

*Why would I want this baby to ever see the light of day? No child deserves to be born out of hate and lust. No baby deserves a father like him or a mother who wouldn't be able to look at her own child. And I can't give it to another couple knowing that it was made from pure evil. No, this poor little bean must go back to heaven or the ether or wherever it is unborn souls congregate.*

*My only problem at this point is money. It will cost thousands of dollars. I have $36. I will have to tell him.*

*April 27, 1966*

*I have my money. It was not pleasant, making him face up to the fact that his actions have consequences, but $6,000 is not an issue for him. He's rich and it's a paltry sum. So paltry, in fact, that I asked for more money than the procedure will cost. He doesn't care about money, not like Lydia does. He wanted to know when the appointment was, and how soon afterward I would be able to have sex again. There was no* *talk of what he could do to prevent this from happening again. I think I'll have to get on The Pill. I have to get a guardian's permission, but that shouldn't be too hard.*

*I feel sick, just thinking about going to the hospital next week to have this done -sick about the whole situation. Bridget is going to go with me, though. Dr. Armstrong said that with this type of procedure she can stay in the room for most of it. I guess the baby is so small at this point, that there isn't much for the doctors to do except get my body to "expel the fetus". I can't wait for this to be over.*

*April 30, 1966*

*Sometimes, when I'm all alone, I wonder what it would be like if I was pregnant in different circumstances. I wonder what it would be like to be married to someone I love like Mama was. I remember how happy she was to have my little brother inside of her. Both of us were so excited that he would be coming to live with us, as poor as we were. I wonder what it would be like to live with a good man and be his wife and take care of him and our child.*

*I wish that this baby was anyone else's baby, that it had been created with love and not evil. I wish I could not be afraid to look down on it and see its father's face looking back at me. I hate him, I hate him so much. I can not hate this baby. It needs to not be born. Then I won't have to hate it. Poor, innocent baby that never did anything to deserve being born in such bad circumstances -there is no way I would ever put a baby through that kind of pain.*

*May 14, 1966*

*Nothing ever goes the way we want it to. Nothing is ever gained without a cost. There were some complications with my abortion. I went with Bridg down to the hospital and checked in, nervous, anxious and sick to my stomach. The nurse led us to the procedure room and gave me a dose of some chemical; I still have no idea what it was. She explained to me that the medicine would make my body think it was time to have the baby and I would basically deliver everything that a woman would normally at the end of her pregnancy.*

*At first I started bleeding like I should, but then it was like a river came gushing out of me. My vision started to get blurry and I don't remember anything after this point. I remember Bridg screaming out the door for a doctor and I remember crying, "Don't tell Lydia, don't let them tell her. Make them call HIM. Don't tell Lydia."*

*Everything turned gray, it really did. Nothing was colored anymore and I was fading, fading out.*

*When I woke up, I was surprised. I almost expected to see St. Peter or something. I was in a hospital room and Bridg was there with me.*

*"What happened?" I asked, my voice weak.*

*"You almost died. I guess the baby was down too low and it messed everything up. The doctor... he saved you. He didn't call Lydia. We called him. He told them to lie to Lydia, he told them that he didn't want her to know -it would distress her.*

*"The doctor asked him lots of things. I heard some of them. He made you sound like a tramp. He said you'd been dating a boy on the football team and that you'd started sleeping with him. If I didn't know, if I didn't know what he'd done to you, I would have believed him. Honey," she leaned in to whisper, "we have got to get you away from him." She sat up as the doctor pushed into the room. He was not as kind to me as he'd been before.*

*"I wish you'd been honest with me before," he said.*

*"She was honest," Bridg told him, glaring.*

*He harrumphed and continued,"If only you'd chosen to go to a home. A problem like we ran into, with a low-lying placenta, resolves itself over the course of the pregnancy in most cases. You wouldn't have hemorrhaged. As it is, I'm sorry to tell you, we had to perform a hysterectomy."*

*Bridget started crying, and grabbed my hand.*

*"I'm sorry, I don't know what that means," I said, feeling dread send a chill shivering through my body.*

*"It means you can never have another child again. We saved your life, but the cost was significant."*

*The cost was significant. I couldn't even take that in.*

*May 15, 1966*

*They told Lydia that I had to have my appendix taken out. That's what we told everyone. And now I don't have to figure out how to save myself from this happening again. It never will. I will never have a baby. I will never have a family. I will never escape him.*

*Sometimes, I wish I had never been born. Everything good shrivels up and dies when it comes into contact with me. Sometimes I feel like my life is a swirling and dark pit that I will never flounder my way out of.*

*May 20, 1966*

*He didn't even wait till I was done healing before he took me. I lay there in my bed, the deep night casting shadows around his rhythmically moving form, wishing for his death. My anger was a burning coal inside of me, licking me with heated waves and building a slow fire that licked away at my sanity.*

*I would kill him. I must. He had ruined my life and he deserved to pay. But as he grunted above me, I had to accept my inability to fight back against him physically. It wasn't possible for me to tell anyone. Even the doctor at the hospital believed his lies about a boy at school being the father of my baby. No one will ever help me.*

*After he was gone, I lay in bed, staring up at the dark, blank ceiling. A thought had occurred to me, born in the furthest, deepest parts of my mind. I suddenly had a flashback of when I was very young, living in the deep hills of Appalachia. I could see distant scattered images of a woman, a witch, casting spells and muttering words. I remember being afraid of her, but my mother and father were also there. I had the feeling she was struggling to a purpose, which is what I needed for myself. I needed to struggle for a purpose. I would cast my own spell.*

*I don't know why I thought it would work. I don't know why it occurred to me to even try it. There must have been a part of me that thought I could harness the evil around me and use it for my own purposes. I lay there, in the dark and felt powerful in a way I had not before. I felt a growing confidence in myself and a determination I had not felt since being adopted by the Wakefield family. I would start my work tomorrow.*

*May 21, 1966*

*I could have asked Bridget about spells and castings. She knows a lot about the Eastern Religions of the world, which according to her from previous conversation contain many aspects of chanting, power transfer, and deep practices from the dawn of time. But I did not. I told no one of my new grand design.*

*Bridg could tell something was going on at work today.*

*"You look black with power," she said. "Like when the evil queen has made the poison apple, in Snow White. What are you up to, honey?"*

*"Nothing, just making definitive plans for my escape."*

*"I didn't think you had much money," she commented, waiting.*

*"I got some extra when I asked for money for the*

*abortion, " I commented. "It wasn't much, a few hundred, but that should be enough to get me a bus ticket out of here and a apartment until I can find a job."*

*"Elicia, that's great!" she said, smiling.*

*"Well, I'm not leaving yet. I have plans to make. I have decisions to settle on." I frowned as I considered what my next step would be.*

*At home that night, I had time to plan. He would not be home till late that night. So I sat in the middle of my room doing that meditation that Bridg showed me when I stayed at her house that night which seemed so long ago now. That was back when I still had endless possibilities of escape, when I could still have the chance at a family of my own.*

*I closed my eyes and hummed tonelessly, letting go of all the day's events and feelings. Instead I latched on to the pulsating anger in the core of my body. I held it and let it flow over me, till I felt myself becoming a vengeful dark being full of malevolent purpose. I let myself dive down deep into that molten center of splashing lava-like hatred.*

*Suddenly I burned and stiffened, shocked by the power that I encountered. It was almost as though I were rubbing a golden lamp and I could have anything I wanted, all I had to do was ask. My every whim was at my fingertips and I all wanted was for him to die. I wanted him to suffer as I had. I wanted him to pray for release, but he would find none. I wanted him to burn in Hell.*

*With each pulsing wave of anger I felt my mind cry out, "He must die. He must suffer. He must die. He must suffer."*

*I said the words again and again, the anger, pain and suffering I had endured fueled me with the fire I needed to keep my deep concentration in the face of the foreign feelings I was faced with.*

*Then, the fire left me. I looked up and standing before me was the ghost of my dead father. It was smiling down at me, an evil so palpable emanating from it, that I feared for my life. I shrank back from it, clutching myself and shivering in fright.*

*"Fear not, child, your command is assured. It will be carried out this night." It disappeared and left me in the cold silence.*

*I woke up on the floor in the morning, the sunlight streaming down on my face, uncertain whether what had happened was indeed a dream or maybe better described as a nightmare. I thought of climbing into bed and drifting back to sleep, as it was Saturday, when I heard the doorbell ring downstairs.*

*I knew that l would have to get the door, as Lydia is not an early riser at the best of times. To my surprise, I heard her steps hurry across the marble foyer and listened as she flung open the door. There was a man at the door, his voice low and inaudible. I peeked down the stairs and watched as Lydia let out a hideous shriek and collapsed on the shining white floor. I knew then what had happened.*

*Victor Alexander Wakefield III was dead. I had killed him.*

## Chapter 18

*June 22, 1966*

*Whatever light at the end of the tunnel I had figured on, died as I watched Lydia sink into a deep depression. You'd think she'd be thankful to be rid of the slime-ball, but despite his many faults, Lydia must have harbored an eternal love for him. I come home from school or work to find her hunched over a glass of anything alcoholic. She's always plastered and morose, sobbing and moaning his name.*

*Of course when she sees me, she says, "Cia, Cia, why did he have to leave us? Why?"*

*I want to say, "Well, I for one am glad he's gone," but I don't want to push my luck.*

*The past few weeks have been peaceful and even the always inebriated Lydia can't make me regret what I did that night. To fall asleep unmolested at night, is a treasure worth having. If only I didn't have this nagging feeling that I've unleashed something that was better off staying locked up wherever it had been.*

*June 28, 1966*

*Now that school is out, I fill my time with work and think about my future. I only have a year left until I go off to college and I've been trying to figure out what I want to do with my life. I think I'll have to go to a local school, as I don't think Lydia can make it without me.*

*I'm worried about her. She's dropped Ladies' Aid and Garden Club and Southern Belles -all clubs that she used to chair- and has given up on her appearance altogether. Her pristine toilette has sunk to that of the local bag lady: limp greasy hair, runny mascara, smudged lipstick, mismatched clothing, comically exaggerated sense of loneliness. I don't know what to do to snap her out of this. We got the insurance check in the mail, you'd think that would have her breaking out the bubble bath and pedicures, but instead it sent her straight to the liquor cabinet.*

*I told Bridg about my concerns and she sighed,"I think Lydia is one of those people who can't function without being under someone's thumb. It's always a surprise what happens when those people are forced to be independent. Sometimes they turn out wonderfully -look at you, hon- and sometimes they go in a different direction."*

*I still hold onto the hope that she will recover.*

*July 5, 1966*

*I got home today and I just couldn't take it anymore. It's been almost two months now and she's worse than ever. I stomped over and snatched the glass away from her, spilling scotch all over the floor.*

*"Lydia," I said, "You need to snap out of this. He's not coming back. You smell like an old shoe and you don't look much better. Go take a shower and try to put your life back together."*

*She shoved me away.*

*"It's easy for you to shay," she slurred, "my life is over and you don't even sheem to care. It's like you're glad hesh gone."*

*She stood up, glaring at me. I met her gaze full on.*

*"I am glad. He made my life hell and I am glad that he's gone forever." I put my hands on my hips.*

*"Monster!" she yelled. "You have no feelings!"*

*She ran from the room and stumbled up the stairs. I'm surprised she didn't kill herself by falling right down them.*

*July 6, 1966*

*The house was quiet this morning as I left. I had to work late, and when I got home, I slipped on my pajamas and slid into bed. A few minutes later, my door crashed open, and Lydia flipped on the light switch. I squinted at the sudden light and gasped. Lydia stood there, perfectly made up, in her best suit, sober as a stone. She glared down at me and dropped something on my bed. I looked down at a battered old suitcase.*

*"I want you out of my house," she said, calm.*

*"Lydia, what..."*

*"This is your fault. I never wanted you, but Victor insisted. I didn't know then what he wanted was your body and your youth. So I gave in. And then he abandoned me, for you, you ungrateful little bitch. But now I don't have to tolerate you any longer. You can go live on the street for all I care. You ruined my marriage and I never want to see you again."*

*"Lydia, please, it's the middle of the night," I pleaded. "I never wanted his attention. I never wanted him."*

*This confession only seemed to anger her more. Her hair almost seemed to crackle with wrath. "Of course you did, you whore. I saw you make eyes at him, and wear those tight little sweaters. You were always enticing him! You are a tramp and a witch and you're the one who should have died, not him!"*

*With every syllable her voice got louder and more shrill. I felt the world close in around me. I had not prepared for this, and her words stung like knife slashes. The world started to blacken and fade out as I tried to catch my breath, but all I could hear was her screaming voice condemning me to hell.*

----

*The world faded out and I felt myself float above it all, seeming to look down at myself curled into a ball on my bed with her standing over me shouting. Then I moved away to another place, a dark place, more evil than what I had endured at his hands for the past four years. I stood in a dark room with my father next to me and a horrible, ugly woman in front of me.*

*She had a knife in her hand and pressed it to my flesh. I watched in horror as the blood ran down and I heard my mother screaming. Then I floated off again and this time I was hiding under the bed in my room, listening to the sound of two people arguing, and I prayed with all my heart they would stop. Then I heard a gun fire over and over, then one final time and there was a metallic clatter as the gun dropped to the floor. I screamed, "Mama!" and crawled out from under my bed.*

*Once more I floated above myself and then back to another time and I was walking along a road, towards some end, shivering and sobbing. My hands were slick with blood and I kept crying for my mother. I got to the end of the road and waited till I saw a vehicle approach. It was my school bus and when the door opened I screamed, "Please, help! Please help my mama! She's hurt, she's hurt so bad." I started crying again and everything faded back to black.*

----

*When I woke, it was still dark, but Lydia was gone. My suit case was open on the bed and she had thrown all my belongings on the floor. Books were flung from the shelves, dresses dumped from their hangers in the closet, and socks and underclothes were scattered over the floor instead of neatly sorted in their drawers.*

*I shoved a few things in the suitcase, not much, but then there wasn't much I loved in this place. I packed my journal and a few of my favorite books. I pulled my money from between my bed mattresses, and made sure to pack winter things as well as summer. Then without a backward glance I walked down the stairs and out the door. I found a phone booth and placed a call to Bridget. She answered the phone, sleepy and mumbled, "Lo?"*

*"She threw me out, Bridg. She flipped out and blamed me for everything, and then she just threw all my stuff on the floor and told me to get the hell out. Can I stay at your place for a few days until I figure out where to go next?"*

*"Of course. Come on over and I'll put on some water for tea. We'll talk this out."*

*I walked all the way to her house and she was waiting at the door when I there.*

*She hugged me and opened the door to let me in.*

*"Now tell me exactly what she said." And I did.*

*July 10, 1966*

*I'm off to New York City. If anyone can get lost there, it's me. I can't stay here, it's toxic. I have enough money to buy a train ticket and rent a cheap apartment to get me by until I can find another waitress job. There should be plenty of them in a city that big. Bridg is heartbroken, but we both knew this day was coming. I'm free, embarking on a journey that will bring me to the best years of my life.*

~~~~~

Paul interrupted my reading.

"Just one more second, I'm almost done," I said, before finishing the last paragraph.

"Okay," I said.

"Take a look at this," he said, sliding a black and white photo across the table to me. The picture featured a man and woman dressed in nice clothes. It looked like a wedding photo. The woman looked similar to Elicia, but she was much shorter than the tall man in the photo who stared out at the camera with a smile on his face. I flipped the photograph over and on the back was written, "Jediah and Charlotte Campbell, January 1947."
~~~~~

"Who are they?" I wondered aloud.

"Who cares, did you notice anything about the picture besides the couple?"

I turned the picture back so I was staring down at the couple again and then it occurred to me.

"That's the cabin we saw in the woods that day, with Kinsey," I said, excited. So there was a connection.

"So now the question goes back to yours, who are they, but more importantly, how are they connected to Elicia?"

I leaned over to look at his pile of photos."Are they in any more of the pictures?" I asked.

"Just this drawing," he said.

Absent the man, the sketch showed the woman sitting in a rocking chair with a little girl in her lap. There was no date on the back, it merely read, "Charlotte and Leesy."

"Leesy? Wait, that's in the journal," I said, turning to the beginning to read the first sentence, "'Mama always said to me,'Leesy, when you grow up, you're gonna meet a nice man...'"

Paul nodded. "So Leesy is Elicia," he said.

"It seems that way," I said. "And I'm going to guess that the couple in the photo are the parents who died in a hunting accident when she was eight. If it was an accident. Maybe Elicia wasn't the start of the curse, maybe she was its final victim."

I felt my stomach flutter.

"You know what this means," I said. "We have to go back to the cabin."

"No, no way. That place was evil. Look what happened to Kinsey after we went there!" Paul said.

"I can't help that. There is something missing in all of this and that cabin is part of what we're looking for. We need to enter that house and find out what is going on inside. We need to search it for any clues or for an idea of what could have caused the curse."

"Just promise me we'll exhaust every other lead before we go back there," he said.

"I'll do you one better. I'm going to make sure we go back with protection next time. We need to get something that's going to nullify all those Witch Balls. Trust me, we have plenty of work to do before we get to that point in our mystery novel."

"It's starting to feel more like a horror story to me," he said, staring down at the picture of the cabin.

~~~~~

File, Biography: Bridget Monahan

Bridget really doesn't have much to do with me, except for that brief period of time where we were both working at the same restaurant. But it had been so long since I'd talked to her, that I thought I should look her up.

Bridg was part of the original nuclear family. They lived in the suburbs, had 2.5 children, a dog and cat and an in-ground pool -this I found out from Bridg herself. She was the rebel, who left home after high school, met Stan, and moved in with him. After I left town, she worked at the restaurant, until Stan heard about a commune in Oregon and they moved there. They never married and they eventually moved to Michigan where Stan got a job at an automobile assembly plant. They still live there.

After I married Jackson and had money, I tracked her down and then flew out to Detroit to see her, the one friend I had during my horrible teenage years. We visited for a long time, and during a pause in our long game of catching up, she looked at me and said, "You're still as strong as you ever were. Look at you, orphaned as a young girl, abused as a teenager, abandoned by the woman who adopted you, made your way in the world at 17. And you did it! You showed them, you could do it.
~~~~~

And now you're rich and married and look at them. Victor is dead and Lydia is a recovering alcoholic. I knew that you would do more than anyone would give you credit for."

I thanked her and we said our goodbyes shortly afterward, but she asked me one final question that haunts me still. We were at the rental car and she was leaning over the windowsill, saying one last goodbye, when she seemed to think of something, and she said, suddenly, "Hey, whatever happened with that man, anyway?"

"What man?" I asked her, caught off guard and mystified.

"The man with you in the picture of Victor's funeral. I was cleaning out the bird's cage a few weeks after you left and I never got to ask you about it."

"What? I don't know any man from Victor's funeral."

"That's funny," she said, "He was standing right next to you. I figured you knew him."

## Chapter 19

File, Biography: Charlotte Susanne Wheaton

This entry is hard for me to write. Mama. My memories of her are strong, still, so many years later. There is a part of me that wants to write this entry "just the facts". Where and when she was born, when she got married, and when she died, those are the easy things to write. But the facts would not tell the whole story about the wonderful woman that is my mother.

They would perhaps convey that she was a spoiled and rich young woman who became infatuated with one of the young gardeners who worked at her house. They would outline her impetuous runaway, her elopement, and her eventual downfall into abject poverty. They would mention her eventual death by being stabbed in the chest by a stag she and my father were hunting. Finally, they would show how the rifle in her hands went off, and shot my father straight through the head. Those are the facts.

The truth, as she told me, was that she was bored and spoiled when she met my father. She saw him out in the yard one day and made it her business to torture him, flirting shamelessly and ordering him around the yard. He proceeded to ignore her. It took her months, but he came around and started paying attention to her. That is when my mother fell in love with him.

It's true she was young and spoiled, but she

and my father loved each other. I'm sure that it must have been hard for her. She probably didn't know how to cook and yet she used the cook stove up at the cabin. She was used to electricity and comfort, but I still remember her lighting the lamp in the middle of the night to take me out to the outhouse. Underneath the facts, is the love story of a man and woman, who lived a hard, but good life. It is the story of the beautiful baby girl they created and loved. Unfortunately, they died before they could watch her grow up.

My mother was born on April 16, 1932 to Jacob and Elicia Wheaton. She met my father when she was 17 and they were married later on May 27, 1949. They moved up in the hills to the cabin owned and still inhabited by his mother.

Nanny welcomed them, taught my mother how to cook and live without life's conveniences (that is something of an assumption on my part, but if she knew nothing before marriage and she lived with Nanny up until then, she probably learned everything from her).

Nanny died when I was 4 or 5 years old. My mother had one other child, a boy, who died at birth from prematurity. She died when I was 8 years old, on a cold winter's day, after having tried without success to hunt down a deer, when we ran out of meat.

Most of these details I had long forgotten, but were run to ground in newspapers and such. The story of my mother and father I remembered most of, but all the other details, such as my father's job as one of the many gardeners on her family's estate and the ensuing whirlwind romance were told to me by the maid. What I do remember of my mother is clearer than what I remember of my father or my grandmother.

I spent most of my days with Mama, mending my

father's clothing, gathering kindling, feeding our chickens and gathering the eggs, making biscuits, and watching her prepare dinner. The one thing I remember most was her singing.

She sang me out of bed in the morning, sang me through breakfast, serenaded me as I got ready for the day, sang me off down the long road to the bus stop, and welcomed me home to her arms, singing one of the many happy songs she knew. Sometimes I wonder if she was aware that she surrounded herself almost constantly with music: humming, dipping, rollicking notes giddily pouring themselves from her lips.

I remember brushing her long gold hair, the same color as mine. I remember her gentle fingers, brushing and braiding my hair for school. I remember that she was the last thing I felt before falling asleep. She would sit next to me, humming, holding my hand and lean down to kiss my goodnight. Sometimes I would pretend to be asleep so I wouldn't miss that moment, when her soft lips would touch my cheek or forehead or lips, and I would smell her lavender soap, handmade, and the scent of the ashes from the wood-stove.

It is almost 50 years later, and I still miss her. Mama.

~~~~~

File, Biography: Jediah Mitchell Campbell

I don't remember my father very well. He was born just a year before my mother, on September 22, in the old cabin and on the same bed that he and my mother later shared and that I, too, was born on. He was the only child of his mother and father. He and his father did not have a good relationship, and so consequently, he left home when he was 14 years old, panhandling for a while, then, when he was collared by the local law
~~~~~

enforcement, he was given a job as a gardener at an estate near to my grandparents.

His father died when he was 16, but by then he had completely cut himself off from his family and he was unaware of the change in his family's circumstances. By the time he was 18, he was gainfully employed by my grandparents, but not making enough money to support a family or the selfish young girl that was professing her love for him.

Swallowing his pride, he wrote his mother to feel out the waters of his home situation. When he found out his father was dead, he took his young bride home to his mother and went to look for a job, since he'd been fired by the Wheatons.

His life was a hard one, wandering throughout the hills and valley, trying to keep food on the table for his mother, his wife and his young daughter. Jobs were scarce at the time of his marriage, what with the Great Depression just making its way out of the country at the time. He tried to avoid getting jobs with the coal mine, though they were plentiful, because of the way the workers were treated and how often workers were injured and killed. Even then they knew what black lung was. I'm sure my mother had no wish for him to become victim to the disease.

I remember little of my father. He was a tall, dark haired man with the saddest eyes. I remember him making me little animals out of wood to play with. I also remember walking with him in the forest and hunting for birds' nests. He taught me how to dig for worms and fish with them. He used to pull me up on his shoulders and carry my giggly little body around the cabin.

~~~~~

File, Biography: Jediah Michael Campbell -father
~~~~~

to Jediah Mitchell Campbell

I have little information on my grandfather. He died when my father was 16. I have birth and death records, but they tell me nothing about who he was and why my father felt he had to leave home when he was just a boy.

I don't remember Nanny talking about him, much. I do remember asking her once, when I was young, why she wasn't married like Mama and Daddy. I remember I was sitting in her lap, watching Mama and Daddy in the kitchen talking and laughing and smooching. I remember her saying, "If you find love like that, Leesy, you run toward it. I never had it, and I always wished I had."

I still remember that, and now I do nothing but wonder.

~~~~~

File, Biography: Jacob and Elicia Wheaton

I was not able to find much about my grandparents. Charlotte, my mother, was their only child and they left no relatives behind for me to question. Everything I found on them was the basics, birth records and such. From what I was able to gather from a former maid, they were a well-off couple that had Charlotte late in their lives.

They spoiled her and she disappointed them in the extreme by falling in love with my father, Jediah Campbell. They objected and told her that they would cut her off if she married him, but she did anyway. She ran off with him and never got the chance to talk to them again.

She tried to go see them when she was pregnant with me, but they refused to see her. The maid said that they were afraid she had come to ask for money, but I don't think that is why she tried to see them. I think that
~~~~~

she wanted them to get a chance to see me. I think she wanted to build a bridge of communication so that they could have a granddaughter. According to my mother I was named for my grandmother.

This is all projection and speculation, but I think they were afraid to open up a relationship with her after all that time. I think they were afraid that she only wanted them for their money, that they would end up supporting Jediah and his family. No one wants to be loved for their money.

Whatever happened to them after that, I know they lived a lonely life, left with the memories of their sweet little girl, but her memory could only be a mere ghost of the lively and loving girl who had once graced their lives. And of course, my mother died, and when I was left alone, no one came forward. The maid knew nothing about it. Maybe they were already dead then. Or I was just being punished for my mother's sins.

~~~~~

"Mom," I said, cutting off the lecture and the tskings, "I know, I know, I've neglected you and you've been worried sick. I'm fine, I've just been busy with my big hobby these days," I continued, filling her in on the latest details.

"Oh, Sibby. This is not good. You can't go involving yourself in a blood curse. Those are the nastiest things out there. You need to stop this and run as far away from the mystery of Elicia Ford as you can go."

"Not an option, Mom," I said, putting all of my determination into my voice. "So instead of taking the next twenty minutes to convince me you're right and I'm wrong, let's just skip to the part where you tell me all I need to know about releasing a blood curse without getting myself killed."

She was silent for a number of minutes. "Let me get my notes," she said, sighing.
~~~~~

I heard a rustle of papers over the phone. "Now, none of this is book knowledge. You won't find this hunting around some internet search engine. This, my dear Sibilant, is the old lore."

I suddenly got a perfect picture of her sitting at her desk in the den, dark auburn curls brushing her shoulders, diamond rimmed reading glasses perched on the end of her nose. This was how I saw her so many times, growing up, usually with a client at her table, but it was a timeless image in my mind.

"Okay, let me just read all my notes and then you can feel free to ask me all the questions you want. It's a bit of translation from an old family spell book -it was all in Italian.

"'When a true evil is done in a family line or when a deep hatred, a hatred that moves not with the ages or vanishes with the passage of time, is born for another person, the seeds of a blood curse are put in motion.

“When the seed is planted, through ritual and sacrifice, the curse becomes a seedling. When the seedling is fostered and grown through each generation, the seedling becomes the healthy plant of the blood curse. A blood curse must fulfill its roots, it must grow from the hatred or the evil that has born it. Without the source to feed it, the blood curse will shrivel and die.

"Woe to the man who is victim of the curse involving hatred, because he can not escape until he wins the forgiveness of the one who created the curse. If the person has died, he will have no recourse but to fulfill the curse's hatred with the sacrifice of his own life. Once that blood price has been paid, the curse is broken.

"The curse borne from evil is harder still to break, because the price is not known. The one who wishes to release it to find out why the curse was created, and make recompense for it.

"Releasing a blood curse involves the same four

elements that were used to create it. The canticle must be written for the specific curse and should mention the intent of release and include the person to be released. If the blood curse follows a family, then it is wisest to speak of the family, as well as the person to be released.

“The binding must be of unblemished materials -in a word, pure. The best for a blood curse is white linen string, cleaned hand-spun from a lamb of the first year, or a complex drawing made of charcoal fresh from the fire. The belonging must come from the person to be released, but it must be personal in a way that even the darkest secrets can not penetrate it. It can be as simple as the line of a favorite poem or as meaningful as a ring made from the person's hair.

"If all the other elements are as perfect to the situation as they can be -a match in every way to the original conditions of the curse- then the sacrifice can be as small as a drop of blood from the Practicioner. If the cure has not been well planned, the sacrifice might be the life of the Practicioner, perhaps even the lives of the Practitioner's family members.

"It is important to remember that the sacrifice is the drawing of accounts. It is the one element that makes all the other elements mean something. Without the sacrifice there can be no binding, the accounts must balance in order for the release to happen. If there is an overbalance in either direction, the results could be disastrous.'"

I mulled over her words, after she finished speaking.

"In other words," I said, "I need to be damn sure of what I'm doing before I leap into this or it could mean the end, period."

"That's what I gather."

"Well, thank you, Mom."

"I'll see if I can find out anything else that might be of use to you. Sibilant, honey, please be careful. You're the only daughter I have and I don't want to lose you."

"I know, Mom.  I love you too."

## Chapter 20

It was another dream. I could feel it pulling me in and dread crept over me, filling my bones like ice water in a lake. I stood outside the cabin, staring at it, waiting for it to swallow me. Then, the door burst open and a shining figure floated down the steps to where I stood, knees knocking. I gasped. It was Elicia, thought not as I had seen her before.

She seemed to be changing in front of my eyes, becoming younger, shorter, childlike, but at the same time, she also seemed to be moving forward in time, becoming stooped and old, with gray hair in the place of the golden hair of the younger girl's. She was in front of me, moving backward and forward, becoming younger and older, but somehow I was able to focus on her essence and move past the constant transitioning of her glowing form.

She leaned in, inches away from my face with her own.

"Sibilant," she said, "I'm so glad you've come here. You're close. So close. Don't let him stop you."

"Who?" I asked.

"The Key Keeper," she said, lowering her voice.

"He wants to keep collecting the debt owed to him. None of us has been able to stop him, Sibilant. We need your help."

She took my hand, and it was warm and tingled, like electricity. She pulled me toward the house, but I stopped at the steps.

"No," I said, shaking my head,"I don't want to go in there. It's cursed and dark in that house."

"I must show you, or you'll never know," she said, insistent, yanking on my hand. "Please, Sibilant, get past your fear and come with me."

I followed her, reluctant, holding back as much as her hand would allow. She pulled me through the door and walked over to the wall. She took three steps from the wood stove that sat in that side of the room and knelt down, placing her hand over the wooden plank there. She looked up at me, beckoning.

"It's over here," she said, pointing at the board. She reached down with her fingers and pulled at the board, yanking it up with a loud creak. "Ah!" she exclaimed, bending over it. She reached in, and I woke up.

~~~~~

“Ah!” I said, in an unconscious echo of Elicia. Sitting up in bed, my mind was a seething mass of excitement and fear.

Paul turned over and I debated whether or not to wake him. Sighing, I reached over and shook his shoulder.

“Paul. Paul, wake up,” I said.

He mumbled and turned his head toward me.

“Sib? What's going on? Why are you awake?”

“I just had another dream, Paul. I know what I have to do,” I said.

He sat up and switched on the beside lamp.

“What is that?” he asked, rubbing his eyes.

I took the plunge.

“I have to go back to the cabin, Paul,” I said.

“What?” he said. I had his full attention now. “Sibilant, I thought we decided it was too dangerous.”

“That was before I had my dream about Elicia,” I said. “Paul, she took me to the cabin and showed me something that is hidden in the floor. We need it to solve the case, I'm sure of it.”

“So we're driving up to the cursed cabin to retrieve
~~~~~

some mysterious thingy, because you had another *dream*? Am I still sleeping or does that sound absolutely crazy?"

"Look, Paul, I'm going up there and you can whine about it or you can come. The choice is yours."

He was silent for longer than I cared for.

"Paul!" I said.

"I'm thinking," he replied. "Can I just have another few hours to considering it?"

I finished pulling on my jeans and sweater, and hunted for a hat. It was cold out today and I doubted that the cabin would have heat. Paul stumbled out of bed to use the bathroom, then joined me in dressing for the day.

We drove with the music on low, some easy listening station and my thoughts boiled over like an overfilled pot. All the dreams, events, and strange occurrences of the past weeks were invading my life -some sort of disease it was impossible to fight off. I believed in fate, the straight path of life, my destiny. Was it my destiny to meet Elicia? Was it my destiny to release her from the curse that bound her? These were only two questions I had no answer to, but there were so many other questions pushing in on me, questions I had no desire to find the answers to.

After a bit of navigating, we found the correct side road. It was only a few minutes from there that we found the lonesome little road going up to the cabin. My heart was pounding and I felt the blood rushing through my body. I took a few calming breaths, Paul reached over to grab my hand, and slowed the car as I saw the old shack sitting in its place.

I sat in my seat, staring out at it for the longest time, trying to work up the courage to face whatever demons awaited me through that doorway.

"This isn't me," I said. "My life isn't about chasing horrors like a ghost hunter gone mad. I'm the cute but chubby girl with the mousy brown hair somewhere between curly and straight who, to make a living, spends her days taking money to tell fortune and future. A situation like this requires a stronger, better, more talented person than me."

"First of all, you're not chubby, not at all. Secondly, you *are* strong enough and more talented than anyone I know. You are right for this task and you are the best person for it. Now come on, let's go find the mystery object."

In the dim morning light, the house looked like one of those abandoned homes on the side of the road. It seemed innocuous and ordinary. I heard the birds making their noises, calling their friends in raucous voices and behind that there was rustling and the breeze blowing. Anywhere else, I would be enjoying early fall, but not here.

I flung open the car door, frustrated and terrified, and Paul did the same, shutting the door behind him. I walked up to the steps, stopping right where I'd had to plead for Kinsey to come down. My toe hit a Witch Ball and I looked down at all of them scattered over the stairs and the ground in front of the cabin.

"You sure about this?" asked Paul. "We can get in the car right now."

I shook my head, and moved forward. It was probably procrastination, but I circled the cabin, following the trail of hairy spheres. The cabin was tiny, it couldn't have been more than two rooms. There was an outhouse and a tool shed and a falling down chicken coop. I circled the house, Paul following and shaking his head all the way, back to the front porch, making certain not to slip on any balls. I recalculated my original estimate -there were thousands upon thousands of the little curses scattered around, and I repressed a shiver when I thought about what they meant in terms of bad energy.

I was back where I started, staring up at the steps, but I wouldn't let myself stall out this time. I put my foot on the first step, then the second, then as, my foot hit the third and finally fourth steps, I realized I was going to do this. I was going to make it into this house, against all reason, the question was, would I make it out?

~~~~~

It was anticlimactic, how easy it was to walk up those steps, push open the creaky wooden door, and walk into the main room of the cabin. We stood in the doorway looking in at the empty room. On the right side of the room was a wood stove with a couple of carved wooden rocking chairs in front of it. There was a wicker basket, empty sitting next to one of the chairs. I pictured knitting or mending previously residing in it. There was a battered rag rug under the chairs. I wondered how much of the house had been emptied out after Elicia's parents died. Anyone could come up here and take what they wanted.

Looking at the floor I saw scrapings and dust balls, but no evidence that anything had been taken. The cabin was sparse.

On the other side of the room was a small round wooden table, with four chairs surrounding it. I walked over to the table and saw a roughly carved hutch opposite of it.

Once upon a time they had lived here. It hadn't been perfect, or opulent, but they had been a family, they had loved each other. Somehow that had been destroyed and Elicia had been on a tragic and lonely road ever since. I sighed and knew that I should go back out and look for whatever it was Elicia was trying to show me in my last dream.

“It's pretty empty in here,” said Paul, and opened one of the cupboard doors and we looked at the dishes inside. They were nothing special, chipped and mismatched, most of them.

“It's heartbreaking,” I said. “A family used to live here.”

The kitchen, if it could be called that, was an extension of the rest of the living area. It had a few wooden cabinets and a large wood topped counter where I guess the chopping was done. There was a metal washtub in the corner, hanging from a
~~~~~

hook and a slop bucket near the door. All of them were covered with dust.

I left the kitchen and opened the only other door in the house, into the bedroom. There was a small cot in the corner, with a mattress -no blanket- on it. A larger bed filled the rest of the room. It had a dusty old quilt on it, and a chest rested at the end of the bed. I opened it, knowing it too would be empty. I sat on the bed for a minute.

"The house feels different today," I said. "There's no menacing presence."

"Maybe Elicia was here for real, and she cleared out all the bad juju," said Paul.

I whirled to look at him, surprised.

"You know, Paul, that is a really insightful statement. Maybe she did."

I walked out into the great room and stood at the door.

"Okay, so Elicia made three steps over this way," I said, pointing for Paul's benefit.

Mirroring Elicia's steps from the wood stove, I counted one, two, three, then stopped, looking down at my feet. I knelt down and Paul knelt down next to me. Running my finger along the board until it touched what felt like a small crack, where the board was pushed up maybe half a centimeter above the floor line, I curled my fingers using the leverage and force of my fingertips to pry the board up. It took some effort and I tore off part of my nail, swearing, but I got it up.

I peered down into the dark hole that was left and saw a white gleaming. Saying a silent prayer against the creepiness of putting my hand down a dark hole in haunted cabin, I reached down and felt a square paper packet. I pulled it out and looked down at it.

The packet was a thick envelope, faded brown with age. It must have down in that hole for years. I wondered how Elicia -if it was her I had seen in my dream- knew to look there for it. There was no writing to indicate what was in the envelope, but on the back was an old fashioned glue-on seal with the symbol of a dove and olive branch on the back. I hesitated, but then broke through it and opened the envelope. I pulled out several sheets of paper and saw a letter, which read:

*To Whomever finds this Account:*

*After the death of my son, it was clear to me that the man I once knew as my husband had become a creature residing in the devil's pit. In all of our years together, our secret meetings when I was but a teenager, our hasty wedding in the face of my parents' disapproval, our relocation to this ramshackle mountain cabin, and our inevitable destitution, I have never felt such ambivalence towards Jed.*

*Through all of his married life, he has been a good husband and father. He has tried his best, through sometimes villainous circumstances, to provide food for our table and a roof for our heads.*

*It's the horrible curse that has done it. I never gave it credence before, and I thought he did not either, until the day he came back from the woods behind our cabin, pale, shaken and bleeding from the corner of his mouth. He stumbled into the main room, tripping over the floorboards, swaying on his feet.*

*"Jediah," I cried, "whatever is the matter?"*

*"My father's curse has laid hold of me, Charlotte. It found me, today in the woods and I met my dark twin." He shivered and sank on his knees to the floor. I saw the blood dripping from his mouth to the rough floor planks and went to fetch a rag from the rag box. I pressed it upon his mouth, and taking care because of my awkwardness, wiped the floor as well. I used his shoulder to help hoist me back to my feet.*

*My babe was heavy in my womb at this point, we were convinced it was a long awaited boy. I stood looking down at him, fear clutching at my throat, and watched as the warm and intelligent man I had married melted away before my eyes.*

*"Surely you were just imagining things, Jed. You've told me many times how silly the old stories were. We laughed over them in our bed on cold nights, as though they were children's rhymes."*

*The old stories were things to frighten children, surely. They told of a family curse that had wandered down through the Campbell men of each generation, haunting each man with his own darker self, until he weakened and died full of terror and pain. I covered my belly with a hand, my instinct to protect my son. My glance went to the front window where I could see Elicia playing on the porch. I resisted the urge to go and gather her inside, instead leaning over to place a hand on my husband's shoulder.*

*"A more evil man than my father never walked this earth, Charlotte. He died when I was but a young boy and all the memories I have of him were of dark ceremonies and twisted nightmares. He was always mixed up in some devilish business. His greatest desire in life, besides being the most powerful man in the county, was to figure out how to rid himself of the curse. He was not successful, and in the end, he died just like all of the ancestors he claimed had been taken by the curse.*

*"I can not die like him. Mama told me when they laid him out for the wake, he was a twisted semblance of the rugged mountain man he'd been. His face was drawn up into a fearful grimace that gave her nightmares for weeks and his limbs were oddly placed and misshapen. Though my aunt tried, she could not lay him out in a properly decorous manner. I can not die like him. I can not."*

*"Hush," I whispered, and ran my fingers through his tousled hair. "Tell me what happened."*

*"I was out in the back parcel, checking my snares, and*

*suddenly I felt the most peculiar sense that I was being watched. I stood, slowly, and looked behind me and there to my infinite dismay, I saw my own self, yet darker and with a loathsome smirk upon its face.*

*"The dark twin walked toward me, laughing at my growing shock and horror, and said, "What? Did you think you would be the most fortunate of your kin, Jediah Campbell? I tell you this, both you and your unborn son are cursed, and when your son is grown and has his own sons, they will also be cursed."*

*At this, Jediah broke down sobbing, head in his hands.*

*"Then he reached down and grabbed my rabbit from the snare, broke its neck and took a snarling bite out of its flesh. I saw its blood running down its face and hands, Charlotte. Then I ran, tripping and fumbling through the woods. At one point, a branch hit my face, which is why I am bleeding."*

*He looked up at me, tears in his eyes.*

*"What did we do? What did my family do to rouse the anger of such evil? Why are we being so foully punished? Have I not always been a good Christian man? Have I not gone to church and read the word of the Lord? Why is there no salvation for me or for my son?"*

*I did not know what to say. Little did I know that my good husband had left out much of his conversation with his twin. I did not find out till much later, the sinister plot of escape my husband had hatched for himself at the expense of our unborn child. I found out when I lost the son I had carried for some months. It was then I started to understand how perverted my husband had become, because of the fear inside him.*

## Chapter 21

The letter continued:

*Some weeks later, I was preparing the bread for supper when I felt a stab of pain and a rush of water and blood left me. I looked down in concern and realized that my time was commencing. It was far too early, and Jed had taken the long walk into town to look for work. Leesy's bus was due to arrive in minutes, and her miles long walk would result in her appearance in an hour or so following that.*

*I was alone. Another pain rushed over me, and I feared for the life of my son. The pain was crippling and I stopped what I was doing and focused on the pain that was pushing my son out into the world. It seemed my second labor would be a quick one. If only I wasn't by myself.*

*I waddled to the bedroom and leaned over against the headboard rocking my way through another wave of pain. I moaned and remembered my first birth. Elicia had taken her own sweet time coming into the world and the pain had been significant. This felt more urgent to me and I knew my anxiety was mounting. This was not right.*

*I can not speak of when my daughter arrived, only that by the time she had done so, I was kneeling on the floor with my skirt hiked up over my shoulders and a pile of clean rags underneath me.*

*"Mama?"*

*I heard her call, but I could not answer at this point, my son's arrival was imminent. I grunted and pushed and I heard her footsteps run over to where I was.*

*"Mama?"*

*She sounded so uncertain. I know she was old enough to realize that there was still a span of months until the time I had told her that her brother would be born.*

*"Is it brother?" she asked.*

*I nodded and pushed again. I could feel his head, so small, leaving my body and then quickly, slick and smooth came the rest of his tiny form. I started sobbing immediately when I saw his blue skin and wondered if he would even take a single breath.*

*I had underestimated my son's will, even at such an early age. I picked him up and tucked him under the bodice of my dress to keep warm against my skin and he gave a quiet squawk. It wasn't much, but enough to give me futile hope. I tried to nurse him, but he had not the strength for that, the little lamb, and instead he breathed slowly and looked up at me with jet black eyes. I was still crying, tears pouring down my cheeks.*

*"Why is he so small?" Leesy asked.*

*"I'm afraid your brother came too early into life,"I said, "He will not last the night I fear."*

*My breath caught over the words and she started to cry along with me.*

*"Why, mama, why did he come so early? Why can't he be bigger? Why does he have to die?"*

*"All things die, Leesy," I said, trying to figure out how to explain death to an 8 year old. "It is merely a question of when they die. I think we would have been happy to have your brother in our lives, but for whatever reason, God has willed that it should not be so."*

*She touched his cheeks and leaned forward to kiss him.*

*"I love you, and I wish you could stay with us for always."*

*He kept his eyes on me, his breathing slowing. I leaned forward to kiss his mouth and smell his skin.*

*"Good bye, my son," I whispered, and we watched his last breath.*

~~~~~

*By the time Jed returned home from a fruitless search, Leesy and I had wrapped the baby in the blanket we'd made for him and some of the clothes, though they were much too big. I knew that Jed could easily fashion a box for us to place him in, for burial.*

*My heart weighed heavy and my thoughts were low. None of that, however, was to compare with Jediah's reaction upon coming home that night. As I said, the child was wrapped and laying in my arm; I had long since delivered of the afterbirth and Leesy had taken it to the outhouse. We'd cleaned me up as best we could, and then we sat, staring down at the baby's still, blue face.*

*Jediah stomped through the door in a foul mood, and I judged rightly that he'd had no luck finding a job.*

*"Charlotte," he called, and I answered back that I was in the bedroom.*

*He gasped as he came through the doorway and saw us, in the lamplight, huddled around the still figure.*

*"Charlotte -what..."*

*He couldn't finish, though he knew as soon as he looked upon his son's face, why we were sitting there with wet faces and darkened eyes.*

*"He just came, I had no control. My waters broke and he just came, he just came."*

*I started crying again, but I stopped as Jediah let out a long moan.*

*"No, no, it can't be! It wasn't supposed to happen like this. He was supposed to live. He was supposed to* live*! He lied to me. He lied."*
~~~~~

*Saying this, he rushed out and I hear the cabin door slam. Leesy and I looked at each other and I felt in my heart that something was amiss in Jed's reaction.*

*He came back hours later bearing a small wooden box that he'd made from scraps in the yard. I could tell he'd been crying and his face was almost as pale as the baby's. He looked ill. He set the box before me and we laid the tiny bundle inside. Leesy had fallen asleep by this time, but I knew she'd want to say good-bye, so I woke her.*

*She kissed the baby with such a soft touch I still can't be certain her lips made contact with his skin. Then my husband and I took our son and buried him under the fir tree, near the west corner of the cabin. We held each other and cried and I almost believed that his grief was over the loss of a child.*

*"We can have more children, more sons," I said.*

*He shuddered and turned away from me.*

*"I don't know if I have enough time," he muttered.*

*I stood alone at my son's grave, worrying over my husband.*

~~~~~

*Thus began the end of my trust and love for my husband. After the death of our son, he became strange and secretive. He muttered to himself constantly, and spent much of his time locked in his shop. He also started making more trips into town.*

*I would have thought he was looking for a job, except that he would leave at odd hours of the night, only to return directly before dawn. He came to bed and curled on his side, away from me. I stopped sleeping, waiting for what was to come next. I had no idea what it would be, but I knew it would ill-begotten. I did not have to wait long.*

*One night, when I was laying in our bed, pretending to sleep, as I did most nights, Jed came in and took Elicia and left*
~~~~~

*the cabin. Dread rising in my heart, I slipped on some boots and a shawl and followed his lamp through the dark woods to a dimly lit shack that I knew about, though I had never seen it.*

*It was the hovel of the witch woman, Myrtha, hung with all manner of charms and foul oddments. I sneaked up to the window to see what was happening and I heard Leesy's muffled cry, "Where's Mama?"*

*"Be quiet, child," Myrtha said, while my husband stood anxiously looking on. She looked up at him and said, "The key here is substitution. The curse is bound to pass from father to son, by right of the blood and the originator -your many great grandfather. But now you see, your son is dead, and the curse haunts you, chases you. In order to substitute your daughter for your son, we will have to perform the same rite as your great grand sire, but with a change for the child here."*

*Leesy sat there, good child that she is, staring with fearful eyes at the hag and then her father, waiting for him to step in and take her home to comfort.*

*Instead, he leaned forward and muttered, "We don't have to hurt her, do we?"*

*"As with most spells, we need something that belongs solely to the child, such as a lock of her hair, and for this particular spell, something that you share, such as your blood. First I will get your blood."*

*She ran a blade's edge along my husband's finger and caught the drops in a wooden bowl. Then she turned to Leesy.*

*"Daddy, don't let her cut me. I want to go home. Where's Mama?"*

*The witch ignored her and cut off a perfect gold curl and placed it in the bowl. It was at this point I realized what was happening. My husband was trying to place his curse on own daughter. I had to stop this.*

*I ran into the room as Myrtha grabbed my daughter's hand. Leesy was crying and asking for Jed's help, but he only stared at her.*

*"Jediah Mitchell Campbell, stop this at once!" I cried, and pushed aside the witch's hand. "What are you doing to your poor daughter? For shame, both of you."*

*I reached to grab Leesy up in my arms, but I was yanked back by Jed, who turned his face from me, while holding me with arms like bands of iron.*

*"Do it," he told the witch.*

*"No!" I shrieked, kicking and screaming. Leesy screamed as the woman cut her finger and let the drops fall into the wooden bowl with her father's. "I won't let you do this, Jed! Let go of this foul purpose. Nothing is worth hurting your child in such a way!"*

*He ignored me and watched as the witch took her bowl over to the table and started mixing various ingredients into it. Leesy scrambled down from the chair that she'd been sitting in and ran over to me.*

*"Mama," she said and hid her face in my skirt.*

*I relaxed my body, now that she was with me, and I felt Jed's arms loosen. I elbowed him with all the force I had and heard the air that came from his lips as I picked up my child and ran for our lives.*

~~~~~

*Somehow, though I am not sure in the dark how we made it, we arrived at the cabin, lit only by the waxing moon. I stumbled on the steps, Elicia was a heavy load, and managed by sheer will to steady myself and go inside.*

*The cabin was dark and empty, but I knew my way around from years of using the outhouse in the middle of the night and I went to where the lamp was and lit it. A dim light filled the room and I took down the rifle from the mantle, checked to make sure it was loaded and told Elicia to go hide under the bed. Then I sat in the old chair that I used to rock her in as a babe, and waited for the appearance of my*
~~~~~

*husband.*

*I heard his slow steps on the porch minutes later and tensed, raising the rifle to my shoulder. He pushed open the door and I heard the long moan of the old hinges as it scraped across the floor. His shadow filled the doorway and I saw the moonlight glint off the knife he held in a clenched hand.*

*"What gives our daughter the right to live an unfettered life while I am doomed to a horrible death? I was born as innocent as she. I never did a thing to deserve what my father did to me, so why should she not be as cursed as I am?"*

*"Leave us, Jed, or you will join your father in hell tonight," I said, holding the rifle steady as I cocked it.*

*He moved forward and I saw his features become clearer in the lamplight. His face held an ugly sneer and his eyes were wild, like an animal's.*

*"What are you going to do to me, Charlotte? Are you going to shoot me, your husband, like a dog? You promised to love and obey me, once. Put down the gun."*

*"I have said it once, and I will not say it again. Get out of this cabin, Jed, and do not return. I will shoot you to save our child. I have already lost one child and I will not lose another."*

*"I'm not going to kill her, you silly woman. I'm just going to save my own life."*

*I stood.*

*"Yes, at the expense of her peace and sanity. I heard it all, Jed. You want to put your curse on her. It is not right and I will not be a part of it."*

*He moved forward another step, looking into my eyes, gauging my determination. Then he stepped backward. He turned, and sighed, hunching his shoulders and walked back toward the door. I relaxed, just a bit, and that is when he turned back, throwing the knife at me. I felt a slow burn spread instantly over my abdomen and a shriek escaped my lips. I did not need to look down to know that he'd skewered me. Jed was skilled with knives, every aspect from skinning a hare, to throwing at a target.*

*Still, even as I felt the blood start to leave my body in a slow drip, I knew I could not be weak, for Leesy's sake. This wasn't about me anymore, it was about her. I took aim, in the dim light and shot him right in the chest.*

*"Charlotte!" he cried and his eyes widened, his hand reaching up to touch the wound I'd created.*

*I shot him again, and reached down to load the shot gun two more times, from the shells in my pocket. Then I walked forward until the rifle was touching his scalp. He brushed feebly against it with his hand, but he was much weaker than I at this point, and I pulled the trigger and blew a hole in his head.*

*As soon as my task was finished, I let the gun slide from my fingers and clatter on the wooden boards then I turned back to the bedroom and called Elicia to come out to me.*

*"Mama," she cried and ran to me, but I held up a hand.*

*"Go fetch some of the clean rags from our bedroom and the whiskey your father keeps in the side cabinet over there."*

*I sat back in the rocking chair, and felt weak. I knew that I would not live much longer than my husband. I could see dawn starting to paint the edges of the leaves outside. I reached down and slid the knife from my side. I knew that it had damaged a vital part of me. I cleaned the wound, however, and pressed my hand into it as hard as I could.*

*I told Leesy to pull the old table toward me, and then had her run to the bedroom for paper and a pen. I wrote out the majority of this story with her standing next to me, laying her head against my shoulder. Then I turned to her and ran my hand over her head, caressing her hair -it shone like silk in the early morning light. Poor little one, such a hard life she will live, losing three family members in such a short time.*

*"Elicia, I need you to go down and meet the bus and tell them that I'm hurt and you need help," I told her.*

*"Mama, I want to stay here with you," she pleaded.*

*"You can not, my love. I need a doctor or I will die as surely as your father did. Be strong, Leesy, and always, always remember I love you."*

*"Mama," she sobbed and nuzzled her face in my chest.*

*I winced at the pain, but relished the affection all the same. I kissed her head and cried silently, wishing I didn't have to leave her, wishing for just a few more minutes. It is a hard cold world we live in, and so I knew I had to let go of her.*

*She walked past her father's corpse and into the sunlight, glancing back at me one last time before she walked out of my life forever. I will miss her, but I hope we will meet again in heaven.*

*I go to hide this letter in a secret place, dear reader. Even now, I feel the life slipping from my limbs, a delicious weakness washes over me.*

*Elicia, if it is you that has found this letter, do your best to end the curse. Don't let your father's dark deeds that night win the day. I include the poem passed down in the family that tells of the curse of Jediah. I feel that it must hold the key to breaking it.*

*-Charlotte Campbell*

I finished reading the letter to Paul, and stared, with trembling hands, with disbelief at the story that had unfolded around me. It was Elicia's father, all along, the man who looked so normal in the photos I had of him, who had loved Charlotte with all his heart at one point in his life, until the blood curse had turned him from a loving and compassionate man into a grief stricken monster.

Paul and I traded glances.

“Well, at least we know what happened now,” said Paul.

"That poor family," I said.

"It's hard to believe that a curse could do all this damage," said Paul.

This was the worst part of a blood curse. There was no end to the suffering that it caused while it ran its course. Without my help, the curse would figure out a way to move on and hurt someone else. Somewhere there was a force driving this evil, and I had to stop it. I still had no plan for how I was going to do that, but my task was ahead of me, nonetheless.

"The curse didn't do all of it," I said, "These people turned on each other. That was their choice."

"I don't see that Charlotte had much of a choice," said Paul. "Listen, I'm going to go find the outhouse. That was a long drive."

He left the cabin and I set the letter, and its accompanying poem on the floor in front of me, as I tried with little success to push aside the overwhelming feeling of dread washing over me. I thought of everything Mom had told me yesterday about curses. There had to be a way to find the heart of this one, if I could only find some kind of divine inspiration. Some little part of the letter I'd just read nagged at me, I was trying to think of what it was, but it continued to evade my grasp, to my frustration.

Time to leave this horrible place behind, I thought. It really was a shame. The cabin had been the heart of a family and now it was twisted and evil, just like what had happened to the mild-mannered Jediah Campbell. I walked out the door, shutting it behind me -why, I have no idea- and as I turned back I almost jumped out of my skin, for standing there in front of me was the oldest and ugliest woman I've ever seen, leaning against a gnarled and pockmarked walking stick.

## Chapter 22

Her stick was an oddity, wrapped in multicolored leather straps, braids and whorls. I could not see how they were attached -if they were glued or tied. Little glass beads peeked out here and there and I found myself thinking that it was a vain piece of equipment for an old woman to use. At the same time, I felt power emanating from her. Not active or impinging, but old and knowledgeable. She was the type of woman who young women sought out for advice on the old lore. She knew things I didn't know, I could tell just at the sight of her and that cane.

"What are you doing here, young woman? Can't see the warning I placed here for all to see?" she waved her stick about with some difficulty, gesturing toward the Witch Balls scattered hither and yon.

"So these curse balls are yours?" I asked, it was an obvious question, but I was hoping it would lead her to explain her unexpected presence out here in the woods.

"Didn't I just say as much? Are all young women as stupid as yourself these days? Why are you here at this cursed place?"

"I'm here on behalf of Elicia Campbell. Do you know of her?" I asked.

She sighed and walked over to where I stood on the porch, and settled herself into the step. "Indeed, I knew the girl as well as anyone around these parts did. She was the daughter of the unfortunate Jediah."

"Yes, the unfortunate Jediah and his wife Charlotte, who did not die in a hunting accident," I said, coming to sit beside her.

"And you figured that out, did you? So proud of yourself, are you?" she cackled.

"I didn't figure it out. I read it in this letter, " I said, holding it up so she could look at it. Although, I guess that I was assuming her eyesight was good enough to read. She nodded.

"Ah, well, it's too true, all of it, I'm sure. Written by Charlotte, was it? Had to be. Elicia was too young and Jediah was dead by the time I got to the house. It was a horrible mistake, that night. I've paid for it over and over again," she sighed again and looked down at all the little spheres around her feet.

"You aren't... you can't be Myrtha?" I asked, astonished. "You must be... ancient!"

She laughed.

"Not that ancient. I was not so young then, true, but I was young enough then to be merely eighty-seven now. I am Myrtha, and before that night I was the resident witch woman. I could make some minor spells, charms, and curses, for a good price.

"I knew it was a mistake to take money from Jediah. I knew that I didn't have the power to fix the curse. But Jediah was convinced that there had to be a way to lift it. He came to me weeks before, and promised me money if I could help him figure out a way to lift his curse. I didn't know then it was a blood curse. I set up a simple transition spell. My idea was to move the curse onto someone else.

"I didn't know then he was going to sacrifice Elicia. I didn't know that she was the intended victim in his plot. By the time he told me he was crazed and out of control. I went through with it, because I was afraid of what he might do to me, or the child or his wife. I can protect against some things with my charms, but they are no match against a large hunting knife."

"So he realized that he was going to die and he came to you to try and release the curse. Did he mention seeing a mirror image of himself?" I asked.

"He never mentioned anything except his father, who I remembered from time past. It was rumored that his father had a mirror man, who served him and did his bidding. Until now I gave it no credence, but it seems as if you know something about another mirror man, so perhaps the stories were true," she said.

I thought about Elicia and her mirror, the photos I'd found of her after her death. I thought about the entry in her journal where a vision of her father came to her, as though called, and killed Victor on her behalf.

"His father performed the same ritual on him at some point in time. That was where we came up with the idea for this spell. His father was an evil man with a bad reputation. Everyone tried to stay on his good side, as those who crossed him found themselves dead."

"If he had so much power, why did they live here?" asked Paul, who had come around the corner.

"I suppose that was part of the curse. No man in the Campbell line has ever been successful, in fact, they seemed to have a rash of bad luck -or so the rumors say."

"So when he revealed his father's curse to you, you realized that it wasn't a simple matter to release it?" I asked.

"Indeed," she answered. "And I have never been more sorry that I didn't listen to my inner voice and stay far away from that mess. When I worked that curse, and Charlotte came in to seize her child away from us, I saw the look in her eyes, that of a mother and wife in torment. I realized that I had ruined her life, perhaps forever, and also altered the life of her child.

"When he left my house with his knife, I was too afraid

to move, another thing I regret. By the time I had worked up my courage to go down the hill Jediah was dead, Elicia was gone to get help and Charlotte's life was moment's from slipping away. I knelt at her side, and she looked up at me and whispered, 'Don't let him take her away from me. Don't let the Keeper have her.' And then she breathed her last.

"I worked an illusion over the bodies and the house, that whoever came to the house would see what appeared to be a tragic hunting accident, rather than the murder that it was. Even Elicia seemed to be affected by it, though somehow she must have remembered something, since she felt compelled to send you back here."

“She didn't send us,” said Paul.

"She's dead, " I said. "Another victim of the blood curse. I came back here on my own. I have one other question, something you mentioned earlier. What do you know about the Keeper?"

She looked at me for a long moment, as though sizing me up. "It is an old legend, passed about among young children as a bedtime story. The Key Keeper is a fallen one, who has been given 6 keys, the keys to the kingdom no less, to watch over and also use when required. The Key Keeper is an immortal without feeling or conscience, meting out powers, pleasures or punishment, whatever his whim might be."

"And this Key Keeper might grant some sort of request to a mortal, in return for payment?" asked Paul.

"So the story goes. There is even a story about such a one, who asks to use the keys, and in return must give his soul to the keeper. Many would think such a payment would be too high a cost, but for some, access to that much power in a lifetime would be worth any sacrifice."

"I've been wondering what evil could be at the heart of this mess. I know it isn't a curse borne from hatred, so it must come from another source. There is a powerful force out there working this curse toward its own end and I'm at a loss as to what kind of creature could have that power. Do you think the Key Keeper could be real?" I wondered.

"Anything could be or not be. It's not my fate to end this tale. I'm forever sorry for the small role I played. After that night, I refused to practice again. I'm just an old woman now, scrounging a living out of the forest and my own small garden, taking the charity others bestow on me. It's my own punishment, and I'll die alone, with hell as my reward. I do not doubt that."

"What do you remember about Elicia?" I asked.

"She was a happy girl, like a little ray of sunshine in her parents' lives -sweet as pie and smart as a whip. I felt bad seeing them take her away like that. Never heard what happened to her afterward and never figured I would.

"I locked that house away in spells and curses to keep people away from it. Anyone round these parts knows that if you see a Witch Ball, you turn around and walk away. You're just ignorant, I guess. Pity. Whether you found that letter or not, you probably weren't meant to. This whole business is nothing but trouble."

She heaved herself up off the step with the help of her cane.

"I wash my hands of this mess, and if you want my advice you both will too, though I can see in your eyes you have no intention of doing that.

"You, girl, must go off and put an end to this, and may the Lord's mercy follow you. There is nothing else that will protect you from this madness. Be careful, I can see death's shadow on you. You haven't much time."

Saying this, she hobbled off on a path leading into the woods and disappeared.

She left us standing there, in the woods with the wind blowing through the trees around us.

~~~~~

The first story my Nanny always told me was this:

Deep in the hills of the Moorelock, lived a demon who fancied himself a king of his own kingdom. He dipped and wallowed in the affairs of mortals, giving gifts, for a price. Many a human found despair in a possession given by the demon, for his gifts required a high price. He kept a tight grip on the affairs of those insignificant beings around him and interfered in them like the veriest potentate.

But the demon had a secret, as such power beings are want to. He had a secret to his powers, a set of keys that he kept hidden from the curious eyes of men. Legend says, that as long as he possesses those keys, he has the power to control all and on the day he loses them, the sky will crumble and evil will lose its foothold on the world.

~~~~~

The second part of the Key Keeper legend is regarding the keys of power and it goes like this:

One day a man came to the Key Keeper and asked for a boon from him. The demon looked at him and said, "I see the make of thee, little man. Thou seeks a gift bigger than that of a normal mortal."

"Aye," said the man, a smug grin lit his face,"I seek the keys of power."

The demon looked at him, surprised, and exclaimed, "From whence hast thou heard of the keys, mortal?"

"It matters not," said the man, "only that I wish to make use of them."

The demon was serious now. "To use the keys will exact a dear price. Art thou ready for that cost?"

The man nodded,"I know the cost and I will pay it."

And he did pay, with his life.

~~~~~

File, Biography: Millicent Campbell (Nanny)

I barely remember anything about my Nanny. She lived with us when I was very young, so young that all the memories I have of her are pieces. I can remember the smell of her skin, the sound of her voice singing to me every night, the feel of sitting in her lap while we were rocking in the rocking chair, and the cookies she used to bake -they tasted of nutmeg.

She was my father's mother, and she was responsible for my dad turning out better than his father had. Thanks to her, he was loving and tender with my mother and I, where his father (my grandfather) was abusive and given to sudden rages -this was according to Mama. She didn't talk about her father-in-law much, I never knew if she met him or if he was already gone. It's been much harder researching this side of my family, because everyone tended to live up in the hills, hidden away.

The cabin where my parents lived had been Nanny and my grandfather's. When I researched land ownership, I was able to find that it had been owned by my father's family for generations.

~~~~~

I looked over the information on the next few pages, tucked into the folder. The next piece of paper was handwritten in pencil in childish script -kind of hard to read.

*The Tale of Jediah*

*Jediah was born on the 7th day of the 7th month. His parents named him Jediah. Jediah was a strange child. He never wanted to go out at night. He said that the bad shadow would get him. When he was 20 years old, he went out one night with his friends. They brought him home later and he was screaming and yelling. His parents asked what was wrong and he told them the bad shadow had spoken to him and told him that he would die. He died a week later. Ever since then, when a boy child in the family was born, they name him Jediah. The Jediahs never live long.*

*The End.*

The writing was almost like that of a child doing a homework assignment. I didn't know if the story was true or not, but it could be one explanation for the reason why the Campbell men were all named the same.

~~~~~

Paul and I were eating soup and discussing what we'd found at the cabin, as well as Myrtha's side of the story.

"What I want to know is, what is this about?" he asked, holding out the poem, "besides the obvious."

"I'm not sure. It seems to offer up an explanation of how the curse began. I think I'm starting to put these pieces together. Somewhere in the past, Elicia's ancestor made a bargain with an evil being to exchange earthly power for the life of his first born child -who wasn't born at the time.

"Somehow the bargain went awry and the curse took the man, his son, his grandson, and so forth. It's always passed through the men in a family. There is some part in here I'm not getting though, and that is how the curse kept passing down. It almost seems like a person realizes he still carries the curse and then he bargains to make it pass from himself to his son, yet the transfer never works.

"Jediah's father performed a ritual to give his son the curse and died himself a few years later. Jediah had planned on using his son as the vessel, but then the baby died at birth. So he changed the curse to transfer to his daughter instead. He died the same night. And then it became Elicia's burden."
~~~~~

"And she died of it," finished Paul.

"Now, it seems like, though it has consumed every last person in Elicia's family line, it's still hungry for more. Kinsey is gone, so is Lyle, and I've already been threatened with more if I try to release this curse.

"From what Mom told me, a blood curse never ends, it just moves on to greener pastures, which in my case means that everyone connected with me or Elicia is in danger: you, Jordan, Mrs. Ford, Francis, and possibly even my mom. The evil presence who set the curse in motion, the being I suspect is called the Key Keeper, is looking for its next victim and I have to stop it before it succeeds in hurting someone else."

"So just come up with your magical elements, or whatever, set the spell, and voila, the curse is broken! I mean, you must have enough information now to break the curse, right?" he asked.

"Well, I know the origins of the curse, yes, but what else do I have? I have no canticle, I have no binding, no belonging and no sacrifice. I'm flying blind here. So maybe what we should do is try to figure out what we could use, and set up a location, that's very important too," I said.

"Well, let's get cracking!" Paul said, and pulled out a pen from his pocket. We started making notes on our paper dinner napkins, but we didn't make much headway. We tried endless combinations, but nothing seemed to come together for us. Finally, I threw down the pen.

"Something is still missing. I just don't have the motivation that I should to figure this out. I think what I need is a good night's sleep."

~~~~~

I was flying over the dark earth -trees, houses and roads passing in a blur beneath me. The world was dim and hard to see, but that wasn't the point. The point was the glowing lights of all the souls beneath me. Each person was a glowing ball,
~~~~~

with an individual color and light size. It was strange how I could tell what they were, even though I was moving with reckless speed through the air. It was almost as though I had seen them so many times before, they were a routine part in my existence.

And now I realized, I wasn't just flying around like some sort of floating specter. I was looking for something, or someone to be more specific. I floated over a house, pausing, I recognized it as Paul's house. I used some other sense to glance in, with my mind, trying to find him. He wasn't there, so I moved on.

The next house that I stopped at was the tall Edwardian that belonged to Phyllis Ford and her son. I looked in, but something kept me from going inside. I could see them, their auras glowing before me -green and soft, and I wished I could go inside, but it wasn't the right move. They weren't what I wanted.

I moved on past Jordan's house, it wasn't what I needed, either. I was starting to get frustrated. I needed to find someone. Why wasn't everything falling into place? I felt impotent and irritated and nothing I did seemed to bring me the result I wanted. I flew around, nudging a consciousness here and there, feeling out what I might be looking for.

Finally, there it was, just... there! I saw it -her to be exact. She was innocent and hopeful, and her soul glowed like a beacon. She would give me power, and all I had to do was reach down and grab it.

That's when I realized, I was not me, Sibilant. I was him, the Key Keeper, and I was somehow able to see what he was doing. What he was doing, was hunting someone, and I had to stop him, but I couldn't. Helpless, I had to watch him hunting down this poor girl.

He was closer now and excited. He could smell her, and she had power, I could tell that because he could tell.

Suddenly, he had her in his sights and he swooped down, hovering over her, before pouncing like the predator he was.

As he zoomed in closer to her face, I felt sick to my stomach and I realized like a sock to the stomach, that I knew her. I knew her. It was Sophie.

He reached down, and she looked up, screaming.

# Chapter 23

It was when her screams turned into a strange ringing noise, that I realized what I was seeing was a dream, and my dream was being interrupted by the jangling of the phone on my bedside table. Heart pounding from my nightmare, I fumbled around in the dark for my phone, glancing at the clock at my bedside. 1 AM.

Paul stirred beside me as I picked up the phone and mumbled, "Hello?"

"Is this Sibilant?" a harried female voice said.

"Um, yes," I said, "Can I help you?"

"This is Danielle King, Sophie's mother. Please, I was wondering if you'd seen her at all today? She mentioned dropping by after school."

I felt sick to my stomach.

"Mrs. King, has something happened to Sophie?" I asked.

"I don't know," she sobbed. "She's gone missing. We've called the police and they're out looking. They made us run through the events of the day and call everyone we think might have seen her today. You're all she's talked about lately; I found your number on the bulletin board by her desk."

"I am so sorry. I haven't seen her for a few days. We had talked about her coming over at some point this week. I had some pictures for her to look at. I'm sorry," I said again. I felt awful. This was my fault.

"It's okay," she said, and I heard the tears clogging her throat as she talked. "I knew it was a long shot. I mean, why would she still be at your house at this time of night without calling? She's a very responsible girl. She's never given me a bit of trouble."

"Is there anything I can do to help? Do you need help making fliers or canvassing the neighborhood? I'll do whatever I can."

"At this point, we're waiting till the morning to start rallying everyone. Maybe if I could have someone call you then?"

"Of course, please don't hesitate." She thanked me and said good-bye. I sat silent in the dark for a few moments, considering.

"What are you going to do?" Paul asked, making me jump.

"I didn't realize you were awake. You heard all that?"

"Yes, and unlike Sophie's mother, I know you aren't the type to sit around waiting for something to happen, good or bad."

"It's my fault, Paul," I said, tearing up. I couldn't handle this. This girl was in mortal danger because of me.

"What do you mean, it's your fault?"

"I had another dream, Paul. This time I was seeing the world through his eyes and he was hunting for a target. He looked for you, but you weren't home, thank God. Then he found someone else. He found Sophie and as I woke up, she was screaming. It was horrible."

"Oh my God, Sib. Then her mom called you right after that? You think it must be real or she wouldn't be missing."

"I just keep picturing what I saw in my dreams about Kinsey and Lyle. It was the most disturbing thing I've ever seen. I can't stand the thought of Sophie being like that. I can't deal with it," I said, flinging back the covers.

I turned on my bedside lamp and flinched as the dim light hit my eyes. I pulled a pair of jeans and a sweater out of the dresser, remembering that I wanted everything as light as possible for what I planned on next. White sweater and pale jeans. I don't own white jeans, I just don't. I grabbed white socks, white boots, white underwear... you get the picture. I pulled my hair back in a white hairband, and tried to gather my thoughts. Paul got out of bed and started dressing and I turned to him.

"No, Paul. You can't come this time," I said.

"Like hell I can't," he said, all eyebrows as he frowned at me.

"Do you not get the idea of what a sacrifice is?" I asked, "I can't take the chance that the Key Keeper will just pluck you from the land of the living as easily as he did the others."

"Sibilant-"

"No, I just can't, Paul. I know it will kill you to let me walk out that door and try to face this thing by myself, but I have to." I walked over to him, held his face in my hands, and stared him down. "This has always been my battle, not yours, love. Please don't put yourself at risk, you don't have the skill set that I do."

"You don't even know what you're going to do!" He protested, pulling away from me.

"I'll improvise. It's how I've figured out most of this anyway. And I was thinking, I'll use that poem for the canticle," I said over my shoulder, moving in the living area of my little apartment.

I put a piece of charcoal from my cold coal bucket into a plastic sandwich baggy, as I hadn't had time to do any wool shopping. My next items came from the table: the drawing of Elicia and her mother on the front porch of the cabin and the faded piece of paper the poem was written on. Paul stood in the doorway to the bedroom, looking at me.

"What makes you think I'll be safe here? If that Keeper guys wants to hurt me, he can do it anywhere."

"True," I agreed, "but I'm counting on the fact that I'll be a sufficient enough distraction for him -he won't have time to go hunting for other mortals to terrorize."

"If that's the case," Paul said, "I'm coming."

I rolled my eyes. "Paul, if you're right there, distraction won't work. He'll just grab you, like some sort of hostage situation. Bad idea."

He crossed his arms and looked like a sulky boy. Instead of being irritated, my heart welled with love for him. The stubborn man was willing to put his life in mortal danger in some kind of misguided bid to protect me. I didn't have the heart to tell him that I had no choice on the sacrificial aspect of this spell.

It didn't matter. I wasn't going to let Sophie get killed because of something that I had foolishly gotten myself tangled up in. Whatever it took, I would save her.

~~~~~

I left Paul sitting in my living room, I knew he wouldn't sleep until whatever I was going to attempt was over. I got in my car and instead of driving to the cabin, I drove to Elicia's house. It was where the curse had taken her and therefore, it was where the curse needed to be released.

My stomach was a roiling and simmering cauldron of worry. Nervous was too small a word for what I was feeling, sitting behind the wheel of the car. I drove down the long driveway, willing myself to breathe slow and deep. It was an exercise in futility. After a few minutes of this, I gave in to the the anxiety and let it become a part of what I was hoping would guide my underlying intuition.

I pulled up in front of the door, grabbed my purse from the passenger seat, and ran up the stairs, heart pounding. I used my keys and alarm code to open the front door. The house was dark and empty. All I was missing was the stormy part, but thank goodness there was no rainstorm to go along with my
~~~~~

terror.

Now that I was in the house, my steps slowed. I knew the path that my feet were pacing, but each step seemed to drag as I walked through the dark entry, flipping on lights as I went up each stair, almost counting them out, so intent was I on making myself reach the end of them.

I turned left at the top of the stairs, clutching my purse close to my chest. I took a deep breath, put my hand on the knob and turned it. I pushed open the door, and flicked on the light, releasing the air I'd been holding. I don't know what I expected, some presence maybe? Some sign that I was on the right track -a demon to guard my way or Elicia's ghost to lead me.

The empty room was as I had left it weeks ago. I flipped on the light residing by Elicia's dressing table and stood for a few moments, scouting out where I would begin. There was Elicia's bed, where she slept every night, haunted by horrible dreams and then there were the nights she didn't sleep at all, so consumed by fear was she. She was found at her dressing table, so I could do it there, or maybe in the closet where she hid all the photos in the shoe boxes. In the end, I decided the center of the room would be the best place to work my spell, drawing on the power of all the objects together. They were all used by Elicia before she died, and would continue to hold the power of her essence.

Then, squatting on my toes, I drew as perfect a circle as I could around me in the soft Berber carpet with my black little piece of coal. I tsked to myself that I was ruining such an expensive floor, but I knew she wouldn't care in the least, living or dead, as long as she was free from the curse placed on her. I decided to leave my binding as a mere circle, rather than complicating it with a bunch of symbols and glyphs.

A circle was a powerful symbol in itself, representing birth, death and rebirth. Never starting or stopping, it remained endless, a perfect binding as long as I didn't pick up my chalk from the carpet as I drew it. As soon as I had lifted my blackened fingertips holding the charcoal from the carpet, Thadius appeared before me.

I was so startled I almost fell backwards in fear and surprise. I kept my balance so as not to disturb my circle. I was not expecting any protection from a circle in black on a carpet, and indeed I would have been foolish to assume such a thing would protect me from an immortal. It's a common enough misnomer from literature. If you are casting a spell, put yourself in a protected circle and you will be safe.

While it's true there are many simple protections against demons and other uncommon immortals, for a being as strong as the Key Keeper there is no good protective measure, except to rely on the deep magic and its rules and hope everything turns out okay in the end.

I stood with care so as not to smudge the inky line surrounding me, maintaining my composure while he stared at me. I pulled out the piece of paper I'd brought, unfolded it and opened my mouth to read.

"You seek to end the curse," he said before I could begin.

It was a statement, and as such I felt there was no need to answer him. I opened my mouth to read again and again he interrupted me.

"Do you really believe that your black circle and your silly poem will end the spell I worked so many generations ago? That circle can not protect you. Let me demonstrate."

He lifted a finger as thought conducting a gentle waltz, and I felt pain in every cell of my body. I screamed, dropping the paper, and my hands went down to brace myself. The pain ended and sobbing, I grabbed the paper in trembling hands and tried to read the poem once more.

"You see? I can end your pitiful life at any moment.

Do you believe I am so weak that I know not how to work my craft with care and deliberation? Elicia is gone, Sibilant of the sacred line. You see, child of light, I know of you and your family of women. I know that you are the least powerful among them. How is it you expect to defeat me, an immortal with power that you can only dream of?"

"I pretend nothing, Key Keeper," I said, trying with all my might not to throw down the paper and run from the room. "I only seek peace for my friend and protection for the child you have imprisoned."

His perfect black eyebrows arched and he walked close enough to me for his polished shoes to touch the line of my circle, almost as if to prove to me that he could ruin my spell at any time with a careless movement of his foot. He leaned down to look into my eyes and touched my skin with a finger.

I couldn't help wondering how such a being could be both beautiful and cruel all at the same time. It seemed like such a waste. Then again, there was no telling if his true form resembled human at all, much less the form I saw before me.

"I have not your child. It is Sophie of which you speak, is it not?"

His glance measured me, taking in my shaking hand and my breathless voice.

"I know you have her, or one of your minions does. I saw you hunt for her. You seek to destroy me by hurting those that I care for. Yet if I lift this curse, your power in my life will end. You can't search for me if there is no connection between us."

He was surprised for a moment, but his face slid back to bored once again. He stood, stretching out his hand, lifting his finger again.

"I may have underestimated you, child of light. Yet, I tell you truly, lifting the curse will only delay the inevitable. You have meddled in an affair that is not yours to meddle in, and thus you must give restitution for it."

The pain was back, lacing around my bones like binding ropes. I couldn't help the sobbing scream that came again from my mouth, but somehow, I managed to hold onto that poem with a death grip.

"What about you?" I gasped, when the pain subsided again.

"By which you mean..." he wondered.

"You are collecting on a debt that has already been paid," I said gathering my strength. "And there must be an accounting for that."

Anger flared over his face, giving way to an otherworldly and thunderous wrath. I started shaking so hard I could barely hold the paper, but I still hoped to extend my life for another few minutes to release Elicia from her spell and hopefully save Sophie as well.

"You are mistaken," he hissed, spittle flying from his mouth.

"I have read the history, Key Keeper. I know the truth of your hellish bargain. When the original Jediah made his bargain with you it was for the life of his son, which you collected on, and yet, you collected *his* soul as well. What bargain was in play there? Why did you take the extra soul?"

"I did not collect any more than was owed me. Jediah's firstborn passed his curse onward toward the first of his line, and so it went, from father to son, for many years. I gave what was bargained for."

I smiled.

"You didn't answer my question. Jediah bargained his son's soul and then he tried to put himself into the bargain instead. One or the other of the men was payment enough for the bargain, and yet you took both. Why?"

"A bargain cannot be amended. Jediah presumed to change the original terms of our agreement. Such presumption is costly."

"A bargain cannot be amended and the punishment is death? I don't think so."

"Who art thou to question me, mortal!" He was enraged and I shook with pain again, a leaf in a storm, but continued to speak, my voice coming out in a raspy squeak.

"I am, as you said, a child of light. I demand my turn to right this wrong. You have been paid for your gift many times over and Elicia, by the fact that she was not part of the bargain and she wasn't even a firstborn son, should be released from your curse. You've had her life and her blood, but you do not need her soul."

"She called on my powers! She called on me to kill a man." He was triumphant.

I shook my head.

“A bargain has terms, Key Keeper. You never gave her the terms, you never bound the bargain. You had no authority. Let me release her."

"She is mine and she will stay mine!" he shouted.

I shook my head and knelt down inside my circle, hunching over to read the poem aloud.

*Jediah was a wicked man*
*Jediah was a fool*
*A fickle man who sought*
*the power of kings, that he might rule*

Part of me wondered why, as I read the poem aloud, he did not try to kill me as he had before. There was much deep lore at work here, and I found myself believing that there were other factors at play than the words I was reading and circle I was sitting in. Or perhaps he was waiting for the sacrifice, and the ending of my life.

*So he called on demon power*
*He called on evil bold*
*the darkest deepest spawn of*
*hell, of which men never told*

*The demon promised sacred trade*
*an old forgotten barter*
*power for Jediah's soul,*
*one thing for another*

*Yet Jediah wanted more*
*to keep his soul intact*
*and so he bargained*
*his son's own life -could*
*never get it back*

*The demon, true to his word*
*gave the man 6 keys*
*each gave Jediah a part*
*of the power he sought -easy*
*as you please...*

"How do you know this?"

The Key Keeper shouted blazing at me in his anger again. He reached for me, but for some reason could not seem to grab ahold of me, like I was made of water and he was oil.

"Stop speaking those words. Give me that paper!"

I saw him reach for the paper, power curling from his fingertips, but nothing happened, and I knew that what I had said was right. The balance of good and evil had been shifted when he took that extra life so long ago.

I may not know much about the old lore, but I know this: magic seeks homeostasis. It doesn't like to pull to the right or the left, but rather likes to find a resting state. That could have been what was happening in this case.

*The first key was intimidation*
*The power to strike fear*
*in the hearts of men*
*to make them cower*
*the benefit was clear*

*The second key, manipulation*
*made everything a gift*
*he would take from men*
*and twist up their words*
*to cause a greater rift*

*The third key gave charisma*
*a charm above all charms*
*he could seduce, coax*
*or implore a woman*
*to his ready arms*

As I reached the middle of the poem, I knew that I needed to get the belonging and prepare myself for the sacrificial element -which I prayed with all my heart would not be my life. I reached into my purse and took out the drawing of Elicia and her mother, but looking at it, I knew that it was not the belonging I needed and I felt sick to my stomach. In my haste to save Sophie, I had grabbed the wrong thing.

I had ruined the ritual and I wouldn't be able to finish it. I would be in Thadius' grasp and Sophie would die.

*Inspiration was the fourth*
*As any leader knew*
*he needed words to*

*tell his warriors*
*watch as their fervor grew*

*Accomplishment, the fifth of these*
*the power to attain*
*whatever lay within*
*his grasp, the wealth*
*all wanted to gain*

*The final key, it had no name*
*power so arcane*
*calling spirits for*
*his own uses, to*
*drive enemies insane*

I paused in my reading, realizing that I had only moments to find something, anything that would fit the end of ritual.

"Oh my God, oh my God, oh my God."

I panicked and set the picture down, shoving my hand in my purse, searching but knowing, deep in my heart, that it was futile.

"Silly child. You did not make proper preparations and now all your work will be for naught," he said, rising and gathering his power in a blinding beacon of light. It flooded the room and started to pulse. I gasped and the purse started to slide from my grasp, but not before my hand snagged a familiar object. It was the All-Inside and it felt right.

Not only was it connected to Elicia, but I could feel in my gut it was personal to her family line in a way that would remove the curse back through all the generations of Elicia's family.

Ripping off the ziploc baggy with my teeth, I held the statue above me in one hand as I stood, trying to appear stronger than I felt, and recited the end of the poem, and all the pleasure on Thadius' face vanished when he realized what I had in my hand.

"No!" he screamed as his powers snuffed like a candle blown out.

*Jediah took his keys of power*
*he made them all his own*
*his greatness pleased him*
*powers increasing*
*yet he was alone*

*And when his wife bore him a son*
*he realized his wrongs*
*power in its place*
*is fine, but only*
*love made him belong*

*To his credit, he tried to fix*
*the wrongful barter made*
*he called the demon*
*he made a new pact*
*but it was too late*

*For his conceit, he paid the price*
*and his soul was captured*
*to his great sorrow*
*his bargain remained*
*his family line was shattered*

The last words slid from my tongue and the drawing at my feet burned from the outside edges to the very center. The sacrifice for the working had been paid and the small statue pulsed with a power that I could barely hang on to. It outshone the power that the Key Keeper had been able to summon and blasted through the walls of the room, and outward past the house. I felt a series of whispers, quiet at first, then growing in strength, like a hundred voices were shushing me in a hundred different tongues.

Suddenly the light that had flown out from the All-Inside, came rushing back toward it and pulled the Key Keeper with it. He screamed and fought the light with all the strength he had, but it wasn't enough. The magic was about to be properly balanced, if I could hold onto the figurine long enough for the spell to be completed. It was no easy task, considering how shaky I was with the fatigue of working such a major releasing spell. My arms struggled to hold the All-Inside above my head, my muscles were beyond fatigued and I was ready to collapse.

With a rush like a forest fire, the light, the Key Keeper, and the magic all disappeared into the center of the little statue. My hands trembled for a moment and I dropped the figurine to the carpet, panting.

# Chapter 24

The room was still lit by the table lamp in the corner, but the room itself was glowing with the shapes of many souls, eager to move on to the hereafter that had, until now, been denied them. Each one of them bowed to me and floated away, some upward, some just disappeared and others faded slow, smiling. The last to leave was Elicia, who floated over to stare at the figurine on the floor.

"It's such a small thing to have done such a mighty work. I suppose it's always that way." She turned to face me. "I have to go now, but there are two things I wanted to tell you. First, thank you. You've released my family from the curse that has haunted us for generations. You have cleared up the mystery of why my life was so twisted and horrible. I'm eternally grateful. Many blessings on you and yours.

"Secondly, there is a reason you are here, and I want to help you with that. I think I can."

"How can you help me with Sophie?" I asked.

"Let's try it like we did when I came to you the first time. Hold out your hands," she told me.

I held out my hands, uncertain what a ghost would feel like and how I would be able to read her. She laid her hands on top of mine, but all I felt was a warm rush of air. I concentrated, closing my eyes, and she was right, I could feel where Sophie was.

"Thank you," I said, leaning down to pick up the All-Inside and my purse. She stopped me.

"Leave that to me, it's been in my family for many

years," she said and reaching out a hand, she enveloped the statue in a golden light where it seemed to explode into a hundred thousand prickling golden star bursts.

"Never stop helping others," she whispered, and then she was gone in a blaze. I blinked and scrambled to grab my purse and my keys, which I realized I had dropped on the floor in my haste to cast the spell. I ran down the stairs, through the hall, and out the door, praying I wasn't already too late.

~~~~~

I called Paul on my way down to the park. I'd seen a picture in my mind as clearly as if I was there with her. I saw Sophie's broken body stretched out in front of me, each shuddering and shallow gasping breath moving through her lungs.

He got there as I did, which must have been some crazy miracle considering we were coming from different parts of town. His car door slammed as he got out.

He ran up to me, yelling, "I called the police and gave an anonymous tip. Hopefully they should be here soon. I told them to call an ambulance."

We were a small valley town, closely linked with wandering wilderness that meandered from the hills above us and flowed throughout in a series of city parks. This particular park, McKinley, was the most wild and overgrown, and even with a specific location, I knew we would still have difficulty finding her.

"Did you bring the flashlights?" I asked as he reached me.

"Yeah," he said, handing one to me. I took the long skull-cracking instrument from him and flipped it on.

I closed my eyes for a moment, trying to get my bearings according to the vision I'd seen in my head.

"This way," I said, and ran off through the trees.

We stumbled over tree roots and most of the time
~~~~~

avoiding smacking into branches. At one point my ankle twisted and I went down, yelping in pain.

"Are you okay?" Paul asked, reaching down to help me up.

"I'm fine. Just feeling a bit foolish," I said, wincing a little as I stood.

"Maybe we should slow down. We don't want to kill ourselves out here."

"Paul, I can't. I just can't," I said, looking for a familiar landmark in the darkness. "I saw her as clear as you see me. She needs us. She needs help."

I closed my eyes again, playing a mental game of hot and cold. Warmer, for sure now.

"Come on," I said, leading the way. The air was chilly and I saw my own breath come in puffs of white in the dim flashlight's beam. We trudged further and I started to feel more anxious, as if we were almost... there!

Paul and I became alert as we heard a scrabbling and scraping sound to the left of us, in the brush. We focused our flashlights on it and I expected to see a deer or other woodland creature, but instead standing with her knife at Sophie's throat, was Myrtha.

"Myrtha!" I shouted and she jerked her knife against Sophie's skin.

Sophie was hovering on the edge of consciousness, she looked so lethargic that I suspected she'd been drugged. Her body must have been nothing but dead weight to an old woman like Myrtha, and yet the hag had no trouble holding her up.

"Stay back!" she screamed, and seemed so altered from the last time that I had seen her, that I felt my heart clench in fear for Sophie.

"What have you done?" I asked. Paul was so tense I thought he might snap like a string if Myrtha wasn't careful.

"Don't move yet, Paul." I said, under my breath.

“There's a chance we can reason with her."

"I've found my salvation," she said, "and your nosy self isn't going to keep it from me."

"How are you going to be saved, exactly?" I asked.

"Wouldn't you like to know," she cackled, "Like to take my secrets for yourself, I suppose. Too bad. The girl is mine. The Key Keeper promised me her youth if I killed her for him."

"Myrtha, he was lying. You can't believe anything he says. In any case, killing her won't do you any good. The Key Keeper has gone to the hereafter. I helped send him there."

"I don't believe you," she shrieked. She jerked Sophie's head by the hank of hair she held in her hand and I gasped as I heard a little moan come out of Sophie's mouth. I prayed for strength.

"We've called the police, Myrtha. After I killed the Key Keeper, Elicia told me where to find Sophie and we called the police and her family to come help us.

“How do you think we knew you were here? I'm a *Reader*, not a *Seeker*. If you hurt Sophie, they're going to take you to prison, and then how would you enjoy this supposed youth?"

"I don't care, I need it too much. You don't know what it's like living in this body."

She raised the knife to plunge into Sophie's heart as I screamed, "No!" and Paul lunged toward her, when all of us were startled by the baying of a hound nearby.

Myrtha released Sophie's hair and shrieked, "You'll pay for this, you meddling bitch."

The words sounded familiar somehow. She thrust the knife through the sash at her waist and ran off into the woods, where I hoped she would spend the rest of her days, away from people.

I heard more noise behind us, and yelled, "Help! We're over here! Please help!"

Paul and I ran over to where Sophie laid, still and cold on the ground. I knelt down and pulled her head into my lap, brushing the dead leaves and dirt from her riotous curly hair.

"Is she breathing okay?" asked Paul.

"Yes, but it's pretty shallow. I don't think Myrtha spared the drugs. Go find the police and lead them here, will you?"

He ran off down the hill, faster than I could credit, as I continued to gaze down at Sophie. I needed to know she'd be okay. I just needed a sign. I slid my hand into hers and closed my eyes, searching for a message. I saw Sophie, at the prom with a tall dark-haired boy, laughing and dancing. I opened my eyes, giving a great long sigh. And looked up to see a bunch of people headed our way, their flashlights bobbing like fireflies on a summer night.

~~~~~

A few days later, Paul and I were cleaning up the remnants of my investigation, sorting it and putting it into boxes for Jordan.

"Are you sure you want to give all this stuff to him?"

"Yes, he's really the only one left in the world who is still thinking about Elicia, besides us. He was so in love with her. I thought he'd appreciate reading some of this stuff. Oh, make sure you put that other one in the box going to Mrs. Ford. I swore to her that I wouldn't let anything about her family be seen by eyes other than mine."

"She didn't turn out to be that bad in the end, did she?" he asked, stacking some of the Ford biography files into the smaller box on the table.

"I think once I got a chance to talk to her face to face, we understood each other better. When she realized I wasn't trying to dig up dirt on her family, she warmed up quite a bit."

"I still can't believe how much Jordan paid you," he said, shaking his head.

"No kidding," I said. "He gave me some nonsense
~~~~~

about the amount being at the discretion of the executor. Most of the money still went to Elicia's favorite charities. Mine is more of a small nest egg. I've been wanting to get a cozy little house to settle into. Maybe a cat."

"A cat?" he asked, "A cat? How about a dog? Dogs are so much nicer than cats."

"Really?" I said, "I've never thought so. Cats are so... clean. And they smell nice. And they don't slobber everywhere."

"I am shocked by this revelation. Shocked."

I laughed and leaned over to kiss him.

"Don't be silly, I love dogs."

He sniffed, mollified, and kissed me back.

"So this house will be dog friendly?" he asked and I nodded. "Will it be accountant friendly?"

"I suppose so." I said.

"Want a roommate?" he asked.

"Maybe... how long are we talking here?" I asked.

"Um, I was thinking maybe forever?"

"Oh!" I said, looking at him with a calculating eye. "How soon can you move in?"

~~~~~

I knocked on the door of Jordan's office and he opened it moments later, smiling at me.

"Sibilant! I didn't expect to see you. Was there anything wrong with the check? What can I do?"

"No, no, nothing's wrong. I wanted to give this to you," I said, holding out the box.

He took it, looking down at the contents, then set it on the desk in front of him.

"What is it?" he asked.

"It's the stuff I got from Elicia's house. I wasn't sure what to do with it, but somehow I got the feeling you might like to look through it. There are a couple of journals, some
~~~~~

pictures, and files."

He pushed a hand through some of the items in the box and looked up, eyes watering.

"Thank you, Sibilant. I really appreciate this," he said.

"No problem, Jordan. I'll see you around," I said, and waving good-bye, I left his office. Looking back once as I walked away, I saw him pull one of the photos from the box, sitting in his chair to stare at it.

No matter how much more peaceful the world was without the Key Keeper, the remnants of the blood curse still remained. It was like that in life, bitterness and sweetness mixing together to become a world that was sometimes wonderful to live in and sometimes unbearably hard. I promised myself to bring light into the world at every opportunity.

Now it was time to go home, put my sign back up, and get to work. It was a new day.

# Epilogue

The world around it was gray, as it always was. It could see the swirling mass of fog spinning around like a typhoon with a large eye, still in its center. Floating along with the current, ever watchful for a certain presence, a meal to feed on. Always hungry and waiting, a painful knowledge gnawed at it like a disease that could never be cured. So it hovered and fed, in an eternal cycle, waiting for a target to pop up on its searching radar.

Now was such a time, another swoop of the world's cycle brought a new meal into its sight. It moved against the currents now, down, down down toward the center place, where time stood still and the stormy chaos was but a mere ripple. It floated down until it saw a little being, a child of light standing innocently as a new fawn, and it leaned in to take a sniff.

"What are you?" asked the little being, backing away and emanating the delicious scent of fear it loved so well.

It circled her and stopped, cocking its head in interest and as it repeated her gibberish back at her.

"What are you?" it asked and watched, fascinated, as the little mortal shrank back. It could feel her pulse quicken, which made its mouth water. What a tasty treat.

"What are you? What are you? What are you?" It asked, and then once more, "What are you?"

She raised her hand as if to touch it and it resisted the urge to bite her hand off. The meal would be more satisfying if it waited until fear filled her to completion before killing her.

It raised a hand in a mirror of hers and lowered its hand when she lowered hers. She started to turn away, and it cut her off, feeling almost tender towards her in her frailty.

"What are you?" it asked again, and felt pleasure at her sudden pulse of fear.

The little being backed up, and it followed. "Go away! Back off!" she screamed.

It grabbed her arms, continuing to mimic her, and enjoyed the sound of her screams as it bit into her neck, savoring the meaty taste of blood and terror.

It was too bad this was just the spirit world, it thought as it consumed the shadow of her real self before it felt her presence leave altogether. It would have to go and look for her out in the world where mortals resided. Her light was a beacon, pulling it to her.

It was only a matter of time before it found her.

# Acknowledgments

Every book has a list of people involved in its inception. Mine is no different. My biggest thanks go out to my gigantic family for reading and giving input. Here they are in order of reading (no favorites here, guys!): Bethel, Aunt Cathy, Christine, Hope, Mom, Promise, Jordan the Girl, Amber, Aunt Bambi, and Mary.

To everyone else who encouraged, loved, hugged, and congratulated me on my small step into the world of writing, you have as much gratitude as I can give -especially you, Jo, for being my very first reader and Mom, for doing all that nit-picky work.

Finally, I would like to thank my husband Garrett -the love of my life, and my best friend. Thank you for our life together and thanks for my baby boy.

Made in the USA
Charleston, SC
02 December 2010